A Very Private Murder

a&b

A Very Private Murder

STUART PAWSON

First published in Great Britain in 2010 by
Allison & Busby Limited
13 Charlotte Mews
London W1T 4EJ
www.allisonandbusby.com

The moral right of the author has been asserted.

a ,

This not,
by v t or
(
writt than
that ir lition

A CIP catalogue record for this book is available from
the British Library.

10 9 8 7 6 5 4 3 2 1

Hardcover 13-ISBN 978-0-7490-0794-2
Trade Paperback 13-ISBN 978-0-7490-0818-5

Typeset in 13/16 pt Adobe Garamond Pro by
Allison & Busby Ltd.

Paper used in this publication is from sustainably managed sources.
All of the wood used is procured from legal sources and is fully traceable.
The producing mill uses schemes such as ISO 14001
to monitor environmental impact.

Printed and bound in the UK by
CPI Mackays, Chatham ME5 8TD

STUART PAWSON had a career as a mining engineer, followed by a spell working for the probation service, before he became a full-time writer. He lives in Fairburn, Yorkshire, and, when not hunched over the word processor, likes nothing more than tramping across the moors, which often feature in his stories. He is a member of the Murder Squad and the Crime Writers' Association.

www.stuartpawson.com

Available from
ALLISON & BUSBY

In the DI Charlie Priest series

The Picasso Scam
The Mushroom Man
The Judas Sheep
Last Reminder
Deadly Friends
Some by Fire
Chill Factor
Laughing Boy
Limestone Cowboy
Over the Edge
Shooting Elvis
Grief Encounters

To Doreen

*Many thanks to the following for their
unflagging assistance, advice and encouragement:
John Crawford, Dave Mason, Dennis Marshall,
Clive Kingswood, John Mills, Hazel Mills
and, as always, Teresa Chris.*

PROLOGUE

The horse could smell their ill intentions. Three hundred years of inbreeding had produced a neurotic, nervous wreck of an animal that was good for only one thing: it could run like the wind. White-eyed, head swinging and teeth snapping, it strained and twisted to reach the hand gripping its halter.

'Hold him steady,' the older of the two men urged.

'I can't,' the other protested as the horse, ears flat against its head, pulled away from him, almost jerking him over the half-door of the stable. He dropped the flashlight he was holding and took a two-handed grip on the animal's leather halter strap, flinching as teeth clashed millimetres from his wrists and spittle sprayed his face.

'Easy, boy, easy.' The older man's voice had calmed a hundred similar animals, but tonight the words were edged in fear and came up from his throat like a corncrake's call. He was a dwarf of a man, small and bent but with shoulders like a weightlifter's, topping out a body twisted by years of hard work. He was wearing overalls and wellington boots, and his hands and face were the colour of the saddles that he'd spent his lifetime polishing, fitting and adjusting and, years earlier, sitting astride. 'Easy, boy. Good boy. There's a good fellow.' He slowly raised a hand and gently rubbed the horse's nose, marvelling, as he always did, at its softness. The horse made a snuffling sound and the ones in the stables on either side snorted and their hooves clattered on concrete.

'Now,' the other man whispered when everything was quiet. 'Just do it.' He was dressed in a sports jacket and cavalry twill trousers that marked him down as a countryman, and his tan didn't extend beyond his shirt cuffs and fastened collar. He could easily have passed as an auctioneer at a cattle market.

The older man lowered his hand from the horse's muzzle and slowly bent down without removing his gaze from the animal. He groped on the ground for a second until he felt the cold metal of the humane killer he'd laid there in preparation, and his fingers closed around the grip. It was an Entwistle heavy-duty horse killer, loaded with a single .32 calibre soft-nosed bullet and fitted with a silencer, as required by Jockey Club rules. He laid his trigger finger alongside the barrel and slowly raised himself upright.

The horse was edgy again, flaring its nostrils, but soon settled as the older man crooned his false reassurances.

He lifted the heavy gun and placed the end of the barrel against the horse's head, but the angle was wrong. He wasn't tall enough. He stretched upwards and lifted the gun as high as he could. Horses have tiny brains, and a brain shot was essential.

'Do it!' the younger man urged. 'Pull the trigger.'

'I...I can't,' the older man protested.

'You're lined up. For God's sake do it.'

The horse was called Peccadillo and was the finest-looking animal he'd ever worked with. His hands were shaking, partly from the weight of the gun, more from nerves, but mostly from the sense of betrayal he felt. 'I can't do it, *meister*. I just can't.'

'Jesus friggin' Christ!' the younger man cursed. 'This is a fine time to back out. You know what this means, don't you? We'll never be able to run him.'

'I'm not backing out,' the older man protested. 'It's just that...just that...I can't do it. I can't pull the trigger.'

'But you'll hold him while I do it? Is that what you mean? You're still *in*?'

'Yeah, I'm still in.'

'OK. So give me the gun.'

The horse pulled away as they argued, but the older man coaxed him back and the two men swapped roles. In a couple of minutes Peccadillo was settled again and the younger man raised the killer. He placed the muzzle between its eyes, at the top of the white stripe that ran down its face, and raised the back of the gun.

'How's that?' he asked.

'Perfect,' he was told.

The crack of the gun was hardly more than the snapping of a dried branch, but the effect was devastating. Peccadillo's body was shocked rigid for a moment, then his head fell and his legs collapsed under him, front ones an instant before the rear. In the neighbouring stables horses whinnied and their hooves rattled on walls and feed boxes as they kicked out. The older man unbolted the stall's lower door and pulled it open so they could survey the results of their crime.

'Shine the light,' the younger man ordered. The horse's eyes were wide open and blood was bubbling from the hole in his head.

'Where are his legs?'

'Jesus, he's fallen on them. They're under him.'

'We need a leg.'

The two men entered the stable and tried pushing the dead weight of the horse to one side. It didn't move. The older man knelt down and groped under the front of the horse. 'I can feel a shoe,' he said. 'Help me with it.'

The younger man curled his lip in distaste as he knelt alongside his partner in crime. Together, they felt the horse's left front leg and managed to pull it free from under the steaming but inert body.

'That'll do,' the older man said. 'Let me get the crowbar.' A moment later he was telling the younger man to pull the leg as hard as he could.

'One blow,' he was told. 'You only get one blow.'

'I know. Are you ready?'

'Ready.'

The crowbar sliced through the air and smashed into

the dead animal's cannon bone, shattering it in two.

''Tis done,' he said, wiping sweat and blood from his forehead.

'Yeah, well done.'

Both men were panting with exertion. They looked for a moment at the scene, horrified by the enormity of their deeds, until the younger man said: 'Now, you let the other horses out, then go home and put your pyjamas on. I'll start the fire and talk to you again after you ring me. OK?'

'Right, *meister*. It's been a good night's work.'

'We've hardly started,' he was told.

CHAPTER ONE

Like all self-made men, Arthur George Threadneedle worshipped his Maker. He flexed his face muscles and watched approvingly as the reflection staring back at him bared its teeth and arched its eyebrows. Tilting his head backwards to catch the light from the mirror of his dressing table he applied the nasal hair trimmer to his left nostril and heard the faint hum of the instrument turn to a buzz and rattle as the blades dealt with the bushy growth that had accumulated since its last application, nearly a week ago.

Four suits were laid out on the bed, chosen – suggested – by his wife as being suitable for the occasion. Each one was blue, two-button, single-breasted, with slight variations of lapel design, in varying weights of cloth. As he would be indoors he chose the lightweight Pierre Balmain, which had the added advantage of an extra security button at the top of the zip fly. Nothing could be left to chance today, and he lived in mortal dread of his zipper failing at an inappropriate moment. Today, he reminded himself, was the day of his ascension, his incarnation, his entry into Jerusalem. OK, so he wasn't sure of the expression, but today he would put the town of Heckley 'on the map', as he liked to say, and in doing so make his own modest space in history. He poured Karl Lagerfeld cologne into the palm of his hand and dabbed it on his cheeks, blinking as the astringency stung his eyes. Today was the day that he, Arthur George Threadneedle, would leave behind the jokey bonds of small-town local government and join the Establishment.

Ghislaine Curzon breakfasted in her hotel room on fruit and green tea and waited for the call to say her car had arrived. She was bemused rather than nervous, although she'd never opened a shopping mall-stroke-conference centre before. It was something she may have to get used to, as widely accepted but still unofficial girlfriend to one of the royal princes, and the people's favourite – in Yorkshire if nowhere else – to be a future queen of England.

She knew Arthur Threadneedle as an acquaintance of her father from his horse racing days, and that he was now a bigwig in East Pennine. He'd contacted Ghislaine's father and suggested that *Curzon Centre* would be a good name for the new, high-profile development he was involved with on the outskirts of Heckley. If Ghislaine could possibly come and cut the ribbon that would be the icing on the cake.

'He's a crook,' Mr Curzon had told his daughter, 'and I'd normally advise you to stay well clear of him, but it might be fun and you'll get your picture in *Yorkshire Life.*'

Ghislaine was five feet ten tall, with a natural grace that eclipsed anything seen on a catwalk. She had dark curly hair, contrasting with the bland, straight-haired blonde clones that stared at the world from every teen magazine, tabloid and TV screen. When she met the prince she was working in northern Kenya, at a field hospital set up to cater for the refugees flooding across the border. She was gaining work experience the tough way, before a postgraduate year studying medicine at St Andrew's University.

The prince was on a whistle-stop tour of East Africa and never stood a chance. The staff and walking wounded lined up to meet him as he crouched and ran from the helicopter that brought him, and Ghislaine picked up the little boy who'd lost a leg to a landmine and joined the end of the queue. The sun was on her face and she had to screw her eyes to see the prince's features as he approached. When he was opposite her, in her white coat, stethoscope sticking out of the pocket, looking ridiculously young to be a doctor, he was momentarily lost for words.

'Hi,' she said, holding out her hand. 'My name's Ghislaine Curzon, but everybody calls me Grizzly.' Her wide mouth was set in a smile and the sun had brought out the spray of childhood freckles that stretched across her nose and cheeks. He never stood a chance at all.

* * *

Arthur George Threadneedle had a small dilemma. Normally he would wear his mayoral chain of office, but he wondered if it would be more appropriate if he left it at home today. Miss Curzon was the main attraction, and he didn't want to do anything to detract from her presence. He wouldn't wear the chain, he decided. It was her day and he wanted it to be perfect. He telephoned for his car to take him to the Curzon Centre and studied the sky. The clouds were high and the chances of rain looked slight, confirming what the TV weathergirl had said. Mrs Threadneedle appeared and asked how she looked.

'Fine, you look fine,' he replied with barely a glance. She was wearing one of her hats, he noticed. Being mayoress had truly gone to her head.

The doorbell rang. 'That's the car,' Threadneedle said. 'Let's go.' He cast a glance back at the chain of office draped over the back of the settee, then turned and picked it up. He was the mayor, after all, and the people deserved to be able to see what they were getting for their money. He adjusted it in the hall mirror and followed his wife to where the chauffeur-cum-town macebearer was holding open the Rover's rear door.

Fifteen minutes later they were in the mall, finding their way through the crowds who were hoping for a glance of the girl who could one day quite easily become their queen. They visited the central atrium, where the unveiling ceremony would take place, and Threadneedle checked that the area in front of the plaque was roped off and the curtains hiding it were intact. He'd spent much of the previous evening opening and closing them until they moved with silky precision.

'Everything fine, John?' he asked the chief of security who stood with five other employees, wearing their dark uniforms and LAPD-style caps, looking like the chorus line from a Midwestern production of *Pirates of Penzance*.

'AOK, Mr Threadneedle,' came the reply. 'It's been under constant surveillance and is just as we left it last night.'

The mall had been doing business for a week, but this Monday was the official opening. Its building had not gone without objections from several quarters, including the RSPB, several local protest groups with silly acronyms, the Ramblers' Association and Friends of the Earth. A sizeable patch of moorland had been sacrificed for the buildings and car parks, and several miles of footpath lost or rerouted. There'd been no threats of disobedience – civil or otherwise – but a large police presence was on show and an even larger one was posing as the shopping public.

Threadneedle checked the CCTV monitors in the basement and received another favourable report, so he made his way through the throng to the Green Room, where all the dignitaries would meet. Mrs Threadneedle, who was only five feet tall, fought gallantly to keep up with him, wondering if the wide-brimmed hat had been such a good idea. As he walked, Threadneedle went through the wording on the stone plaque that he himself had composed, wondering if it could have been improved upon, if he ought to have called himself *Councillor* Threadneedle. It said:

Opened by
Miss Ghislaine Curzon
In the presence of
A.G. Threadneedle, Mayor of Heckley
Architect: W.H. Jones & Partners
14th May 2007

The Green Room was crowded although Miss Curzon's party had not arrived. The chief constable and the local MP, plus wives and management, were already in there, sipping sherry and waiting. She was understood to be bringing along her younger sister for moral support and would be accompanied by the Lord Lieutenant of the county and two police bodyguards. Officially she wasn't authorised to have a royal bodyguard, but when any high-profile dignitary was in a police force's area it was the custom to pass on notification and a weather eye would be kept on them.

She arrived without her sister ten minutes later, via the back door and was smuggled into the Green Room without the public realising. Everybody stood to greet her, mouthfuls of Pringles were swallowed, hands discreetly wiped and proffered, smiles fixed.

Ghislaine Curzon conquered the room with a glance. She was wearing an ivory suit in Shantung silk, with recklessly high stilettos, and carried a small purse the same shade of green as the shoes. No jewellery, gloves or hat and hardly any make-up. Every man in the room fell in love with her with varying degrees of lust, and all the women gave envious sighs.

Arthur George Threadneedle conferred with the Lord Lieutenant and they counted down the last few minutes. The Lord Lieutenant was in full dress uniform, medals and all, and Threadneedle was glad he'd taken the decision to don his chain of office. He'd had a short chat with Miss Curzon, offered her a sherry (declined), enquired about the health of her father (he was fine, thank you) and left her talking to the MP, happy that she knew who he was without monopolising her company. He caught the eye of his macebearer-cum-chauffeur and indicated that they'd leave in two minutes.

On the stroke of eleven the macebearer hammered the carpeted floor of the Green Room three times with the mayor of Heckley's symbol of authority and everybody fell silent. Threadneedle positioned himself alongside their guest of honour and glanced round to see if his wife was still with him. He saw her gulping down a schooner of Amontillado, hat already askew, and wondered if he'd done the right thing bringing her along. The macebearer opened the door and led the phalanx of dignitaries out into the airy vaults of the mall and through the pressing crowd who'd come to see this beautiful young woman whom the tabloids had already elevated to royal status and whom one day they would probably destroy. The people looked at her as she walked amongst them and any cynicism they may have harboured was shed like wool off a moulting sheep. Cameras flashed and Ghislaine stopped for a few seconds while a flustered woman came to grips with her mobile phone camera. The woman mumbled a thank you and turned away, hoping she'd pressed the right buttons.

A little girl offered a bunch of freesias and Ghislaine crouched down to speak to her.

'Where's Kevin?' a youth asked as she pressed forward, trying to keep moving without being too impolite.

She smiled back at him and said: 'He couldn't make it,' over her shoulder, glad of the banter with someone nearer her own age. Kevin was her pet name for the prince, as revealed in one of the celebrity magazines.

It took fifteen minutes to walk the thirty yards to the podium, but nobody minded. Threadneedle watched her work the crowd, glowing with pride. He was keeping a low profile, staying out of the limelight, but he'd reminded her that he knew her father and asked to be remembered to him. This was a day, God willing, that would go into the town's archives and would be the high point, the apogee, of Heckley's romance with royalty, and it happened during his year in office.

John of the security company parted the ropes that surrounded the ceremonial area and let the party through onto the dais. Ghislaine walked over to where the embroidered curtains covered the plaque, like a child's theatre set halfway up a wall. Threadneedle shuffled alongside her, running through his speech in his mind.

It was to be a short speech. He wasn't famous for short speeches. Behind his back his fellow councillors referred to him as Gobshite. But he'd taken advice, given it some thought, and today wasn't a day for a policy statement. The spoken word was ephemeral, wasted on an occasion like this. What mattered was carved in stone behind those curtains. What it said there would be read and noted by visitors to the mall for the next fifty years. Today he'd introduce their distinguished visitor and step aside. She could do the rest.

The macebearer pounded the floor again and the babble of the crowd fell to a murmur. He half turned and nodded to Threadneedle, inviting him to start the proceedings. Threadneedle cleared his throat and tapped the tiny microphone on the lectern with a fingernail, sending a thousand decibels of electronic noise crackling around the mall like a jet fighter.

'Good morning, ladies and gentlemen,' he began, adding 'and children' as an afterthought. He congratulated himself for remembering the children and forgot what he'd intended to say next. His mind was blank. *Just do it*, he thought. *Get on with it.*

'Today is a great day for Heckley,' he improvised. 'Today it's my pleasure to introduce to you a young lady who has stolen all our hearts...'

This was better. It was starting to flow, until somebody in the crowd shouted for him to hurry up and he lost it again. *Never mind*, he thought, *it's my name on the plaque behind those curtains*. He looked straight at the YTV camera that was recording the occasion and said: 'Ladies and gentlemen, I'd like to call on Miss Ghislaine Curzon to open the Curzon Shopping Mall and Conference Centre. Miss Curzon...' He turned to her, holding out a solicitous arm, and she stepped forward.

'This one?' she silently mouthed at him, taking hold of the silken rope.

Threadneedle confirmed it was with a violent nod of the head.

Ghislaine took hold of the rope and leant forward towards the microphone. 'Good morning,' she said. 'It's lovely to see you all and thank you for making me so welcome. I know Heckley fairly well because I used to come here walking with my father when I was quite small. You're so lucky to live in this part of the world. We always had tea and scones in a tea shop in the town. My only hope is that a super new development such as this won't be to the detriment of small, more traditional businesses in the town centre, such as that tea shop.'

The smile slipped from Threadneedle's face. He didn't know that she'd ever been within twenty miles of Heckley. 'Sod the tea shop,' he hissed to himself, 'just pull the frigging string.'

'So now...' Ghislaine continued, 'all that's left is for me to declare the Centre open...and...pull...like...this...'

The curtains parted to reveal the legend they were hiding. The crowd stood in shocked silence for a second before exhaling a collective gasp, followed by an explosion of camera flashes. The Curzon Centre was well and truly open.

CHAPTER TWO

'Fuck?' I echoed.

'That's what it said,' Superintendent Wood repeated.

'In red paint?'

'I told you.'

'In foot-high letters?'

'For God's sake, Charlie, how many more times?'

'Ha ha ha ha!'

'It's not bloody funny.'

'Oh, it is, Gilbert. It certainly is.' The tears prickling my eyes were confirmation.

'The chief constable was there. Everybody was there, and the TV cameras recorded the whole thing. It's embarrassing, Charlie. Makes us look like a right bunch of turnips.'

'So what did the glamorous Miss Curzon think of it?' I asked.

'That's the worst bit. She had a giggling fit. They're

trying to say she was hysterical, but I'm told it looked more like she thought it hilarious.'

'Ha ha! Good for her. Well thanks for that, Gilbert. I'll be glued to my television tonight when *Look North* is on, to see what they make of it.'

'Oh no you won't, Charlie. You'll be at the Curzon Centre. The chief constable was adamant: he wants you in charge of the investigation.'

I was on holiday. My garden was overgrown and I'd had a letter from the council saying that the neighbours were complaining. I'd borrowed a strimmer and had attacked the worst part at the front and was having a well-earned rest and a glass of shandy when I'd heard the phone ringing.

'I'm on leave,' I protested. 'And I do murders, not graffiti. Give it to young Caton. He's a royalist.'

'It's more serious than graffiti. It was a breach of security. It could have been a bomb. You're on it, Chas, whether you like it or not.'

'Tell him I'm on leave, paddling a canoe down the Loire Valley.'

'He knows you're at home, gardening.'

'Damn.'

'I'll see you there in an hour.'

'OK. Hey Gilbert...'

'Yes, Charlie.'

'Did he say he wanted Charlie Priest on the job or did he tell you to put your best man on it?'

'Just get your arse down to the Curzon Centre, asap.'

'Right, boss. I'm on my way.'

* * *

I lingered under the shower until I was rid of all the pollen, creepy-crawlies, dead leaves and other items of flora and fauna that had attached themselves to my body parts like burrs to a sheepdog. I dried myself off and finished the shandy that I'd taken in with me. Suddenly, I felt good. I was clean and refreshed and the little bit of gardening I'd managed to complete had raised my pulse rate out of the lethargy zone. The rest of the garden could wait. I pulled on new jeans, white shirt, jacket and leather slip-ons over the socks with little anchors on them. I didn't want to look as if I was trying too hard, but there was always the chance that Miss Curzon was still around.

I'd watched the shopping mall and conference centre being built with a mixture of admiration for the vision of the developers and horror at what they were doing to the landscape. This was the first time I'd actually been in the grounds. A big sign welcomed me to the Curzon Centre and another announced that Monkton Civil Engineering were working with the People to build a better Yorkshire. I drove around the perimeter road, past several turn-offs and eventually found a parking space within a reasonable hike of the entrance. I noted the location but had already forgotten it by the time I reached the automatic doors and made my transition into the never-never land of the out-of-town shopping experience.

The place was throbbing. Steady streams of customers, almost all female, were converging on the exit. They were spilling off the bottom of *down* escalators, rising out of the floor on *up* escalators and approaching from three other directions, laden with big bags bearing the names of exotic fashion houses. Well, they were exotic to me. Craghoppers is about as designer as I ever get. An equal number of eager punters, plastic friends burning holes in their handbags, were fighting their way in. When I reached the main hall I took my bearings, consulted a you-are-here plan of the place and headed towards what was grandly called the Atrium, where I imagined the action had taken place.

The rostrum was cordoned off with police tape and guarded by a uniformed bobby, two female community support officers and four employees of the Centre's security staff. I pushed my way through the gawpers and showed my ID to the bobby. Halfway up the wall were the curtains that somebody had hastily closed again to hide the forbidden word and I struggled to keep a straight face.

'What time does this place close?' I asked.

'Ten o'clock, sir. Ten 'til ten.'

'Ten!' I exclaimed. 'Jeez!' It was going to be a long day. 'So where is everybody?'

'Down in the CCTV control room.'

'Where's that?'

It was in the basement, along a corridor lined with pipes and cables, through a couple of *Staff only* doors. I was the last to arrive. The room was dimly lit with a green light, and one wall was covered with high-definition monitors, some showing the car park, others various views of the interior. A technician sat at a control desk, like the producer of some outside broadcast, except this one lasted all day, every day. I wondered what he did for relaxation in his off periods. Gilbert introduced me to Miss Carol McArdle, the manager of the Centre, who had a surprisingly firm handshake for her size. You have to watch the little ones. She probably developed her assertiveness by giving full-contact karate lessons in her spare time. I told her that they looked to be doing good business upstairs and flexed my fingers behind my back.

It was a normal working day for the troops, so the ones who weren't already mingling with the crowd, looking for terrorists, nutters and overenthusiastic republicans, had descended on the Centre like orphaned schoolkids on a burning sweet shop. I'd like to think it was because of their conscientiousness, but I suspect the chances of meeting the leggy Miss Curzon had more to do with it.

'Has Miss Curzon left?' I ventured. It was the most pressing question I could think of.

'She's gone off to a civic luncheon at the town hall,' I was told.

A SOCO had been sent for and he was eager to be let loose on the plaque and try for an adventitious hit. In other words, he'd swab it, willy-nilly, and hope to collect some DNA. I wanted a look at it myself, too, but I didn't want to wait until ten o'clock.

'We could do with some screens to put around it,' Gilbert suggested, looking towards the manager after I'd voiced my feelings.

'Mr Wood,' I began. 'We're in 2007. The F-word is used on Radio Four almost every day. It's spray-painted on every motorway bridge around town and drawn in the dirt on the back of every white van. I don't think exposure to it will offend or corrupt any good citizen of Heckley who happens to be shopping here today.'

I got my way and we all moved off towards the scene of the crime. Climbing the stairs I asked Miss McArdle if there was an office we could use as an incident room and she said there was.

The SOCO donned surgeon's gloves and mask and had first go at the plaque, followed by the photographer and then me. The crowd pressed forward, watching and photographing every move we made, and no doubt a good proportion of them would have letters in the *Gazette* later in the week complaining about the police wasting public money or, alternatively, not devoting sufficient resources to the case. I studied the offending word and wished I'd brought my magnifying glass to put on a show for the audience.

The office was on the upper floor, tagged on to the business suite, as Miss McArdle called it. The shopfitters had been using it as a canteen, so it was well equipped with chairs and a few tables that had been borrowed from the food court. Industrial-size tins of paint were stacked in a corner, mainly in shades of magnolia, and a thin layer of plaster dust covered everything.

'Will this do?' Miss McArdle asked.

'It's fine,' I said. 'All it needs now is a whiteboard.' Every incident room has a whiteboard.

'I'll fetch one,' she said, and big Dave Sparkington turned to follow her.

'Dave's quiet,' I said to Jeff Caton. 'Is he OK?'

'He thought we were rid of you for a few days, that's all,' he replied.

'This'll be sorted by tomorrow,' I assured him. 'Then you'll all be able to sit around reading the football pages and swapping boozy stories for the remainder of the week.'

When they returned with the board I asked Miss McArdle and John, the security firm's superintendent, to stay and started the meeting in the time-honoured way: 'OK, what have we got?' I asked, raising the marker pen expectantly.

'Not much from me,' the SOCO replied. 'I've no doubt collected a few microscopic samples, but they're all mixed up and contaminated and it would cost a fortune in time and effort to amplify and separate them. And then what do we compare them with? Anybody who's been in the mall this morning could have left a sample. DNA will be floating around like snowflakes in a blizzard. So don't wait for anything from me because you'll be wasting your time.'

'Well thanks for being so positive,' I said, lowering the pen and turning to the photographer. 'Did you get some decent pictures?'

'Yes, boss, but I don't see how they can help with the investigation.'

'No, they can't, but they'll be essential if it ever goes to court. Miss McArdle…'

'Yes?'

'When was the last time we can vouch for the offending word not being there?'

While she was thinking about it John of security said: 'I can answer that, Inspector. Mr Threadneedle was here until about nine o'clock last night, making sure everything was working well. He tried the curtains about a hundred times and then we left the dais roped off with two of my men looking after it with strict instructions not to leave it unattended. Mr Threadneedle was adamant about that.'

'Threadneedle?' I queried. 'Is he the lord mayor?'

'The mayor. He's just the mayor,' somebody told me.

'That's him,' John confirmed.

'I'm sorry, John, but I don't know your second name.'

'It's Brighouse, sir. John Brighouse.'

'Call me Charlie. So the offence was committed some time between nine last night and eleven this morning.' I wrote it on the board. 'I need some information from either you or Miss McArdle. First of all, a full list of all the names of your security staff, with another list of those who were here between nine last night and eleven this morning. And I'd like another list of all the names of the dignitaries present at the opening ceremony.' I looked at the manager. 'Do you think you could do those for me as soon as possible, please?'

She said they could, and the two of them left. I said: 'Right, so now we're alone, what do we know about Threadneedle?'

'He's a crook,' big Dave Sparkington replied.

'He's a pillar of society,' someone contradicted.

'The mayor of our fair town.'

'The economic crime unit have been trying to get their hands on him for years.'

'You mean the department formerly known as the fraud squad.'

'The shiny-trousers branch.'

'The same.'

I could see a spin-off. We might not catch the phantom painter, but investigating our beloved mayor might turn up a few smelly surprises. 'What's he supposed to have done?' I asked.

'He's rich,' somebody supplied.

'Believe it or not, that's still not a crime,' I said.

'It is if you were born in a caravan in Ireland, never went to school, earned a living working the lump and now owned a big share of this.' The speaker wafted a hand around, demonstrating that he was talking about the building we were sitting in.

'He owns shares in this?' I asked.

'Allegedly,' Brendan, one of my DCs said. Brendan is a collector of conspiracy theories, and prone to go off on uncontrolled tangents. 'It's been in the papers, boss. Don't you read them?'

'He owns shares in Monkton's,' I was told. 'They were the major contractors. And he owns part of several of the subcontractors. Him being on the approvals committee can't have prejudiced their chances of lifting the contract.'

'And he drives a powder-blue Rolls-Royce.'

'Ooh, powder blue – how *passé*,' one of the comics commented in an appropriate accent.

'It's not that simple, Chas,' Jeff Caton stated. 'He has fingers in lots of pies. It's not subcontractors – more like subcontractors to subcontractors, et cetera. And, of course, his position on the council will have helped push through the necessary compulsory purchase orders. Fraud have looked good and hard at him, but his affairs are labyrinthine. He made a pile as a racehorse owner, which just about excuses him from normal investigation.'

What Jeff meant was that he could claim to have made his money in any number of ways associated with the industry, from gambling to stabling horses and selling bags of manure, without keeping accurate records. We'd have to give him the benefit of any doubts.

'So how did he get to be the mayor?'

'He was democratically elected as a councillor, and eventually it was his turn. He said the right things that the tosspots understood, and the rest was due to apathy.'

'He's made the buses run on time,' Brendan told us.

'Listen,' I began. 'I know we all think this is hilarious but the chief constable has his teeth into it and he'll want me to keep him informed, so let's cut out the messing about and get on with it. Understood?'

They mumbled their assent and Jeff said: 'Did you find anything, Chas?'

'Not much, but I did notice one thing that I thought interesting: it wasn't done with a spray can. The paint looks like acrylic, as used by some artists, and there were brush marks. I'd say it was applied with a stiff brush.'

'Was the paint dry?' asked Maggie Madison, one of the two female officers in the team.

'Yes, but acrylic dries in a few minutes and sets like concrete. That's why I never use it. If you don't clean your brush every two minutes you ruin it, and they don't come cheap.'

'What are you supposed to clean them in?' Brendan wondered.

'Only water. That's the main attraction of the paint.

What's uppermost in my mind at the moment is who was the intended target? Who was the painter aiming his offence at?'

Jeff held up a hand and counted them off on his fingers: 'Miss Curzon – does she have a jilted boyfriend? Threadneedle – he must have dozens of enemies. The Centre in general – there was quite a bit of opposition to it.'

'Anybody else?' I invited. Dave Sparkington was sitting with his head bowed, elbows on his knees, doing his impression of Rodin's *The Thinker*. I said: 'Come on then, Dave. I can see words of wisdom bubbling up inside you, so let's have them.'

'We're wasting time, aren't we?' he pronounced.

'Go on,' I invited.

'It wasn't aimed at anybody. If it had been, the wassock who did it would have put *Fuck you*, not just *Fuck*. It was some twelve-year-old kid who thinks painting that word is the most daring thing he's ever done. It could have been any one of the kids from the high school.'

'Sounds reasonable,' I agreed. 'Have a word with any graffiti artists we have on the books. One of them might know who it is, and he won't be popular with them for drawing the heat their way. In fact, lean on them, hard. Meanwhile, let's have a brainstorm. I reckon finding the paint is priority. Where do we start looking?'

The ideas came thick and fast. Our starting point was that the culprit remained on the premises after closing time and left whenever he could, probably abandoning the paint and any disguise he'd worn. The finger pointed at an inside job, meaning the security staff or the cleaners who came scrabbling into the place after hours, like the undead hiding from the light.

We went back to the factory and composed a leaflet to distribute to all the shops and businesses in the Centre. It asked them to look anywhere where our culprit could have hidden overnight, and to search for a tin or tube of paint and a brush concealed on their premises. We ran off five hundred copies and I sent the troops back there mob-handed to distribute them and suss out the security in general. While they were doing that I made appointments to see Councillor Arthur George Threadneedle, Mayor of Heckley, and Miss Ghislaine Curzon, Enslaver of Princes. I knew which one I was most looking forward to.

CHAPTER THREE

It was easier than we thought. At eight-fifteen Tuesday morning the manageress of Lucy's Frock Shop rang to say that while putting out a rack of cheesecloth buy-one-get-one-free ra-ra skirts she'd noticed what looked like a tube of paint tucked away underneath one of the marble seats that were a feature of the Centre. I wondered at what stage in their careers manageresses became managers and hotfooted it round there. She was an avid watcher of all the scene of crime TV programmes that flood our late-evening schedules and had done exactly the right thing. She'd cordoned off the seat with a row of chairs and sent for me. The villains watch TV, too, and are becoming more forensically aware, so it's a pleasant change when it works in our favour. She was probably hoping for George Clooney but didn't look too disappointed with Charlie Priest.

It was a tube of WH Smith's own-brand acrylic paint in rose madder, and was half empty. A toothbrush lay alongside of it, the head a blob of hard paint. I put both items in evidence bags and congratulated the manageress on her powers of observation.

The troops were up in the incident room, finishing cups of coffee and sharing out the tasks when I entered, holding the evidence bags high in the air like the executioner with Marie Antoinette's severed head.

'Ta-da!' I called. 'Charlie does it again.'

Jeff Caton was on the telephone and he waved a hand to tell us to make less noise. 'How long ago?' he asked, followed by: 'Give me the address again.'

'Robbery,' he told us as he slipped his phone back in its holster. 'The pit bull gang strikes again, but this time it's on our turf.'

There'd been a spate of robberies in Lancashire by a two-man gang armed with a slavering pit bull terrier. They terrorised their victims, threatening to set the dog on any children present, and stealing jewellery, credit cards and cash. And now they were operating on our patch. Either that or we had a copycat.

'Tell us more,' I said.

'Couple with two children. One of them took the wife to the nearest ATM machine and drew six hundred pounds on her two cards. Left them all tied to chairs but they managed to get loose.'

'I'm supposed to be interviewing Threadneedle shortly, and the Curzons later. You wouldn't prefer to see them, would you?'

He was already stuffing his notebook into his pocket and clicking the top on his pen. 'I don't think so, Chas. You're the acceptable face of the force. I'll stick with the common criminals.'

'Then take Serena,' I said. 'She's a dog lover.'

Serena's our second female member and the youngest on the team. We give her all the jobs involving children and weeping women, and, it goes without saying, any involving denizens of the subcontinent. 'Aw,' she protested, 'I wanted to come with you to meet Ghislaine.'

'Boss's perks,' I said with a grin. 'You get the pit bull.'

When they'd gone I said: 'OK, where are we with it?'

'I've spent the last two hours going through the dumpsters out the back,' Maggie told us, 'and you come breezing in with the evidence, smelling of roses. I smell of yesterday's KFC skins. It's not fair.'

'So that's you and Serena disgruntled. I must be losing my touch. And for the record, it's *He* by Armani, not roses.' I turned to Brendan. 'What about you, my little leprechaun assistant? How gruntled are you, this bright morning?'

'I'm perfectly gruntled, boss. Never been more gruntled.'

'So what conspiracy theory have you come up with for this one?'

'Nothing really. We've looked for the paint in all the litter bins and in every nook and granny we could find, but you beat us to it.'

'Nook and granny?' I queried.

'Oops, did I say nook and granny? Freudian – it'd be more fun.'

'Go on.'

'This place closes for shoppers at ten but most are winding down before then. Every shop has some sort of grille that closes off the front. At the moment there are five security staff on through the night, including the one in the control room. The CCTV is digital, state of the art, with fully controllable recording, zoom and panning. We've asked for the disks. The cleaning staff come on at eleven and are done by three...'

He droned on and I nodded in what I hoped were appropriate places. It all sounded secure and well organised, except that the security men would do a quick patrol to satisfy themselves everything was as it should be, then crash out for the remainder of their shift, and the cleaning staff were not exactly Mensa material. Well, most of them weren't.

'It sounds like an inside job,' I declared, feeling somewhat self-conscious at using the term. 'Collate all the names and work out a schedule for interviewing everybody. If we lean hard enough someone will crack.'

Threadneedle's house was in the part of town where the new money lived. He was two doors away from the manager of Heckley Town football club on one side and next door to the owner of a string of entertainment venues, like bingo halls and lap dancing clubs, on the other. The doors in question were about a decent nine-iron drive apart.

His driveway was block paved, the grass like velvet,

and dwarf ornamental trees – weeping willows and acers – marked the curves of the approach to the front portico as if delineating a slalom course. No sign of a Rolls-Royce, just a Lexus, shining like a bowl of morello cherries, standing outside the house with its boot lid raised. As I parked behind it Threadneedle appeared carrying a bag of golf clubs which, after sparing a glance at his visitor, he unceremoniously dumped into the back of the Lexus. He brushed his hands together and turned towards me.

'Mr Threadneedle,' I said as I pushed the door of my humble Vauxhall closed. 'DI Priest. Thanks for finding the time to see me.' A collared dove landed on the lawn, looked at us and flew off.

'My pleasure, Inspector,' he replied expansively, arm extended. 'It's nice to see you in the flesh after hearing so much about you. I'm deputy chairman of the Police Authority, you know, and you get more mentions in the minutes than the chairman does. Heckley's lucky to have you.'

'Yeah, I think so too,' I agreed, and he laughed out loud and slapped me on the shoulder.

His wife is a midget. Not a clinically defined midget but she's a good head shorter than he is and he's barely average height. You could tell that she'd been a looker in her youth, but the ravages of high office had taken their toll, and now she looked stressed out and ravaged. Her hairstyle was lopsided and her lipstick, which had been applied with a palette knife, was bleeding at the corners. *Either high office or the booze,* I thought, noting the well-stocked bar in the corner.

We were in what I suppose was a sitting room, surrounded by reproduction auction house furniture designed to prevent visitors becoming too comfortable, and photos and mementos of Threadneedle's career in public life. He'd shaken hands with Freddie Trueman and stood next to Jimmy Savile at a fund-raising event. Big deal. I'd played in goal, one time only, for Halifax Town reserves, but I don't have photographs of it all over the house.

'Tea or coffee, Inspector?' he was asking as I took in my surroundings.

I didn't really need either, but he was wanting to be off golfing and I wanted to cultivate a chatty, man-to-man atmosphere. 'A coffee, please,' I replied. 'It must be nearly an hour since my last one.' He chuckled again, and I wished I had someone like him in all my audiences.

'Do you mind, Janet?' he said, gesturing towards the door.

His wife turned to me, saying: 'Or would you prefer, you know, something a little stronger?'

'Just a black coffee, please,' I said, giving her my lopsided smile.

'Janet, Janet,' Threadneedle chided. 'Mr Priest is on duty. Perhaps we'll be able to offer him our hospitality some other time, in the future.'

'So how is the investigation going?' he asked when she'd left the room. 'Are you any nearer catching the scum who did it? Flogging's too good for them, if you ask me.'

'We've found the tube of paint and it's gone for fingerprint testing. Do you have any ideas who might have done it?'

'Well, I've got enemies, if that's what you mean. Nobody I could name, but I've trodden on a few toes, particularly with the Curzon Centre, and people bear grudges, don't they? But...you know...I'd like to think my enemies were a bit more subtle. I've given it a lot of thought overnight and have concluded that someone was put up to it. Someone young, by somebody else who wouldn't want to dirty their own hands, and we've plenty like that in the town.'

'Anyone you'd like to name?'

He shook his head. 'No, I don't think so.'

'You seem to have taken it personally. You think it was aimed at yourself rather than Miss Curzon?'

'Oh, it was aimed at me, Inspector. Rest assured of that.'

Mrs Threadneedle came in bearing a tray with three coffees and a jug of cream. The cups rattled in their saucers as she tipped the tray and lowered it precariously towards the little table that her husband hastily produced. It landed like a Vulcan bomber on the deck of an aircraft carrier and coffee slopped over the sides of the cups. Neither of them seemed to notice.

We talked for another ten minutes or so without me learning anything of interest. The graffiti had hurt him, that was for sure, so perhaps his enemies were subtler than he believed. Next to money, Threadneedle's guiding light was his standing in the community and his fear of ridicule.

Frankly, my dear, I didn't give a toss. The tabloids would report the incident tomorrow with their usual decorum and by Thursday it would all be forgotten. Then I'd be back to the robberies. Except that the incident, as we'd started to call it, was an opening into another world. A world we only ever glimpsed the fringes of when we visited a stately home, or saw over a high wall as we drove by. A world that guarded its membership jealously. Old money and class struggling against the tide of new money and vulgarity, and I was as intrigued as any suburban housewife with her Aga boiler and *Country Life* magazines.

A big shaggy dog was having a pee against the front wheel of my car when we walked outside. 'Shoo, Wolfgang, shoo,' Threadneedle shouted at it, pointing into the distance, and the animal slinked off round the side of the house. 'Looks like he's staked his claim to your car, Inspector. Sorry about that.'

'It's had worse. Wolfgang?'

'As in Mozart. Blame the wife.'

'Right. He's a weird-looking animal.'

'Yeah. Got him from the rescue place to be company for Janet while I'm away, but he's got a bit smelly in his old age.'

I nodded towards his car's boot. 'Where do you play?'

'The golf? Oh, I'm going down to the Belfry for a couple of days; meeting up with some business associates. You know how it is.'

I didn't, but I nodded sympathetically. It was a chore, but it had to be done. We shook hands...I made the usual noises about seeing him again...if he thought of anything else...please thank Mrs Threadneedle for the coffee...and that was that. Duty done and the sun was shining like fury. I hung my jacket behind my seat and pointed the

car towards the motorway and East Yorkshire, abode of
the Curzon dynasty. I was early, so for a relaxing hour
or so I was just another anonymous rep driving his bog-
standard fleet car between appointments. I flicked round
the radio stations and caught Bonnie Tyler's 'Total Eclipse
of the Heart', singing along with her for the few words I
knew: 'Turn around, bright eyes...'

I'd made enquiries and the best anybody could tell me
was that the occupant of Curzon House was simply a
mister. Mr James Sebastian Curzon. I didn't know why
– the British aristocratic hierarchy is a mystery to me.
Perhaps an older brother inherited the family title, if
there'd ever been one, and ran off to Tasmania with a
chambermaid, taking the title with him. I saw the sign I
was looking for and turned into a narrow lane. A mile
further on it was left again past a raised barrier and
through some open ornate gates. A painted board told
me that I was at Curzon House and the tea shop and
gardens were open every day except Monday, from Good
Friday until October.

The house was a three-storey cube, made of yellow
stone with raised pointing, topped off with a confusion
of chimneys and dormer windows. The chimney pots were
tall and crenellated, like the crowns worn by wise men in
a Greek Orthodox nativity show. One of the roof windows
was catching the sun and reflecting it into my eyes, as if
some mad relative imprisoned up there was signalling for
help. Beyond the house, round the back, I could see more
buildings – glasshouses and what looked like the outside
of a walled garden. Presumably the tearooms, plant sales

and gift shop were round there, too. Gravel rattled against
the underside of the car as I approached the front door
and wondered where to park. I felt I ought to be driving
a brougham drawn by four chestnut mares, or at least
a Humber Super Snipe. I stopped right at the entrance,
yanked the handbrake on and swung my legs out.

The door opened after the first push of the porcelain
button and I found myself gazing into the gloomy interior
of Curzon House. When I lowered my gaze I saw her. She
was about the same height as Mrs Threadneedle and was
wearing thick spectacles and an Adidas tracksuit. Estimated
age: about twelve, but I'm no expert.

'DI Priest,' I said. 'I've an appointment to see Miss
Curzon.'

'You're the cop?'

'I'm a police officer.'

'I'm Miss Curzon.'

'Oh. I was expecting you to be older.'

'A common mistake. I'm Brains, she's Looks. You want
Looks. Actually, she's got the brains, too, but I have to
fight back, don't I?'

'I'm sure you've both got a fair share of each...either...
both...whatever.' For God's sake, I thought, she's a kid.
Pull yourself together.

'I think it's *each*.'

'Yes, I think so too. Is...Miss Curzon, um, senior...
available?'

'No. Her and Daddy have gone to see one of the dexters
that's just calved. Grizzly rang to say they'll be about twenty
minutes and I've to keep you entertained till then.'

'*She*,' I said. '*She* and Daddy.'

'Is it?'

'I think so.'

'Oh.' She beamed up at me and I saw that the plain Jane look was just a temporary phase. In a couple of years she'd shed a few feathers, polish those that remained and be pulling the ducks off the water as easily as skin off a rice pudding.

'Who's Grizzly?' I asked as she stepped past me, into the sunlight, and sat on the balustrade.

'Looks, Ghislaine. Everybody calls her Grizzly.'

'Thank you. And what's a dexter?'

'It's a cow. Daddy breeds them.'

'Right. So how are you going to entertain me?'

I was hoping she'd offer to show me round, but she said: 'Do you play tennis?'

'I could, years ago.'

'Would you like a game?'

'Um, if you like.'

'Or would you prefer to see the badger sett?'

'Er, tennis, please.'

It was as if I'd wound up a clockwork doll and set it going. She jumped to her feet and brushed the hair off her eyes. 'You would? Honest? I'll get the rackets.' She dashed into the house and reappeared in seconds, carrying two high-tech-looking rackets made of carbon fibre or some other spin-off from the space race. The last one I used was made of bamboo and catgut. 'It's round the back,' she said, marching off, and I turned to follow her, wondering what I'd set in motion.

It was a proper court, laid in some sort of red composite material, with a high netting fence around it. Dozens of tennis balls were scattered all over, like windfalls in a Golden Delicious orchard. 'Let's get rid of some of these,' I said, deciding it was time to assert my crumbling authority, and kicked the nearest ball into a corner. 'You'd break your ankle if you stepped on one. Six is plenty. I don't know your name,' I said as she joined in the kicking.

'Toby, and don't say it's a boy's name.'

'Is it?'

'Everybody tells me it is. I didn't like my original name so Daddy said I could change it. I chose Tobias, shortened to Toby. Loads of girls have boys' names, don't they?'

'I know what you mean. I'm called Charlie. Now nearly every woman I meet is called Charlie.'

'Ahah! There you go, then. Can I call you Charlie?'

'When I'm off duty.'

'Are you off duty when you're playing tennis?'

'I suppose I am.'

'OK, Charlie. I'll serve first. I have to warn you that I'm a demon server.'

She wasn't joking. It cleared the net at about Mach 4, made a *vvvrriip* noise as it bounced, and rattled against the wire behind me, all before I'd transferred my weight to the appropriate foot. I was in big trouble, so I took the only course left open to me.

'Out!' I called.

Her shoulders slumped and the racket trailed on the ground. 'Was it out?' she asked, forlornly.

'No,' I replied. 'It was a good one. Fifteen-love.'

I missed the next two but she was so surprised when I got one back that it went straight past her. Then she wrapped it up and it was my serve.

Her backhand was hopeless so I played to it and regained some respectability as she continually hit her returns into the net. I was beginning to realise that she spent hours practising on her own, blasting them aimlessly with nobody there to hit them back.

As we changed ends I said: 'Show me how you hold the racket.' It was the standard shaking-hands grip. 'And how when the ball's on your backhand?'

'The same.'

'OK. So from now on I want you to rotate the racket in your grip...like this...' I demonstrated, holding her wrist '...whenever the ball's coming over to your left. It's a lot easier than it looks. Just try it for a few minutes, see what you think.'

We played pat-a-ball for a while and soon her returns were clearing the net and giving me the run-around. I was beginning to puff when a burst of derisory applause behind me caused me to turn and I had my first in-the-flesh sight of the celebrated Miss Curzon senior. And her father. I waved to Toby, signalling that the game was over, and went to meet them.

'DI Priest,' I said, and we shook hands. 'Miss Curzon, Mr Curzon.'

Toby had joined us. 'Charlie's showed me how to hit backhands,' she blurted.

Ghislaine turned to her. '*Inspector* to you, young lady,'

she said. 'And we expected you to offer him a drink, not a game of tennis.'

'My fault,' I said. 'I was offered the option and chose tennis. She's a very talented player. Beat me fair and square.' I winked at her and she gave me a half smile.

'We'll believe you,' Curzon said. 'Let's go inside.'

We walked back towards the house, leaving Toby behind, and a few seconds later I heard the *plunk...plunk...* of tennis balls being smashed pointlessly across the court.

We drank instant coffee from mugs that grated on your teeth, seated at a refectory table in a kitchen that once had buzzed with action. At one end an old iron range stood, a cold and indifferent observer of feasts and orgies in years gone by. Now it was decorated with copper pans and strange utensils for obscure culinary tasks. A two-gallon kettle hung on the spindle that had once held a rotating boar or a swan stuffed with skylarks. Sunlight streamed in through the tiny windows and everything glowed in shades of gold and orange. Ghislaine Curzon wore faded jeans and a check shirt and was everything I imagined she'd be. Freckles spanned her face, I noticed. Why do freckles make my knees go weak?

'How's the dexter?' I asked.

'Fine,' Curzon told me. 'They're both fine. They're hardy little beasts.'

'Heifer or a bull?' All those years listening to *The Archers* hadn't been wasted.

'A heifer.'

'Good. How many do you have?'

'Ten. Eleven now. They're a little sideline, that's all.'

I turned to Ghislaine. 'So who did the graffiti, Miss Curzon? Any ideas?' She looked awkward for a moment, or was it my imagination? Perhaps it was simply the recollection of an embarrassing moment. I didn't allow it any importance.

'No,' she replied. 'You're the policeman.'

'But you know your friends and enemies. Any boyfriends still holding a torch for you?' I would have liked to talk to them separately, but it felt inappropriate to say so, and she'd hardly confess to having sex with half the men in the village whether her father was present or not. Not that I thought for one second that the wholesome Ghislaine – Grizzly, was it? – would do such a thing.

'I can't think of anyone,' she replied.

Now that was a lie, if ever I heard one. She was twenty-five years old, fairly rich and beautiful. Girls like that attract all sorts of attention, plenty of it from nutters and chancers. 'I'd like you to think about it,' I said, then went on: 'How do you feel about the incident? Have you got over it?'

Now she looked sheepish. 'It was hilarious. Embarrassing for everyone, but it was almost worth it to see the expression on the face of that pompous twit who calls himself the mayor.'

'Threadneedle?'

'That's the man.'

'Can I ask how you became involved with the Curzon Centre?' I flapped a hand around and stumbled on: 'You're obviously well connected, for want of a better expression,

but at what point was it named after you? And when were
you invited to open it?'

'About two years ago,' Ghislaine said, 'it became public
knowledge that I was friendly with, you know, one of the
royal princes. Shortly afterwards Threadneedle wrote to
me, saying that he was an old friend of Daddy's and would
I be interested, et cetera et cetera. We thought, why not?
We couldn't stop him calling it the Curzon Centre and I
thought my friendship would have fizzled out long before
the Centre was completed, but it sounded like good fun. I
talked to Daddy about it and then told Mr Threadneedle
I'd be flattered and delighted. He wasn't the mayor then, of
course, but was chairman of the development committee,
or something like that, and wielded all the power.'

'And he probably knew that he'd be mayor when it
opened,' I said. 'There's usually some sort of progression
with the title.' I turned to her father and asked: 'Did you
know him? Was he an old friend?'

Curzon shuffled in his seat and looked uncomfortable.
He was wearing pressed jeans with leather brogues, a
white shirt and a tweed jacket with leather-reinforced
cuffs. It probably cost about three hundred pounds from
Bond Street and had been repaired several times. 'I knew
him slightly,' he admitted. 'Back in the Eighties, early
Nineties, we owned a couple of racehorses. Or my wife
did. I humoured her. She enjoyed going to the races and
we sometimes saw Threadneedle in the owners' enclosure.
Rarely in the winners' enclosure, sadly.' He allowed himself
a wry smile as he remembered the folly and the enjoyment
of those days.

'Mummy died in ninety-six,' Ghislaine explained.

'I'm sorry. I didn't know.'

'She'd been ill for a long time,' Curzon went on, looking out of the window. 'She loved her racing. Christmas Day, it was. We were planning to go to the Wetherby Boxing Day meeting, but she was too poorly. Died later that night. I haven't seen Threadneedle since some time before then.'

We chatted for a while about policing and the weather and the risks of backing horses compared to the stock market. I rounded things up by asking how concerned they were about the graffiti incident.

Curzon shrugged his shoulders and looked at his daughter. Ghislaine looked at me. I went dry in the mouth.

'It's water under the bridge, as far as I'm concerned,' she said. 'Presumably they've removed the plaque and will either clean it up or replace it. Or perhaps they should leave it as it is and call it a reflection of the times. That might be fun.' She smiled at me and the five thousand midget Cossack dancers that live in my nether regions slapped their thighs and shouted 'Hoy!' in unison. I tried a nonchalant smile back but it felt all wrong from my side and probably came out as a cheesy grin.

Curzon said: 'We were quite surprised when we heard an inspector was coming, but presumably it's all part of the chief constable's zero tolerance initiative.'

I didn't know anything about a zero tolerance initiative, but I nodded my agreement. 'That and the fact that it was a breach of security,' I added. 'That's where the criticism will lie. General consensus is that the perpetrator was a malicious youth doing it for kicks, that's all, but we've got

to run with it, just in case.' By 'general consensus' I meant
big Dave and me. I turned to Ghislaine. 'Will you be at
home, Miss Curzon, if I need to speak to you again?'

Her cheeks turned pink under the freckles and she
rotated her coffee mug in her fingers. Curzon stared at
her, his face a blank but eloquent mask.

'I'm not sure,' she admitted, sheepishly. 'I might go
away for a few days.'

I let it sink in. What she meant was that she might
be visiting her aristocratic friend, to do what they'd been
doing to the rest of us for a thousand years. And Daddy
wasn't pleased. I changed the subject. 'Do you have any
trouble with the paparazzi?'

'Here? No, not really. I keep well hidden, and they're
not the types to relish camping in Yorkshire for days on
end. They come, grow discouraged and leave. The people
in the village are used to seeing me around and give them
short shrift.'

'OK. Well, thank you both for your hospitality. And
Toby, too. She's quite a character.'

'I think you've made a friend there, Inspector,' Curzon
said.

Ghislaine walked me to the door and closed it behind
me. The gravel drive led round in a big arc, everywhere
was neatly cropped grass and the only limit to the view
was the wall of heavily laden trees that stood like silent
witnesses as they had done for hundreds of years. I opened
the car door and leant on it for a few seconds, wondering if
Constable had ever painted there. Blackbirds and thrushes
foraged for worms on the lawns, a flock of swallows –

or were they swifts? – wheeled and dived overhead, and behind all the screeching, whistling and cawing, almost lost, was the steady *plunk...plunk...plunk* of young Toby, measuring her skill against a wire-netting cage. I slid into the driving seat and started the engine.

Threadneedle had told me he was going down to the Belfry for a few days, but I didn't think Mrs Threadneedle was present when he said it. I ran the scene through my brain. That was right: he'd walked out to the car with me. He said it after we caught the dog, Wolfgang, staking his claim to my offside front wheel. I pulled into a lay-by just before the end of Curzon's lane and dialled his number. Mrs Threadneedle answered quicker than an Indian call centre, like in about ten minutes.

'Mrs Threadneedle?'

'That's right. Who is this, please?'

'Detective Inspector Charlie Priest. I came to see your husband this morning. I was wondering if I could pop in to see him again, in about an hour? I have a few more questions for him. Nothing important – just background information.'

'I'm sorry, Inspector, but he's gone away on business for a few days. Is it anything I could help you with?'

'Um, that's very kind of you. I'm in my car at the moment. Will it be all right if I call, in about an hour, perhaps a bit less?'

'I'll be expecting you, Inspector.'

Sometimes, I don't know where I get it from. Look for the weakest link, that's my guiding principle. I turned out on to the lane, towards the A64, and imagined the diminutive Janet dashing around the house with her feather duster, plumping up the cushions, waiting for her inspector to call.

Perhaps I did her an injustice. She was upright and coherent and politely welcoming. Or maybe she could hold her liquor. I asked for a coffee again, when invited, and this time she managed to keep most of it within the confines of the cup. She was wearing a pretend-velour jogging suit the colour of unripe bananas and as she lowered the cup in front of me her newly refreshed perfume hit me like an avalanche in a potpourri quarry. I'd found myself a seat in an easy chair; she curled up at one end of a settee.

'How can I help you, Inspector?' she asked, leaning forward, her chin on her fist. Her slippers had long pointed toes, and with a matching hat she'd have made a passable pea pod in a fancy-dress contest. I looked past her and saw the glass and Gordon's bottle on the floor beside her settee.

'I haven't made much progress,' I confessed. 'Trouble is, we're still not sure who was the target of the vandalism: your husband or Miss Curzon. Or perhaps both of them. How well did you know the Curzons?'

'Not too well. We haven't seen them for years. Ghislaine was just a little girl, and look at her now. Quite regal, don't you think?'

'You knew them through horse racing, didn't you?'

'That's right. For a short while we had a small stable near Malton but it burnt down. Arthur had applied for a trainer's licence. Before that he had shares in a horse called Shergar. You might remember it. He introduced Mr Curzon to the right people and he became a joint owner, too.'

'Shergar!' I exclaimed. 'You mean the horse that vanished? It won the Derby, didn't it?' I was taken by surprise but it soon subsided. The two big unsolved mysteries of my lifetime were what happened to Shergar and where was Lord Lucan, but I doubted if I was hot on the trail of either. I decided she was as nutty as a fruitcake.

'That's right,' she replied. 'The IRA kidnapped it. The Aga Khan sold shares in it when it went to stud, and Arthur introduced Mr Curzon to the syndicate manager. I imagine they both had their fingers burnt when it vanished but you'll have to ask Arthur for the details. He doesn't tell me anything.'

'Was it insured?'

'I don't know.'

I was wasting time, heading up a blind alley, so I decided to push things along. 'Did you ever meet Mrs Curzon?' I asked.

'Oh yes. She was a lovely woman, no edge to her at all. Not very well, though. I don't know what was the matter with her but she died a few years ago. We didn't know about it until weeks afterwards, or we would have sent some flowers. I was disappointed about that.'

'Has your husband mentioned any names when you've talked about the graffiti incident? Or does any acquaintance stand out as a suspect?'

She shook her head.

'Any problems with the neighbours, Mrs Threadneedle?'

'No. And call me Jan, please.'

'Right. Jan. Any disgruntled employees that you might know of?'

'I can't think of any.'

'Has Arthur appeared under any extra stress lately?'

'Well, yes. But that's down to the opening of the Centre. There was always the chance that it wouldn't be ready on time.'

'I see. But otherwise, he's been OK?'

'Fine. He's been fine. To tell the truth, he has a bit of a *thing* about Ghislaine. I think it's his age, an older man's crush, that sort of thing. He was looking forward to meeting her more than he'd ever admit to me.'

I knew the feeling. An older man's crush; was that it? As Dave once said: 'If you've got to be an old man you might as well be a dirty one.' I thanked Mrs Threadneedle for her assistance and stood up to leave, saying I'd had a busy day.

'I never offered you a proper drink,' she said, struggling to her feet. 'I'm sure you deserve one.'

It might have been my imagination, or wishful thinking, but I'd swear the zipper on her jogging top had crept an inch or two down towards her navel. 'Not while I'm driving,' I said, rather meekly.

'Are you sure?'

'Positive.'

'That's a pity.'

'Tell me,' I said. 'Is Arthur Irish?'

'He pretends to be. His father was, but he came over here years ago, before Arthur was born. Made a fortune building roads and what have you, and lost most of it. When he died of cirrhosis of the liver Arthur took over the business. We've done very well out of it, as you can see.'

'You certainly have,' I replied, taking in the Ashley Jackson watercolours and the glass coffee table balanced on a tangle of driftwood, but the expression on her face told that the benefits of wealth had bypassed her. She'd gained a fur coat and an architect-designed house, but lost a marriage. 'Threadneedle's not an Irish name, is it?'

She said: 'No. It was his mother's name. I think he wanted to deny his Irish roots. Thought he'd do better in business as an Englishman.'

'There's a local legend that says he was born in a caravan in rural Ireland. Is it not true?'

'Not a word of it. He's a chameleon, changing his colours to please the people he happens to be dealing with. That's his romantic side. He was actually born in St James's hospital in Leeds. You know what they say: the further you get from the Old Country, the more vociferous are the immigrants.'

I nodded. 'He seems to know what he's doing.'

We were standing barely a yard apart, me towering over her, she looking up into my face. She said: 'He hasn't gone to the Belfry to play golf with his business chums, you know.'

'Hasn't he?'

'No. He's said he was going there on several occasions before. Last June it was his birthday while he was away, so I hid a birthday card in his bag of clubs. It was still there when he came home three days later. They'd never been out of the car boot. And there've been other times... other...lies...'

'I'm sorry,' I said, turning to leave, but the little bit of me that I despise was filing the information for future use. *Knowledge is power*, it whispered in my ear.

CHAPTER FOUR

Toby would never make a top tennis player, and that thought made me unhappy. She just wasn't tall enough. Tennis matches, like presidential elections, always go to the taller candidate. I was on my way back to the office before the evening rush started, with both visors down against the low glare of the sun. The lights changed and we moved off. I was disappointed that I hadn't questioned Ghislaine more, but she was in an odd position. I could have gone to any of the celebrity magazines and sold anything she confided in me for a year's salary, so her answers to my questions would have been guarded and worthless. No matter, fingerprints would have it all sewn up by now. They'd have found some prints on the paint tube and matched them against the database. If they hadn't lifted the culprit already it was only because they'd decided to wait until I could be in on the action.

Working the lump, it was called. After the war thousands of Irishmen came over to England to repair the damage done by the Luftwaffe, and, later, to build the motorway network. They worked in gangs, for gang masters, and didn't bother with inconveniences like health and safety, or taxation. It was a hard-drinking culture, with tales of thirty pints of beer per day quite common. If you didn't fit in, you were out on your neck. The smart ones sent their money home and returned to the Old Country as rich men, the dumb and the gullible wrecked their bodies and paid the price. It looked as if Threadneedle senior was somewhere in between, but his son had been more ambitious, had seen beyond where the next drink was coming from, had glimpsed the distant, sunlit uplands and decided he wanted to bask there. And who could blame him?

Jeff Caton was in the office when I arrived back at the nick, looking harassed.

'Tell me about the robbery,' I said. It was closer to my heart than chasing vandals and pandering to high society.

'It's frightening, Chas,' he replied. 'The kids are terrified and their parents are not much better. I don't think there'll be much sleeping done in that household for a week or two. The villain with the dog babysat the husband and children while the other one took the mother to the cash machine. It was straining at its leash and foaming at the mouth, trying to get at them. The tosspot holding its chain was barely in control, they said.'

'Descriptions?'

'Both above average height and well built. Wearing overalls and wrap-round shades, with NY baseball caps pulled down over their faces. And they wore surgical gloves.'

'Great,' I said. 'I'm coming to the conclusion that the general public know more about forensics than we do. How've you left it?'

'Serena's still with them. I'm seeing West Pennine in the morning to compare notes. A couple of neighbours report seeing a Jaguar that might be interesting. Dark grey, no number. We're checking for stolen ones.'

'So nobody local springs into the frame?'

He shook his head. 'No, but it will be interesting to see where the other robberies were. It might give us an idea where they're coming from.'

'Their *locus of operations*. Don't hold your breath. It might be easier to find the dog.'

'I know. Pit bulls are not everybody's idea of a four-legged friend.'

His phone rang and a second later Dave and Brendan came bustling through the door.

'Caton,' Jeff said.

Dave walked to the coffee-making table and held a cup up and I nodded a 'Yes, please'.

'We haven't taken delivery yet, Mr Wood,' I heard Jeff say, then: 'Yes, it's a pity this morning's victims hadn't been supplied with it. OK, I'll chase it up.' He replaced the phone.

'What was that about?'

'SmartWater. Mr Wood wondering if we were any nearer to getting some.'

'Neighbourhood Watch will have complained,' I said.

SmartWater is a magic liquid that you spray on valuable items and around windows, et cetera. We weren't sure how it worked but it made villains glow in the dark, and therefore more easily identified. At least, that's what we'd been led to believe it did. We'd never actually seen any. A neighbouring town, Todmorden, had pioneered its use and witnessed an immediate reduction in home burglaries of eighty-four per cent. I couldn't help thinking that a decimal point had been mislaid, but about six months ago the good citizens of Heckley had forked out ten pounds per household and were still waiting.

'Did you see Threadneedle?' Jeff asked.

I gestured towards the others as Serena came in. 'Wait until this lot join us.'

Dave brought my coffee and collected another chair for Serena as she hung her jacket behind the door. Brendan fetched a chocolate chip muffin from his desk and seated himself next to Serena.

'My, you look smart, Mr Priest,' she said, her eyes sparkling. 'And...mmm...that's a nice aftershave you're wearing. Have you been anywhere special?'

'Oh, you know, Serena, just interviewing witnesses.'

'So, did you see her?' she asked, unable to contain her curiosity any longer.

'Who?' I wondered.

'You know who!' I couldn't see her feet but I suspect she stamped one of them.

'Mrs Threadneedle?'

'*No!* Ghislaine.'

'Oh, her. She's, y'know, very nice.'

'Uh!'

Dave said: 'So did you find anything of interest?'

'Not from Threadneedle or Mr Curzon,' I replied, 'but I had an interesting talk with Mrs Threadneedle, after he'd gone. Apparently he was a racehorse owner and she reckoned he had shares in Shergar.'

Jeff looked sideways at me and Dave gave a polite cough. Jeff said: 'And did they buy these shares from the same Nigerian diplomat who sold them the ones in the London Eye?'

'OK, OK,' I responded. 'I'm only reporting what she said, and she was slightly under the influence at the time.'

'She likes a drink?'

'Or the drink likes her. She also told me that her husband had an Irish father but he changed his name to Threadneedle because it sounded more English. Does that make sense?'

'Probably,' Dave agreed. 'If he had business ambitions he may have wanted to join the Freemasons, and I doubt if they admit Irishmen.'

'Or Catholics,' Jeff suggested. 'I can't see them allowing Catholics in. Is he one, do you know?'

'I've no idea.'

'Uh!' Serena snorted. 'I thought we were supposed to be the ones with the tribes and cults.'

Jeff turned to his computer and tapped away at the

keyboard. I said: 'I've been thinking, Dave.'

'Go on.'

'There was a documentary on TV a few years ago about the Kennedy assassination.'

'There've been dozens,' Serena declared.

'I know, but this one was a bit different. The Dealey Plaza, where it happened, was lined with spectators wanting to see the president. And the first lady, of course. About half of them had cameras, and as the cavalcade drove by they all snapped merrily away. But as well as photographing Mr President they made a record of all the people in the crowd at the other side of the road. The FBI appealed for the photos and eventually identified almost everybody there. I remember that they came tantalisingly close to getting a snap of the top of the grassy knoll.'

Dave said: 'So it's Shergar and who killed Kennedy, is it? Don't you think you might be aiming a little too high for a small-town DI?'

'Listen, buggerlugs,' I replied. 'Whoever did the painting was probably there, in the crowd. Let's ask for the photos and see who we recognise. It'll keep the boss off our backs if nothing else.'

Jeff swivelled his chair round and bugled a 'ta-da!' as he came to face us again. 'Guess what?' he demanded.

'We're all agog,' Dave growled.

'You're not going to believe this. According to Google, Shergar won the 1981 Derby and three other classic races, before being retired to stud, which is common knowledge. But this is the best bit: when it went to stud the owner, who just happened to be the Aga Khan, sold thirty-four shares in the horse at a cool quarter of a million each. Your friend Mrs Threadneedle could have been telling the truth.'

Wednesday morning I left Dave in charge of the Curzon Centre massacre enquiry and went with Jeff to talk to our cousins in Lancashire. We took our big map with us and marked on it the locations of the first three pit bull robberies and the whereabouts of the cashpoints they'd used. Ours was way out on a limb. It looked as if they'd decided things were too warm on their side of the Pennines so they'd spread their wings. When we compared descriptions and MOs it was obvious that it was the same gang. A grey or silver Jaguar had been seen near one of the incidents so we alerted the automatic number plate recognition system to look for stolen ones.

'What about the dog?' I asked my opposite number. 'Have you had any success looking for that?'

'We've appealed for information,' I was told, 'and replies have come flooding in. You'd be amazed how many pit bulls – or pit bull lookalikes – there are in Manchester. We're following them all up.'

We stopped for a bacon sandwich on the way back and I rang Dave. 'How's it going, sunshine?' I asked.

'Pretty good, *mon capitaine*. The *Gazette* has agreed to publish an appeal for photographs and Radio Pennine said they'll find a slot for us, too. And guess what – fingerprints have found a partial on the paint tube. Haven't made a match yet, though.'

'That's great. And what about the CCTV tapes? Any joy with them?'

'Ah,' Dave began. 'That's where it all goes a bit pear-shaped. Unfortunately they're all recorded on DVDs. We can play them in the office on a laptop but we've only got one that'll do DVDs. I've left the Spice Girls watching them in the control room at the Centre, but I had to lean on the manager there. He's a bit of a jobsworth.'

'What about Miss McArdle?' I said. 'Wouldn't she overrule him?'

'She'd taken some time off. Not back until Friday.'

Terrific, I thought. I'm dragged in from my holiday and she goes gallivanting off on hers. 'OK, we'll see you back at the factory.'

'How've you gone on?'

'Not bad. It's the same gang, possibly based in north Manchester and using a grey Jag. It should be enough. See you.'

Fierce dogs arouse strong feelings, and Thursday morning the calls started trickling in. It's not illegal to own a pit bull terrier, but there are restrictions. It must be on a lead and muzzled when in a public place, and neutered. I can't imagine why anyone would want one but they are particularly liked by men with beer guts and tattoos. The Aga Khan, we learnt, divided Shergar into forty shares worth a cool ten million, and kept six shares for himself, raising eight and a half million for his pension fund. Unfortunately, the IRA kidnapped the horse one sunny day when a major horse fair was taking place and the lanes and byways of that fine land were clogged with horseboxes and trailers, making the job of the Gardai almost impossible. The popular belief is that poor old Shergar proved too much of a handful for his kidnappers and was killed and buried somewhere in the wilderness, but as there has never been any proof of its death the insurance company – surprise, surprise – has refused to pay out.

'What are we looking for?' Dave asked when I handed him the list of nineteen dog owners.

'Use your intuition,' I said, adding: 'There should be one of those high-pitched dog-scarer whistles at the front desk. I'd take that if I were you.'

'Do they work against pit bulls?'

'I doubt it.'

'In that case I'll settle for a .38.'

As he was pulling his jacket on Maggie shouted for me and we both strode over to her desk, where she was studying the CCTV recordings on her Lenovo laptop.

'Have you found something, Maggie?' I asked.

'I think so. Look at this.'

It was timed at 00.14 on 14th May 2007, in other words, early Monday morning, before the official opening. The system was set to take a snapshot every second and the camera was pointing at the raised dais area, with the curtains in front of the plaque clearly visible. Suddenly a figure appeared, striding jerkily towards the plaque in giant leaps, like someone's early attempts at moving cinematography. He was wearing a security man's fluorescent jacket that engulfed him, a woolly hat pulled down over his eyes and his sweatshirt hood pulled over the hat. Successive frames showed him standing in front of the plaque, then the curtains were open, then he'd painted FUC, then the curtains were closed again and he'd turned towards us, but with his head lowered to hide his face, as if he knew we were watching.

'That's great,' I said. 'Can you get a still off it?'

'Um, I imagine so.'

'Not that it shows us much.'

Maggie said: 'No, but now that we know the time we can race through all the other disks and possibly trace laddo's route through the Centre.'

'Brilliant. Let me know when you have more. Meanwhile, I'll try to placate the boss.'

Mr Wood had gone off for the day so I rang the chief constable's office and his secretary put me through, which was a surprise. I'd been rehearsing my 'tell him I rang' line but instead I found myself relating all about the fingerprint and the CCTV and suggesting that we back-pedal with the investigation in the short term but keep it on the books in case we ever made a decent ID. The newspapers had been reasonably subdued in their reporting of the incident, partly due to bad news from Iraq, and it made sense to let things fade away, like snow in April, and the CC agreed with me. It wasn't a target point, but we were off the hook and I could concentrate on catching robbers. Except that I couldn't help feeling that there was still some unfinished business with Mayor Threadneedle and his affairs.

CHAPTER FIVE

We'd had a warm spring and now the cherry and mayflower trees were bowing down under the weight of blossom they carried, like virgin brides in some Eastern ritual to mark the dawning of the new year. I was driving down the Parkway, away from Heckley, determined to salvage the remnants of my holiday.

The Lake District was my intended destination. I felt in need of a strenuous challenge, dragging some clean air through my coked-up lungs and the feel of a decent altitude beneath my boots. I'd spent the evening before poring over my maps and had decided that the Coledale Round, near Keswick, was worth a revisit. It was a tough walk but had the advantage of several drop-out points if it all became too much or if the weather changed. Then it would be a speciality goulash in the Dog and Gun, a couple of pints

of Jennings and sleep like a zombie in my favourite B&B.
Paradise. I'd had a perfunctory glance at the map for East
Yorkshire, but when it comes to landscapes I prefer the
wild and rugged to the pretty-pretty. I found the stately
home symbol representing Curzon House and drew a
circle around it. The area looked interesting, with miles of
criss-crossing footpaths, but it was in the Yorkshire Wolds,
not renowned for their altitude, and I decided it might be
worth a visit sometime in the future. Not now, though;
today we were heading for the mountains.

So why, when we reached the motorway, the car turned
east instead of west, I'll never know. I didn't fight it or
waste energy justifying the decision; I just settled down for
the drive and looked forward to renewing my acquaintance
with Curzon House and its surroundings.

I did a five-miler in the morning, taking in a medieval
village called Low Ogglethorp, which was just a bumpy
field, and a couple of churchyards, before arriving back
at Curzon House, near the village of High Ogglethorpe.
A painted wooden sign told me that the village was a
regular finalist in the Yorkshire in Bloom competition.
Near the end of the walk I called in the Boar's Head
for a ham sandwich and a pint, apparently arousing the
displeasure of the landlord who was in a deep discussion
with a woman sitting on a bar stool with what could
have been a gin and tonic before her. It could equally
have been a glass of water, although the portion was
rather small for a water. She was furtively dragging on a
cigarette, her enjoyment enhanced by the knowledge that
in another six weeks the anti-smoking bill would come

into force and she'd have to go outside for her nicotine fix.

'Your sandwich'll be 'ere in a couple of minutes,' the landlord told me as he returned from placing the order with someone in a back room. He gave me my change and topped up my drink.

'Is there a B&B in the village?' I asked and the woman cleared her throat in readiness to speak. He beat her to it.

'Phyllis 'ere runs one,' he told me. 'Don't think she's rushed off 'er feet at the moment, are you, Phyl?'

'Not at the moment. Brad and Angelina only stayed the one night. It's twenty-five pounds, if you're interested. En suite bathroom and full English breakfast included.' She stubbed her cigarette in the ashtray, pressing the butt next to her two earlier ones. A spiral of blue smoke climbed from it and I thought that the ban couldn't come soon enough for me.

'Sounds fine,' I said. 'Book me in.'

'Just the one night?'

'For the moment.'

'Will you need an evening meal?'

I hesitated, but the landlord stepped in with his three pennyworths: 'Phyl's the best cook this side o' Market Weighton. Her steak and kidney is worth dying for.'

I wasn't too sure about the recommendation, but I placed my order for seven-thirty. I had a feeling that – what was the expression? – they'd *seen me coming* and ganged up on me, and I'd fallen for the *drop of York,* as my dad would have put it. Never mind, I thought, Phyllis's cooking would no doubt be better than I'd find in a pub, and more wholesome, and I was partial to a decent steak and kidney.

'You're with the press?' the landlord hit me with as I lifted my pint of Copper Dragon to my lips. I took a slow sip, considering my reply.

'Ah, you keep a decent pint. The press? No, not me.'

'You're wearing good gear. A bit over the top for these parts, if you don't mind me saying.'

I looked down at my three-season boots, my Tog 24 shirt and my rucksack leaning on the wall just inside the door. He was right: it was a warm day and I was overdressed for a summer's lowland walk.

'Do you get many press people in the village?' I asked.

'A tidy few.'

'What's the attraction?'

'Your guess is as good as mine.'

'How about a certain Miss Curzon?'

'Curzon? Curzon?' he mused. 'New one on me. Mean anything to you, Phyl?'

'Never heard of her,' she replied.

'Your loyalty is commendable,' I told them, knowing that their loyalty was as substantial as the blossom on the trees that lined the village and, like that blossom, would go whichever way the wind took it. I decided to play a high card. 'I'm police,' I said, reaching for my ID, 'and I'm here for the walking. And the beer.'

The landlord took hold of my card and studied it. 'A detective inspector,' he read. 'Detective Inspector Priest.'

I eased it from his grasp and replaced it in my pocket.

'I'll sit over in the corner, and...' I nodded towards the ashtray '...enjoy it while you can.'

The sandwich was made from locally raised ham cut straight from the bone, which meant it was edged with a thick layer of fat. I prefer it in sanitised slices exactly the same shape as the bread. It came with a selection of chutneys, which helped it go down, but it wasn't the culinary experience I'd hoped for.

The intention was to do another loop walk in the afternoon, but when I arrived back at the car I decided that a pot of tea in the house's tea shop was a more attractive proposition. I'd been the first to arrive that morning, but now there were ten or fifteen cars sharing the huge parking area. Needless to say, one of them had managed to squeeze in about six inches from mine. I checked for dents, changed into my trainers and wandered off to see what was on offer.

I settled for a wedge of fruit cake with a slice of Wensleydale cheese and was dabbing up the last few crumbs when I saw a familiar figure come into the tea room, look around and head in my direction. I stood to welcome him and we shook hands.

'Hello, Mr Curzon,' I said. 'Just thought I'd check out your fruit cake. It's a weakness of mine.'

'Toby saw you from her window. You should have rung ahead. Have you been walking?'

'Hardly, but knowing when to quit is a sign of maturity.'

'The least we could have done is feed you.' He leant forward conspiratorially and added: 'Especially at these prices.'

'They are a bit steep,' I agreed, *sotto voce.*

We chatted for a while about global warming, the economy, weapons of mass destruction and other lightweight topics until I asked how the girls were and the curtain came down. After a few seconds' silence he said: 'Come up to the house, the bit we live in, and we'll have a chat and another pot of tea. That is...if you're not wanting to be away.'

'Actually,' I began, 'I've booked in to a B&B in the village, so I'm in no hurry to be off. I'm not sure if I was wise, but the deed's done, now.'

'Phyllis Smith's? Phyllis will look after you. And tell you all the gossip. Take most of it with a pinch of salt – you know what villages are like. Her pies are legendary.'

We sat in the same kitchen as before, which, I learnt, had originally been meant for the staff. The main kitchen, which was elsewhere, was now a feature of the Stately Home Experience and open only to ticket holders.

'You asked about my daughters,' he began. 'Toby's not very well: having a bad day. Grizzly's gone to see...you-know-who...her boyfriend. She was driving up to Catterick and then flying down to Sandringham. She's certainly moving in influential circles, these days.'

I said: 'It can't have been easy, bringing up two girls and looking after this place.'

He smiled. 'We had our moments. Grizzly was fourteen when her mother died but Toby was only three. We could've gone under but the Country Homes Association saved us. Grizzly took charge: did most of the negotiations; looked after both of us. She's...amazing. I only hope...' He let it hang there for a while, then went on: 'I only hope she's aware of what she's doing, that she doesn't get hurt.'

I opened my mouth to speak, then realised it would sound as if I was prying, so I closed it again. We sat in silence for a moment until he said: 'I'm sorry. What were you going to say?'

'I was going to say that you sound as if you disapprove, but I'm trying not to ask anything too personal. I appreciate that your daughter has a price on her head these days. Sections of the public think she's their property. You're living in a topsy-turvy world, can't possibly know who you can trust and who you can't. Let's change the subject, eh? We've found a fingerprint on the paint tube the graffiti artist used, but haven't made a match. If he steps out of line in the next sixty years, we'll have him.'

'Disapprove?' he echoed. 'Would you approve, Inspector?'

'Probably not. And it's Charlie.'

'Hello, Charlie. Call me James. Sixty years? I've heard about the wheels of justice being ponderously slow, but that's ridiculous.' He was smiling as he said it.

'We have a long memory,' I explained.

'On Tuesday,' he began, 'I believe you said you'd talked to Threadneedle. Did you happen to see his wife, Jan?'

'Yes. I had an interesting chat with her.'

'How is she?'

This is more like it, I thought. I'd been wondering how to steer the conversation towards Threadneedle. 'She's not very happy. I'd say she drinks too much and she's discovered that he's having an affair.'

He looked downcast. 'The bastard,' he said. 'I always said she was too good for him.'

'How well did you know them?'

'Oh, you know. They lived near Malton and we had mutual friends. He enjoyed entertaining and our wives enjoyed comparing furnishings and suchlike. He was a bit of a pest, if the truth's known, but Jan was delightful. She was a concert flautist, but gave it up when she married him. She played like an angel.'

It sounded as if Threadneedle had negotiated his way into the country set behind his wife's talent, on the heels of his new money, but they hadn't taken to him. I could imagine why. I decided to dive in with the big one. 'She was a bit under the weather when I spoke to her, but she claimed that you and Threadneedle had shares in Shergar. Tell me that she was rambling, please.'

Curzon gave a chuckle but it came from deep down and sounded forced. 'Shergar! I remember it well.' The kettle boiled and he jumped up to deal with it. Moments later he returned with mugs and teapot on a tray and lowered them onto the table.

I waited until he'd done the mother thing with the teapot then reminded him that he was in the middle of telling me about Shergar, but he had little to add. He told me about the Aga Khan and the stud fees, stating that Threadneedle had wanted him to join a syndicate for a share, but there was no way he could have afforded to. 'Besides,' he added, 'the pleasure is in watching your horse race, not rutting someone else's mare.'

'Did Threadneedle go ahead with it?'

'Of course not. We used to meet for a meal after a meeting and fantasise about winning a classic. It was my wife's hobby, not mine. She was unwell, and I went along with things to please her. That's all it was: juvenile fantasies. He upset a few people and moved away. To Heckley, I presume. Our loss was your gain.'

'In what way did he upset them?'

'The usual. Paying too much attention to one or two of the ladies. You know how it is.'

'I thought that came under the heading of country pursuits,' I said.

'Ha ha! You're right. Perhaps it was the ones he neglected who were upset. Let's say he rubbed some of the husbands up the wrong way. Not the best behaviour in a small community. And then there was the stable. He bought his way into a small stable when Jonty Hargrave retired, wanted to become a trainer, but it burnt down. A horse died; it was all very unpleasant.'

A car with a sporty exhaust drove by the window with a crunch of gravel and stopped out of sight. The engine blipped and fell silent. 'That sounds like Grizzly,' Curzon said, twisting in his seat. 'I wasn't expecting her.'

'It looked like an Audi TT,' I told him.

'Mmm, that's her. His Royal Nibs must have engagements elsewhere.'

Doors opened and closed and a few seconds later I was rising to say hello once more to the woman who could easily be on the cover of *Vogue* in the near future. I made a mental note to look out for it, for the office wall.

'Inspector,' she said. 'This is a surprise. Have you found the graffiti artist or is it a social call?' She didn't *sound* surprised, as if she'd expected the dumb-struck yokel policeman to come back to stalk her, like so many before him.

'Charlie's been walking,' her father explained, sensing the suspicion in her tone. 'I caught him in the tea shop; insisted he come down here for a cup. We've been chatting about the Threadneedles. You're home early – I wasn't expecting you.'

'I'm working this evening,' she replied.

Curzon turned to me and explained. 'Grizzly helps out at the cottage hospital when she can,' he told me. 'Accident and Emergency tonight is it, darling?'

'Hmm, and talking to the old dears about Edward VIII.'

'I imagine they love that,' I said.

'Yes, they do.'

'The graffiti artist is on the back burner,' I told her. 'We have a fingerprint, so we'll catch him one day.'

'I'm surprised the good citizens of Heckley could spare an inspector for the enquiry. It's not exactly the Great Train Robbery, is it?'

'They couldn't,' I replied, 'but I'm officially on holiday, so I came cheap.'

The steak and kidney pie lived up to its reputation, and there was blackberry and apple crumble with custard to follow. I pushed my empty bowl away with a heartfelt 'Phew' and wiped my lips on my napkin. Phyllis cleared the table and asked if I'd like tea or coffee in the front room. I opted for tea and invited her to join me.

'Will you be in the Whore's Bed, later?' she asked.

I smiled. 'Is that what you call the Boar's Head?' We were sitting in deep armchairs in the front room, where an antique long-case clock measured out the seconds with oiled precision.

'No, the Whore's Bed is Mrs Smethick at number 22.' She threw her head back with a laugh that sounded like a greenhouse collapsing until it turned into a coughing spell.

'I don't mind if you smoke,' I said as she calmed down and regained her equilibrium. My parents were smokers and they paid the price, but I try to avoid coming on heavy with the sanctimony.

'Well you should,' she reprimanded me. 'It's a filthy habit. What did you think of your meal?'

'The meal?' I replied. 'I think you are an impostor. I'd have been happy with something homely and wholesome, straight from your country kitchen. Instead, I got top-notch cordon bleu cookery. Like I said, you're an impostor.'

'What makes you say that?'

'All this,' I replied, waving a hand in the direction of the dining room. 'The linen, the cutlery, the first-class ingredients. The subtle use of spices and herbs. Just enough to enhance the natural flavours without overwhelming them. You, Phyllis Smith, have done this before.'

'Thank you. It's nice to be appreciated, but you make it sound as if I'm trying to seduce you.'

'Aren't you?'

'No,' she replied. 'When I said you could park your car in my driveway it wasn't a metaphor,' and the greenhouse came crashing down around her ears again.

'Damn. I'd rather hoped it was.'

Apparently Friday night was karaoke night at the Boar's Head, and the single street through the village was usually gridlocked for the evening. Knocked-off mirrors and dented doors were the norm. Mr Curzon had forewarned me and suggested I leave my car in their car park overnight, which was an offer I gratefully accepted. It was a half-mile walk from the house to the village, and, he told me, the hospital where Ghislaine worked was another mile beyond that. I explained the arrangement to Phyllis and said I'd probably be in the pub for the last half-hour. As I left to take my car back to Curzon House I shouted: 'Number 22 was it?' to Phyllis in the kitchen, and was rewarded with her giggle again.

It was kerb-to-kerb cars outside, with more arriving by the second. Every make and price range was represented – karaoke night was the social highlight of the week for anyone within twenty miles who was only marginally brain damaged. Cars and 4x4s were parked on the footpaths and verges, double-parked in the lay-by and heaped on top of each other in the pub's tiny yard. I couldn't have put mine in Phyllis's drive if I'd wanted to, but I managed to extricate it from a Land Rover sandwich and thread my way out of the village.

I parked it in front of the house but far enough away for my slamming doors not to disturb them, and sat there for about half an hour, listening to the radio while the darkness closed in. I didn't want to get back to the pub too early. A swift glass of red before retiring was all I needed, and I didn't think East Yorkshire was ready for my Leonard Cohen impression.

Two windows were illuminated upstairs, and remained so while I waited. No silhouettes fell on to them, nobody came or went and nothing disturbed the perfect darkness – not even a shooting star. At a quarter to ten I gently closed the car door and set off on the fifteen-minute amble back to High Ogglethorpe and the grand finale of the karaoke. All around me tiny eyes in the undergrowth would be watching my departure, resenting the intrusion, before resuming their normal nocturnal preoccupations of feeding, fighting and...fornicating. It was that time of year.

It was that time of year in High Ogglethorpe, too, and the activity had spilt out of the pub into the road. 'Eye of the Tiger' was throbbing the walls as some overweight diva from Pocklington enjoyed her three minutes of fame, and a youth in a hooded top sat on the roadside, holding his head and moaning. He looked to be bleeding.

'Wurz fuckin' 'ospittle?' his companion demanded as I walked by, skirting his damaged friend.

I looked at the sign on the telegraph pole, dimly illuminated by light spilling from the Boar's Head. It said *Hospital 1*, with an arrow pointing straight ahead.

'Ah said wurz fuckin' 'ospittle? Am fuckin' torkin' to you.'

'Work it out,' I told him, and turned towards the pub doorway. Before I laid a hand on it someone inside kicked it open and three more youths staggered out, cans clutched in fists, testosterone coursing through their bloodstreams like February fill dyke. I decided that a glass of cheap red was not what I required and turned away. One of the youths fetched a Vauxhall Corsa that sounded like a DC3 Dakota with a dodgy magneto and they bundled the bleeding youth into it, with the driver imploring his friends not to get blood on the seats. They roared off in the direction of the hospital while I wondered where DI Priest of Heckley CID fitted in to this everyday story of country folk.

Up to his neck was the answer. Every day we come across certain misdemeanours that make the blood boil but we appear powerless to do anything about them. Throwing stones at firefighters is one; causing mayhem in hospitals is another. Half the village knew I was a cop, so I couldn't plead invisibility, and the nearest panda car was probably parked outside a kebab shop twenty miles away. Trouble was, I'd no car and no phone. I took a deep breath, turned my back on the pub and started jogging back towards Curzon House, the strains of 'Simply the Best' chasing me up the road.

The furry beasts in the undergrowth paused again in their activities and wondered what the world was coming to. I resisted the temptation to spin the wheels in the gravel and eased the car out onto the lane as silently as possible. Both windows were still illuminated in the house. I wondered if one of them was Toby's.

I arrived at the hospital about twenty minutes after the youths but I hadn't missed the action. Four people were in the waiting room, cowed in a corner like hostages. One man had a heavily bandaged foot; a woman sat with a small boy who looked decidedly green and another woman sat with her leg across a chair. It had been an average night in a country cottage hospital up to the youths arriving. I could hear them, somewhere further inside, berating the triage nurse because they'd been kept waiting.

I followed the noise and found myself in a small room with them all. The patient was sitting in a chair, two youths were sitting on the trolley and the male triage nurse, who looked about fifteen, was trying to examine the wound on the patient's head. The other two yobs were leaning on the wall, smoking, cans of beer in hand. All eyes turned to me and the room fell silent.

'Whose is the Corsa?' I demanded. Nobody replied.

'I said, whose is the Corsa?'

'Wot the fux it got to do wi' you?' one of the seated youths replied.

I miss lapels. You can't get a good grip on a T-shirt, but I did my best. I heaved him off the trolley and slammed him against the door jamb. 'I'm your best friend,' I told him. 'Now give me the keys.'

'The keys?'

'Yes. You're not fit to drive.'

He handed them over without another murmur.

'Right. Now clear off.'

'But...'ow do I get 'ome?'

'You phone for a taxi. I'll leave your keys behind the front desk. You can pick them up tomorrow.' I watched him slink off, through the waiting room, and turned to the others, who'd all been struck dumb. 'Before you follow him,' I told them, 'there's something you have to do. I want you all to apologise to this young man who is trying to help your friend.' I turned to the nearest, who had acne like raspberry ripple. 'You first.'

'Me?'

'Yes, you.'

'I'm sorry,' he mumbled.

'That's not good enough. Have another try.'

'I'm...very sorry. I'm a bit drunk. I'm sorry for being a nuisance. It won't happen again.'

'That's more like it. Now you.'

They all apologised, with varying degrees of sincerity, and staggered out into the cold clear air, which, if the folklore were correct, would have hit them like an uppercut.

It still wasn't closing time and the village was crowded, so I drove back to Curzon House and parked in the place I was beginning to regard as my own. The animals in the undergrowth thought: *Jeez! It's like Piccadilly Circus in here*, and waited for the night to close in on them again.

Mrs Smith cooked me an excellent breakfast and asked if I'd been in the Boar's Head when the fighting started. I said I'd missed it and didn't explain my role in things. I carried my boots and rucksack back along the lane to Curzon House and was putting them in the car when I heard the rustle of footsteps behind me. I'd risen early, told Phyllis I wanted a prompt start, and the sun hadn't burnt off the dew yet. Its rays were catching the facade of the house and Ghislaine was walking towards me, casting a long shadow.

'Good morning,' I said. 'You're up and about early. Your father suggested I leave the car here overnight.'

'It was you, wasn't it?' she stated with a grin. Her face was in shadow but I could tell she was smiling.

'What was me?'

'At the hospital. You sorted out the yobs.'

'It's what I do.'

'Naseem was most impressed. He said you just stood there like Wyatt Earp and told them to apologise. Actually, he said Wyatt...effing Earp. But he didn't say effing.'

I said: 'Can I quote you on that?' and pretended to write it on my cuff.

'Well, on behalf of the hospital I just wanted to say thank you. You could easily have stayed out of it, but we're all grateful you didn't.'

'Very graciously delivered,' I told her. 'And much appreciated, but it was no trouble.' I glanced towards the house and slammed the boot lid. 'How's Toby?'

'She's up and about, much better today, thank you.'

'Am I allowed to know what's wrong with her?'

'Pneumonia. She's prone to it. Antibiotics work most of the time. Are you going walking again today?'

'Mmm. I was thinking of Robin Hood's Bay, from Ravenscar. It's one of my favourites.'

'I know it well, from long ago. I'd...'

She let her words trail off. 'You'd what?' I asked.

'Oh, nothing.'

'You'd like to come? I don't mind waiting while you fetch your gear. We could take Toby if it would do her good. It's going to be a beautiful day.' I opened the car door, slid in and lowered the window.

She shook her head. 'I'm sorry, but I have other arrangements. Thank you for asking, though. It sounds delightful.'

'Fish and chips for one, then,' I said, starting the engine. 'Say goodbye to Toby for me, please.' She said she would and I eased the clutch in. Five yards from her I stopped and waited for her to catch up. Now I was looking up into her sunlit face. 'Best wishes for the future, Ghislaine,' I said. 'I hope everything turns out well for you.'

She thanked me, called me Charlie, and I drove out of her life. Well, I tried to.

CHAPTER SIX

The fish and chips were nigh on perfect but my appetite had gone and I couldn't eat them. I was outside the café in Robin Hood's Bay, surrounded by hikers and holidaymakers and hungry seagulls the size of hang-gliders, with beaks like chainsaws. I ate a few chips, picked at the batter on the fish and left most of the meal. The tide was going out and I was able to walk on the beach all the way back to Ravenscar, eyes down, looking for fossils, or up, watching the cliffs for rockfalls. I was hot and bothered when I arrived, so I called in the hotel and a Polish waitress took pity on me and made me a pint of shandy. I drank it outside, overlooking a view that never fails to thrill me, sitting on a seat that was a memorial to a young man who had died while scuba diving in the bay.

An hour later I was heading towards the M62 and

a steady slog home. It had been a worthwhile trip and there'd be no paperwork to complete. That's always a bonus. Monday, if nothing else had turned up, we'd put the file away with a note to review the case in twelve months and concentrate on proper crime, like the pit bull robberies. The shandy was making its presence felt so I stopped at a Little Chef for a pee and a coffee.

I'll never learn. I visualised big Dave lighting his barbecue on their back patio, sausages defrosted, lager in the cooler, wife Shirley tossing the salad and supervising the jacket potatoes. If I'd guessed right I might be in for an invitation. I dialled his mobile number.

Mad Maggie Madison answered it. 'What are you doing there?' I asked, wondering if I'd pressed a wrong button.

'We're on a shout, Charlie,' she told me. 'Your phone was switched off. Where are you?'

'I *am* supposed to be on holiday. I'm in East Yorkshire, heading home, sitting in a Little Chef car park about five minutes from the end of the M62. Are you with Dave?'

'That's right. The grey Jag used by the pit bull gang may have been spotted by the ANPR system. One was picked up on the Manchester orbital about half an hour ago. It's a ringer. Two men believed to be in it. The proper vehicle is locked away in its garage in Formby. Everybody and his giddy aunt are out looking for it. We're assigned to the M621, on our way.'

'Who's in control?'

'They are, until we have a sighting this side.'

'Tell them where I am, ask if I can help.'

'OK. Will ring you.'

I went back in and bought a couple of chunky Kit Kats. My appetite was returning and it might be a long day. I was drumming my fingers, studying the map, when the phone rang.

'It's Maggie. Control will be grateful if you could stake out between J35 and J36, eastbound. They're believed to be on the M62, heading your way. Should be in that area in less than one hour unless they turn off, which is likely. You're the backstop, that's all. Observe and report only. Don't follow. If they leave the motorway before then we'll let you know.'

'Understood. I'm on my way.'

'So where've you been?'

'Walking. Ravenscar to Robin Hood's Bay and back.'

'Alone?'

'Of course.'

'Umph!'

I was on the wrong side. Junction 35 is where the M18 turns off to the south and it was unlikely they'd come that far, unless they were heading for Hull. I ran through the possibilities. They could have been taking the car to the docks, to export. They could have been on a job. They could have been out on a reconnaissance mission, looking for the next job. They could have been visiting their invalid father in Withernsea who had just had his prostate reamered out, and that thought made my eyes water. I didn't care. Police work should be fun, I tell the troops, and this was fun in the sunshine. I put my headlights on and gunned it.

The tyres squealed on the J35 roundabout, which added to the feeling of urgency, but once I was back on the motorway, pointing in the right direction, I eased up, looking for somewhere to stop.

I found a traffic car ramp and gently reversed up it, perching on top. It's something I'd always wanted to do. Once upon a time you could drive straight up them, but a lady driver apparently fell asleep at the wheel and launched herself into space off the top of one, so they've all been modified at a cost of several millions. Now you have to drive past and reverse. I adjusted the door mirror so I could see the traffic approaching from behind and reported to Maggie that I was in position.

My window was down and I could feel the sun burning the right-hand side of my face. I didn't want a lopsided tan so after fifteen minutes I got out of the car and stood with my arms resting on top of the open door, facing backwards, watching the madcap, endless stream of traffic hurtling towards me.

I read the names on the sides of the lorries, trying to get a snapshot of what proportion were from the Continent and what were home bred. Eddie Stobart went by, all the way from Penrith, followed by Longs of Leeds. A brief gap gave way to Norbert Dentressangle from sunny France, James Irlam, Deveraux Logistics and several unpronounceables from the Eastern bloc.

And then there were the contents. What were they all carrying? Wine and window frames; socks and socket sets; chickens and chickpeas? Plastic buckets, frozen fish, plasterboard, steel girders, feminine requisites?

Cargoes. You could write a poem about them. The driver of a Christian Salvesen artic gave me a wave and I acknowledged with an inclination of the head. What was he taking to Hull that they needed thirty tons of in such a hurry? How about:

Articulated lorry in the motorway fast lane
Belting down to Dover with illegal haste
Loaded to the gunnels with tomato ketchup
Jigsaw puzzles and nuclear waste.

Hey, it was fun! An Audi swung into the overtaking lane without signalling and the Mitsubishi he nearly sideswiped blared his horn. Where was I?

Sixteen-wheeler Volvo with a brand-new paint job
Fresh out of Stockholm on the Liverpool run
Delivering machine tools, aero parts and tractors
And complicated circuits for electron guns.

I could've been a poet if I hadn't made it as a cop. I was working on the next verse, about a white Transit loaded with double-glazing, trying to find a rhyme for ultraviolet radiation, when I saw the Jaguar.

He was cruising in the middle lane, not drawing attention. I didn't react: just kept staring into the distance, chin resting on my folded arms as he went by, but my eyes were swivelling to clock his number and my hand was reaching into my pocket for the phone.

'Target has just passed me,' I reported, without turning to watch him go. 'Heading east at about 70.' I pulled out into the carriageway and as I approached the next exit the helicopter came clattering by, closely followed by the East Yorkshire cavalry. The instruction was that I should turn off the motorway, do a U and go home, but the old Captain Scott spirit prevailed and I pressed on. Instructions are there to be broken. I didn't hurry: just ambled along below the legal limit.

Two men were face down on the hard shoulder when I arrived, protected by a phalanx of police vehicles, light bars flashing, as their wrists were cuffed. They'd given up without a chase, trusting that bluffing their way out of trouble would be easier than running from it. Guns were being holstered and all the uniforms were grinning like it was Mardi Gras time. I parked half on the grass and went to introduce myself.

Ten minutes later the Heckley troops arrived; first the ARVs, followed by DS Caton in his hot hatch. We held an impromptu meeting on the hard shoulder and it was agreed that East Riding could claim the collars but Heckley was having the bodies. It's almost impossible to rise to your feet with your hands handcuffed behind your back, so two burly traffic officers kindly hoisted the suspects upright and we shared them between our ARVs, one to go to Heckley, one to Halifax. The helicopter did a low pass and headed off back to base and the rest of us followed suit.

They were half-brothers called Carl and Sean Pickles, and didn't have a dog with them. Carl was taken to Heckley and the clock started. We had up to thirty-six hours to link him with the robberies, but first we talked about the car. They'd bought it for three thousand pounds from a man named Andy who drank in the Lamb and Flag, one of Heckley's more traditional watering holes.

'Three thousand pounds?' I said.

'Yeah.'

'It's worth about six times that.'

'From a dealer, maybe,' he told me, with mock helpfulness, 'but a lot less on the street.' Any moment I was expecting him to say that he was as surprised as I was to find the car was a ringer: 'Straight up, Inspector, I've been 'ad as much as anyone.'

'What's Andy's second name?'

'He didn't say.'

'Isn't it on the paperwork?' I fenced around with him for fifteen minutes or so, and discovered that his insurance certificate was in the post, as was the car's V5 registration document. He thought brother Sean was a pal of Andy's and had taken care of all the legal stuff. Over in Halifax, Sean was saying the same things about Carl. Andy was in serious financial trouble, the implication being that it was with drug dealers, and needed three big ones asap. They'd taken the car off him to help him out of a tight spot.

'Do you have a dog?' I asked.

'A dog? What sort of dog?'

'Any sort of dog?'

'No.' We stared at each other across the table until he broke the silence. 'Andy had a dog,' he said, and almost licked his lips. What he meant was that if we found any dog hairs in the car they belonged to invisible Andy and his amazing talking tripe hound. The detention clock had started at five-thirty p.m. and we could hold him for twenty-four hours, plus another twelve on the super's authority, which would take us to early Monday morning. It was going to be a great weekend, and my name would be mud to several wives and children.

I pushed my chair back and stood up. 'Keep Monday morning free,' I told him. 'We've booked you an audience with a magistrate.'

Serena, meanwhile, had been to see the magistrate and had returned with a search warrant. 'Got the keys?' I asked, and she jangled them in front of my face.

'Right here.'

'OK, let's go.'

They lived in Heckley. So much for geographic profiling, I thought – the experts had predicted they'd live in north Manchester. It was an ex-council house that had been tarted up at considerable expense to make it stand out from the neighbours. There were pretend shutters framing the windows and a rustic arch around the door, covered in a decent show of roses. The neighbours either side had tried to keep up but had finally settled for matching satellite dishes and abandoned the contest. I wasn't mocking them. The houses were tidy and well maintained. They didn't look as if they'd ever had a letter from the council telling them to cut the grass.

We'd arranged for a SOCO to be present and I told him to record the tyre prints on the dirt drive. Serena knocked and pushed the bell button. No dog started barking and eventually a woman aged about twenty-five pushing forty opened the door. She had straggly blonde hair that was brown at the tips and looked as if she'd been disturbed from a hundred-year sleep. She pulled her skimpy top down to cover her navel stud and brushed an imaginary strand of hair out of her eyes. Serena told her who we were.

'Mrs Pickles?' I asked.

'Miss,' she replied, blinking in the evening sunlight. 'It's Miss Pickles.'

'Is this the home of Sean and Carl Pickles?'

'Yeah.'

'Do you live here?'

'Yeah.'

'Can you tell me where they are?'

'Rugby match, I 'spect.'

'Actually, Miss Pickles, they've been arrested on suspicion of stealing a motor vehicle. We have a search warrant, so may we come in?' I was halfway past her as I said it, with Serena hot on my heels.

On the way we'd discussed what we were looking for. The robbers had worn overalls and gloves, with baseball caps. Any of those would do nicely. Then there was the property they'd taken. It was all small items of high value, but they had no reason to expect a visit from the police, so we weren't expecting it to be hidden away in secret compartments.

'What relation are you to Sean and Carl?' I asked.

'I'm Carl's sister.'

'I see.' Although I didn't. We'd need the computer to work out what relation that made her to Carl's half-brother.

Serena looked upstairs while I did the ground floor. When we swapped over she opened her eyes wide in a look of stage shock. I soon found out why. Only two of the three bedrooms were furnished, each with a double bed, unmade, and a couple of free-standing wardrobes. I glanced in the 'robes and probed the pile of jeans and T-shirts that lay on the floor with my toe. Under one of the mattresses I found what is called a hunting knife, with a twelve-inch serrated blade. It probably had nothing to do with the offences but would add some street cred to our black museum, so I slipped it into an evidence bag.

They both had eclectic reading tastes. The magazines on their bedside tables ranged from *Guns 'n' Ammo* right through to *Nympho College Girls* and *Sex Bizarre*. I picked up a well-thumbed volume and spent a couple of minutes flicking through it. I never realised there were so many types of guns.

The SOCO took a few samples for elimination purposes, as we say, but otherwise the search was fruitless. I had a look in the garage but there was nothing there that grabbed my interest. I told Miss Pickles that we'd be holding her brothers until Monday morning and we left. In the car Serena said: 'Boss...'

'Mmm.'

'I was thinking...'

'Mmm.'

'If they are half-brothers and sister...'

'Ye...es.'

'And there were only two beds...'

'Ye...es.'

'Where did they all sleep?'

I said: 'Don't ask, Serena. Don't ask.'

I was disappointed with the search, but there was nothing I could do about it. I started the engine and drove off. We desperately needed some forensics to link the brothers with the robberies. Without forensics we had no case. We'd do them for the vehicle offences but they were relatively trivial. As I slowed at the end of the street an elderly Ford Escort driven by a baseball-capped youth pulled into it, dragging a plume of diesel fumes behind. I paused and saw him stop outside the house we'd just left. Perhaps our luck was about to change, I thought.

The youth climbed out and walked round the back of the car. He lifted the tailgate and a dog jumped down onto the road. It wasn't just any dog. It was of the type sometimes referred to as a fighting dog: all teeth and aggression, with a pain threshold somewhere in the stratosphere. 'Bingo,' I said.

The dog's stump of a tail was wagging like my windscreen wipers on full speed. The youth slipped a chain around its neck and led it into the garden of Chez Pickles, pausing only for it to relieve itself against the gatepost.

'Are we going back?' Serena asked, her voice shaky with nervousness and her big brown eyes wide with alarm.

'Are you any good with dogs?' I asked.

'No.'

'Neither am I. Do a PNC check on him; see if he's legit.'

Two minutes later we knew that the owner of the Escort was called Terence Bratt, age twenty-three, and he lived on the Sylvan Fields estate.

I said: 'That must be him. I can't see how we'd learn anything from a heart-to-heart talk right now. Can you?'

'Not a thing.'

'OK, that settles it. Let's go back to the nick.'

Monday morning, after the Pickles boys had been bailed and sent on their way, we had a big meeting. 'Right,' I began, when everybody was seated, plastic beakers of coffee balanced precariously on any handy level surface. 'We've a lot to get through, so let's stay with the facts and not go drifting off on flights of fancy.' I looked at Brendan as I said the last bit. 'We'll deal with the pit bull robbers first.' I told them about my interview of Carl Pickles and the fruitless search of his house, until Smokey and the Bandit came cruising into the street. There were groans of derision when I confessed to not going back to face the dog.

Jeff's interview with Sean was a carbon copy of mine with Carl. 'They both have extensive but relatively minor criminal records,' he told us. 'Calling them career criminals is probably not an exaggeration. They've had plenty of experience at talking to the police and they are forensically aware enough to keep a firm divide between their home life and the criminal side. Somewhere, I suspect there's a lock-up garage filled with all their robbery gear and proceeds. We need to find it.'

After a few questions I moved on. 'The Curzon Centre incident,' I said. 'I've had a word with the chief constable, who just happens to be a mate of mine from the old days. In fact, I taught him all he knows...'

'What did you do in the afternoon?' somebody interrupted.

'Um, well, let's just say we've been firm friends ever since. As I was saying, I've had a word with the CC and he's content to wind down the investigation to find the graffiti artist. The press have had other stories to bother about and they've given us a relatively easy life, for which we should be grateful. The Curzons aren't bothered. It was just a minor embarrassment to them. However, it would be nice to find out who did it, and how, don't you think?'

Their response suggested that they didn't give a flying fart, but I persisted. 'Brendan,' I said. 'Give us an update, leaving out anything about grassy knolls and book depositories.'

'Right, boss. We've seized...well, not seized...borrowed is probably more accurate...nearly a hundred photographs taken by the onlookers when the incident occurred. So far we've identified about twenty per cent of the people in the background. Only one attracts any attention.' He pulled an A4 printout from the pile in his briefcase and passed it towards me.

It showed Ghislaine out of focus in the foreground, her head turning away from the camera, and a smiling youth beyond her, his mouth open, as if speaking. 'Go on, Brendan,' I said, handing the photo to Maggie.

'The woman who took the photo said there was a brief exchange between the two of them. She thought he said "Where's Kevin?" and Miss Curzon said "He couldn't come", or something similar.'

'Hmm. Any ideas who Kevin might be?'

'Yes, boss. Apparently Miss Curzon and the prince have code names for each other. Let's face it, everybody from GCHQ and MI6 down is trying to tap into their phone calls. She always calls him Kevin. One of the tabloids had spilt the beans a couple of days earlier.'

'What does he call her?'

'Sorry. Don't know.'

'It sounds harmless but he might be a stalker. Let's have him in. Anything else?'

'More CCTV stills of the culprit, that's all. We know his movements but they don't help much.'

'Right. Show me them later. Keep on it but don't spend any money. Is that everything? If so, off you go.'

One of the DCs raised a finger to attract my attention. 'Just one thing, boss,' he said. 'The SmartWater kits have started to arrive. I've one here.' He held up a small Ziplok bag and I gestured for him to toss it to me. It wasn't as big as I expected, consisting of a tube of the magic liquid about the size of a fountain pen and a few stickers for windows, to frighten off would-be burglars.

'How many do we have?' I asked.

'We've ten thousand on order, of which about a thousand are downstairs.'

'How have other forces handled it?' I asked.

'I think the idea is to give it to vulnerable people – those who are burgled regularly – and the rest are on sale. We've had a few thou orders, at ten pounds a time, so we'll have to fill those first.'

'Tell us how it works, please.'

'OK. It's a bit like those marker pens that glowed under UV, except every kit has a unique DNA code, which is registered to a particular address. The liquid is put on any valuable items, or round windows, et cetera, and it stays there for years. If a villain handles the item, some of the liquid residue is transferred to him and can easily be seen under UV light and linked to the address that applied it.

'Doesn't it wash off?'

'Not very easily.'

Someone said: 'It's a pity the houses robbed by the pit bull gang weren't treated with it.'

'That's true,' I said. 'Thanks for that. I'll have a word with Mr Adey about some help distributing it.' Gareth Adey is my uniformed counterpart.

'Like, them doing it.'

'That's a good idea. The important thing is that it isn't left under the front desk gathering dust for evermore. So go to it, my fine young cannibals, and catch us some crooks.'

Dave followed me into my office and sat down in the spare chair. 'How was the trip to East Yorkshire?' he asked.

'Fine,' I replied. 'Just fine.'

'Will you be going again, this week?'

'No. Why should I be?'

'I just wondered.'

'I went for the walking. It's a nice place.'

'Oh. So you didn't see Miss Curzon at all?'

'Well, actually, now you come to mention it, I did happen to bump into her, but it wasn't intentional.'

'And you were on holiday.'

'Exactly.'

'As was Threadneedle.'

'So he was.'

'And Miss McArdle.'

'Mmm,' I agreed. 'That's interesting. I wonder where *she* went.'

Serena poked her head around my door, saying: 'Guess what.'

'The Pope's been done for OPL?' Dave suggested. 'He'd been hitting the green chartreuse a bit hard and ran a few friends home in the Popemobile after midnight mass.'

'Not quite. Miss Audrey Pickles, aka Monique, has a record for soliciting, with a short custodial for non-payment of fines.'

I shook my head. 'Monique! The desirable Audrey Pickles sounds to have hidden depths.' I turned to Dave. 'We suspected that she was probably having it away with her half-brothers or brothers – or whatever they are.'

'Keep it in the family, Serena,' he said. 'An old Yorkshire tradition,' and she tutted and rolled those big brown eyes.

'I'm taking Dave to interview Terence Bratt,' I told her. 'He's an expert with dogs, aren't you, sunshine?'

'Love 'em,' he replied, unconvincingly.

We didn't take a gun, or the high-pitched whistle device, relying on the hound being chained up or silly soft or something. Dave and I used to be in the same football team, and I could run faster than he could, but I didn't remind him of that.

Terence Bratt lived in a one-up one-down back-to-back terrace in a part of town that is awaiting redevelopment. Knock three or four of them into one and you have a reasonable starting point for a desirable family town residence, providing the roof doesn't cave in. They were built a century ago, for the millworkers who lived like rats in the maze of streets that once clung to the hillsides. Now there's only a token few left alongside a cobbled street, like museum pieces. Bratt had lived there since the age of sixteen, when social services found and furnished it for him, to rescue him from an abusive father. All his neighbours are Asian. The Asians killed the industry with cheap imports, then moved in to fill the vacuum.

'I'm Detective Constable Sparkington and this is Detective Inspector Priest,' Dave began. 'We have reason to believe you are in possession of a dangerous dog, namely a pit bull terrier, and may be in contravention of the Dangerous Dogs Act of 1991. Mind if we come in?'

'Er, yeah,' he replied. 'It's a pit bull cross. I always keep 'im on a chain and muzzled when we go out.'

'Where is he now?' I asked.

'Down in the cellar. That's where I keep 'im. Must be fast asleep or he'd be barking 'is 'ead off.'

'What's he called?'

'Bruno.'

'Can we come in?'

I've seen worse flats lived in by the brightest and best that the education system throws up, so I was mildly surprised by Bratt's downstairs room. The difference, I thought, was that he was a long-term tenant, not just passing through. He sat on the settee, which he'd recently vacated if the copy of the *People* strewn across it was anything to go by, and Dave and I made ourselves comfortable on hard chairs that didn't match. There was a faint odour of dog and cannabis in the room.

'Do you have a job?' I asked.

'Not properly,' he replied. 'Barman at the Lamb...the Lamb and Flag. Three nights, that's all.'

'The Lamb and Flag,' I echoed. 'You may be able to help us there. Have you ever come across Andy? He drinks in the Lamb, we're told.'

'No. Never heard of 'im.'

'He deals in the occasional motor, if that helps.'

'No, sorry.'

'Do you draw benefits?' Dave asked.

Bratt coloured up and stared down at his knees. 'Yeah, some. Is that what it's all about?'

'No, we're not interested in your benefits. We're here about the dog. Where was it at about six o'clock on Saturday evening?'

'With me, I think. Yeah, with me.'

'What were your movements?'

He'd driven over to the Sylvan Fields to see his Uncle Carl and taken Bruno along for the ride.

'So who can corroborate that you were there?'

'Audrey can.'

'What relation is Audrey?'

'Sean's half-sister.'

'And Sean is...?'

'Carl's half-brother.'

I grinned at him, asking: 'Can you do us a chart with all these on?'

He grinned back. 'Blame Sean and Carl's mother. She has seven kids from six different dads, including one set of twins.'

'Do you bother with birthdays?' I asked.

'No.'

'So did you come straight home or did you stay?'

'I stayed. She was...you know...upset.'

Yeah, I thought. Upset like the crew of Apollo 13 were when the 'chutes opened. So the caring Mr Bratt stayed to comfort her.

Dave said: 'Is Bruno difficult to handle? Could anyone handle him?'

'No. Just me. They're OK, dogs like 'im, but you can't trust 'im. You've got to let them know who's t'boss.'

'Why do you keep him?'

'Protection. Nobody's touched my car since I got Bruno. And he's a good pet. I like dogs. You know where you are with them.'

'And you don't with people?'

'No.'

Dave said: 'Do you ever lend him out?'

He looked puzzled, then said: 'No, never.'

'Not even to your Uncle Carl?'

'No.'

'Could he handle him?'

'No. Well, only on a lead and muzzled.'

I wondered if it was the dog that wore the muzzle or Uncle Carl. I said: 'So Bruno only goes out with you?'

'That's right.' He looked awkward as he said it.

I turned to Dave, who pulled a piece of paper out of his pocket. 'Where were you on the morning of last Tuesday? That's the fifteenth, if it helps.'

He shuffled his feet and hunched his shoulders. 'No idea. Nowhere special.'

'Try harder.'

'In bed, I s'pose. I don't get up until about ten on a Tuesday. I'm normally still a bit hung over.'

'What about Thursday third of May?'

'No idea. Well, here, I s'pose. I never go anywhere except to Uncle Carl's and the Lamb. Walk in the park, sometimes, that's all.'

Dave read out two more dates and got the same response each time. Terence Bratt's world didn't stretch beyond visits to the pub, a quiet joint and the occasional rumpty-tump with his uncle's stepbrother's half-sister, or something.

'Is Bruno microchipped?' I asked and was rewarded with a shake of the head. He'd grown paler and his eyes had glassed over. If he hadn't recognised it at first he was beginning to realise that this wasn't about his dog licence or his benefits; it was about the robberies. 'So you won't mind if DC Sparkington takes a few specimens of dog hair from your rug, just for elimination purposes?'

He shook his head again and Dave squatted on his heels

to collect some samples. We had a quick look upstairs, with his permission, and drove back to the nick via the sandwich shop.

Maggie had left me a note. *Boss. I was looking down the lists of employees and contractors' staff for the Curzon Centre to see if any name jumped out at me and I noticed that the shopfitters' list ended with an unnamed student. I rang them and their human resources told me that he's called Oscar Sidebottom and he's Carol McArdle's son, working weekends and holidays with them on job placement from college. Just thought you'd like to know. Maggie.*

I read it twice and passed it to Dave. 'Poor sod,' he said and gave it back to me.

'Do you fancy having these in the square?' I asked, holding up the sandwiches, 'watching the girls, catching some sunshine?'

'What a good idea,' he replied, pulling his jacket back on.

Dave bagged a seat while I fetched two large espressos from Starbucks. Several young women strolled past in various degrees of undress, mobile phones clamped to ear, and the inevitable pigeons came waddling by, looking for crumbs. Two teenagers eyed the end of our seat, then gave Dave and me the once-over before deciding they didn't want to share it with two old fogies. I watched them retreat, midriffs bulging over jeans cut so low you could have parked a pair of unicycles in their bum cracks.

'I think I'm growing old,' I stated.

'I know what you mean.'

'Whatever happened to sex appeal?'

'Audrey Hepburn.'

'Kim Novak.'

'Eunice Williamson.'

'Who?'

'Eunice Williamson. Her parents owned the chippy on Silver Street. She used to serve in there when they were busy. The sweat used to come through her T-shirt in all sorts of interesting places.'

'How do you know it was sweat? It might have been chip fat.'

'You spoil everything. You know what your trouble is, don't you?'

'Tell me.'

'You've been moving in higher circles lately. Too high.'

'Could be,' I admitted.

'So how far are we going to take it?'

'Not much further. I'll go see Threadneedle again, to tell him we're winding the investigation down, but really just to…um…needle him.'

'He might cotton on.'

'Shush, or I'll lose the thread. I'll go over to make mischief, that's all. And I wouldn't mind knowing if Miss McArdle went away with him. That's about it. Should be fun – I'll enjoy it. Then we can…um…sew it up – no further action, not in the public's interest.' I looked at my watch. 'The Pickles boys will be enjoying their third or fourth pints, about now, so we can concentrate on them. I'd say some surveillance was called for.'

I'd eaten my sandwich and my coffee was just about cool enough to drink, so I took a precautionary sip. It tasted good. I was having a longer drink when Dave's mobile burst into life. His son Danny is a wizard with all things electronic and he gives his father a different ringtone nearly every week. This week it was 'Ride of the Valkyries'. Dave fumbled with the phone, which was almost lost in his big hands.

'Front desk,' he told me, with a flick of his eyes in my direction. He put the instrument to his ear, saying: 'Mr Sparkington is at lunch. Please call again after three p.m.' After a silence he glanced at me again. 'Yes, he's here. We're over the road, keeping observation in the square.' He listened for a while then emitted a long *Jeeez*.

'OK, we'll be back in a minute. Out.'

He folded the phone and slowly returned it to his pocket. 'Forget interviewing Threadneedle again,' he said. 'Someone's blown his brains out.'

CHAPTER SEVEN

Serena was in the office. 'Right person in the right place,' I told her. 'I have a job for you and it's very important that you do it before the weather changes. Today if possible. I'll try to find someone to go with you. Come and listen while I make this phone call, then I don't have to repeat myself.' I dialled a number from memory.

'Who's that?' Serena asked.

'Scene of crime.' When I'd finished the conversation I dialled again. 'It's Charlie, Gareth,' I said. 'Can you lend me somebody to do some detective work, please? It's important.'

He could. Serena said: 'If I catch rabies I'll sue.'

'You'll catch bigger fish than rabies,' I told her, giving her arm a squeeze. 'Do your best.' Dave was hovering, itching to be off, a bag of paper suits and other detective stuff over his shoulder. Actually, we don't carry much with us these days, because we have an expert for about everything. His eyes and his brains are the good detective's tools of the trade. Together, Dave and I can just about hack it. I led the way, Dave followed.

One of our pandas was parked outside the Threadneedle residence and another one turned into the cul-de-sac behind me. A Day-Glo orange Ford Focus stood on the drive, close to the door, with its boot lid raised.

'Who made the call?' I asked the driver of the first panda.

'Lady of the house, sir.'

I guessed it was her car. I'd taken a quick peep in the boot as I passed it and seen it was full of shopping. 'Where is she now?'

'Inside.'

'Anybody with her?'

His female partner was babysitting her, which was a relief. Having the number one suspect all alone in there wouldn't have been good news. The PC had been told that the body was upstairs. He'd taken a perfunctory look and decided it was murder and radioed for help. I needed to confirm his diagnosis before sending for the cavalry.

I pulled on the full paper suit and padded down the driveway and into the front door. I caught a glimpse of the PC through the half-open door of the room where I'd had coffee six days earlier and assumed Mrs T was in there with her. I'd talk to her later.

My feet, clad in overshoes, sank into the deep carpet as I climbed the stairs and I pulled the jumpsuit's sleeves over my fists to keep them out of trouble. The banister was to the right, so I kept hard over to the left to cause as little disturbance as possible. My own breath sounded like that of a deep-sea diver as it forced its way through the dust mask I was wearing. I paused for a few seconds, pulling it away from my nose as I took a long, slow inhale. Furniture polish and the flower arrangement on the antique pedestal table that stood in the hallway. No bitter almonds; no Gauloises; no Hugo Boss. A trace, perhaps, just the slightest trace, of the smell of blood.

His feet were projecting from behind the bed, pointing away from it. He was face down, and I was grateful. Alongside the bed was a dressing table with naked light bulbs around the mirror, as you would find in a theatre's dressing room. The lights were blazing and a tuneless song was coming from a bedside radio. Polished shoes in two tones of brown, socks with diamond patterns on them. I took a step forward. Grey trousers that looked smart even on a dead man. Thin leather belt. Right hand down by his side, palm upwards; watch strap in yellow metal. Was Threadneedle left-handed? I took another step around the end of the bed.

Left hand flung forward. Something grasped in it. Shirt collar loose with blue and silver tie around it. Head like a big overripe plum tomato. No sign of a weapon.

It was murder. I stooped down to grasp an ankle and lifted his leg. No rigor mortis. The window was open and the first greenbottle had arrived. His *compañeros* wouldn't be far behind. Dead, say, two to five hours. Back downstairs I told Dave to send for the patho and then question the neighbours.

'Hello, Mrs Threadneedle,' I said, easing my way into the sitting room where she was perched on the edge of an easy chair, hands clasped together. 'Do you remember me?' The PC rose to leave but I gestured for her to stay and she sank back into her seat.

Mrs Threadneedle gave me a faint smile of recognition, saying: 'Yes, of course I do. You're Inspector Priest.'

'That's right. You gave me coffee last Tuesday. Do you feel up to telling me all about this morning? We could leave it a while if you like, but the quicker we move...'

I left it hanging, and she said: 'I'll do my best, Inspector. What can I tell you?'

She was remarkably composed, and gave the impression that she hadn't had a drink yet, even though the sun was well higher than Armitage's mill chimney. I said: 'Just go through your movements, then tell me how you found... your husband.'

I was in a tricky position. Mrs T was the number one suspect. Spouses automatically fall into that position – it's a statistical probability – and I knew that she had caught her husband philandering. But if I treated her as a suspect I'd have to haul her down to the station, read her the Riot Act, arrange a solicitor and start the clock. On the other hand, she was unlikely to do a runner or interfere with witnesses, so I could get away with treating her just like one of those witnesses.

She sat staring out of the window for a while, biting her lip, wondering where to start.

'Jan...' I said.

She turned to me with a start. 'I'm sorry. I was...just thinking. Where shall I begin?'

'Right at the beginning. In your own words. It's all off the record. What time did you get up?'

'Hm, about seven-thirty, I think.'

'Go on, please.'

'Well, I had a shower and got dressed and went downstairs for breakfast. Do you want to know what I had?'

'Yes please.'

'Oh, right. I had my usual. That's bran flakes with dried fruit, and camomile tea.'

'Did your husband breakfast with you?'

'No. He's a toast and marmalade man.'

'So where was he at this time?'

'He was in his bedroom. We have separate ones. Have had for a while.'

'Did you see him?'

'No, but I heard him moving around, and his shower. And his radio. He plays Radio Two infernally.'

Played, I thought. *Played* Radio Two. Wogan's audience had reduced by one, and I could imagine how Threadneedle's listening habits would irritate his classically trained flautist wife. 'Did you see him?' I asked.

'Yes. He came down for breakfast, still in his dressing gown.'

'What time would that be?'

'About eight-thirty, perhaps a little later.'

'And then...?'

'I drove into town and parked in the New Mall car park.'

The New Mall is like the New Forest – it's the oldest we have. It opened back in the Seventies when people wanted joined-up shops and local councils sold off all the bus stations and school playgrounds to packs of speculators. No doubt the New Mall was already feeling the impact of the Curzon Centre on its customer base: it's dog eat dog in the retail trade.

'What time did you leave home?'

'Nine o'clock. After the morning rush.'

'Go on, please. You're doing well, but we can stop any time you want.'

'I had a ten o'clock appointment at the hairdresser's. Cindy's on Church Street. I was a little early so I visited a few dress shops in the mall until it was time. Afterwards I went to the supermarket for a few things and then I came home.'

We were nearly at the harrowing bit. She paused as if gathering strength, but before she could launch herself into it she said: 'I never offered either of you a coffee. Would you like one?'

I shook my head. 'No thanks, Jan. I'd like you to continue with what happened, as soon as you feel up to it.'

'I expect you're wondering why I'm not nursing a large G&T, Inspector. Truth is, I haven't had a drink since Friday. You're looking at a reformed character.'

'I'm looking at a lady who was a talented musician, who has had more than her fair share of ups and downs,' I told her. 'We all need a little support at some time in our lives.'

She made a little 'huh' noise and went on: 'I needed some help with the shopping so I went in, looking for Arthur. He wasn't downstairs so I shouted up the stairs, but he still didn't appear. There was a smell. I couldn't describe it but it was sharp on the nostrils. I went upstairs looking for him. The smell was stronger up there, and his bedroom door was open. I walked in and...there he was... on the floor. I still couldn't believe what I was seeing... thought it was some stupid practical joke or something...I told him to get up...not to be so stupid...but he didn't move. Then I realised he was dead.'

'And then...?'

'I came downstairs and dialled nine nine nine.'

After a long pause I said: 'Tell me about the smell, if you can, please.'

She shuffled in her seat. 'I've been thinking about it. Was he – Arthur – was he shot?'

'I don't know.'

'If he was, I think it was smoke. It was what you might call acrid.'

'Right. Did you notice anything else?'

'No.'

'Did you see anyone?'

'No.'

'What about as you drove into the cul-de-sac. Was anybody leaving?'

'No.'

'What was the last vehicle you saw as you drove home?'

It took her some thinking about, but eventually she

remembered that the postman had turned out of the lane as she turned in.

'Did he bring you anything?'

'I...I don't know. I haven't had a look.'

'Could you do that now, Jan, please?'

She left the room, looking, I thought, slightly affronted. I took the opportunity to smile at the PC, who rewarded me with a blush. Had my undeserved and grossly exaggerated reputation gone before me, I wondered?

'I'm sorry, I don't know your name,' I said.

'Judith, sir. Judith Long.'

'Are you enjoying the job?'

'Most of it, sir.'

'Ah, well, we need the miserable bits to make the rest feel better than it really is. *If all the world were playing holidays, to sport would be as tedious as to work.*'

'Sir?'

'Shakespeare,' I told her.

'Oh. We didn't do Shakespeare at school.'

Mrs Threadneedle came back with the information that the postman hadn't even knocked once. No mail today. I said: 'Tell you what, Jan: you make that coffee and Judith and me will bring your shopping in for you. How does that sound?'

It sounded good, so she toddled off into the kitchen and I took Judith outside to fetch the shopping. I spent a couple of minutes with one of the uniformed officers, marking out a path from the street to the front door and appointing him in charge of logging all visitors, then set about the shopping. There was a bootful.

After our second trip Judith said: 'It's good of you to lift all this in for her, sir. Is it all part of the service?'

'Just a little kindness,' I told her, struggling to find a fingerhold on a twelve-pack of Britvic fruit juices. 'It all helps to make things easier. A little kindness goes a long way, as my mother always insisted.'

'I suppose so, sir.'

'And apart from that,' I said, 'there should be a pay and display ticket in here somewhere, and the store's receipt. They'll have times on them. See if you can find them, will you?'

We were drinking the coffee when I saw the pathologist from the General pull up in his Porsche Cayenne and lift his bag of gubbins from the back. I needed a word with him as soon as he'd finished upstairs. Mrs Threadneedle was sitting quietly, sipping her coffee, probably thinking it needed a large slug of Grand Marnier to make it palatable. I said: 'Is there anywhere you can go for a couple of days, Jan? We have to regard the house as a crime scene and will need it sealing off while our forensic people can give it a good going-over.'

She had a sister in Harrogate, which was useful. After a brief discussion she accepted my offer to break the news to her sister and I did the necessary. Her reaction was more or less what you'd expect. Surprise, with a touch of grief and an underlying impression that she thought he'd got what he deserved. Janet would be most welcome to stay as long as she wanted. Sister even offered to collect her and the dog, which I gratefully accepted.

I was explaining to Janet when the pathologist looked into the room and gave me a nod to say he'd finished his preliminary examination and would grant me a few minutes to relate his findings. I excused myself from the ladies as politely as I could and was soon climbing into the passenger seat of the Porsche.

'Thanks for coming so promptly, Prof,' I said. 'I know you're a busy man.'

'Got to when it's a fresh one, Charlie,' he replied. 'Time is of the essence, whatever that means. It's not so important if the corpse has been in the river for a month.'

'So what can you tell me?'

'Shot in the back of the head at close range. Time of death between eight a.m. and eleven a.m. Body not moved. That's about it. PM at nine tomorrow. Will you be there in person or will you delegate?' I could feel him smiling as he said it.

'I'll delegate. Bullet still in his head?'

'Yes.'

'Did you see a gun anywhere?'

'Only had a perfunctory look, but no.'

'He was holding something in his left hand…'

'Yes. It's one of those little nasal hair razors. Wouldn't mind one myself, if they're any good. Do you think that's the clue that will unmask his killer, Charlie?'

'It might be. Did he have hairy nostrils?'

'Yes. It's like a bramble patch in there.'

'Then no, it won't be. Can I send the Munchkins in?'

'I'm done here. It's all yours.'

'Thanks.' I patted the dashboard. 'Nice car.'

PC Long was coming away from the house as I waved the professor off. As we'd talked I'd been thinking about

Mrs Threadneedle. I needed her clothes. There'd probably be blood on them either way, but the pattern of that blood would speak volumes. She'd need to change all her clothes before she went to her sister's, and I wanted the ones she removed. 'Judith,' I called to her. 'I have a little job for you...'

Back at the nick I cleared the walls of the Portakabin we use as an incident room and opened a new diary and crime log. Dave came in with the usual bad news from the neighbours: they hadn't seen or heard a dicky bird.

'A sister's coming to pick up Mrs Threadneedle,' I told him. 'She'll want to change her clothes before she goes and I've asked Judith – that's PC Long to you – to liaise with the SOCO and confiscate her washing basket. I assume she realised I mean the contents and not the actual basket, but I'm not too sure, so keep an eye on her. When the geeks let me in I had a good look for the gun but couldn't find it. He had a hole in the back of his head the size of a satsuma and blood had welled out of it.'

'And if she shot him she'd be sprayed with the stuff.'

'Yep.'

Mr Wood, the super, came to join us and I went through it all again for his benefit. I didn't mind – sometimes, by going over things again and again something jumps up that you'd missed earlier. But not today, unfortunately.

'He had enemies,' Gilbert declared. 'Have you had words with the fraud boys?'

'Not yet.'

'They might have a list of his business acquaintances.

And what about his links with the Curzons? Do you think there's anything in that?'

'I doubt it. Going from graffiti to murder is a bit of an escalation, don't you think?'

'I suppose so. What I really want to tell you is not to let the pit bull crimes slip off the radar. They involve the general public; we're all potential victims. Sad as the death of Mr Threadneedle may be, chances are it's an isolated incident, a private murder.'

Yeah, I thought, and it would only count as one off the clear-up rate, whilst the burglaries were standing at four.

'Do you need any help?' Mr Wood asked. He was about to go for his annual dose of salmon fishing, and I'd be left to fend off the brass and the press.

'We can always use some help,' I replied.

'I'll see what I can do.'

When he'd gone Dave said: 'I wonder if it's painful.'

'What?'

'Slipping off the radar. Do you think there might be a link with the Curzon incident?'

I screwed up my face into an expression of disbelief. 'I can't see it...but, on the other hand, it might be wise to put East Yorkshire in the picture. Pass me the almanac, please.'

They weren't too pleased but accepted what I told them, said they'd keep a weather eye on the house and its occupants. The phone had only been in its cradle for a second when it rang.

'It's Duncan at scientific services, Mr Priest. Those clothes and shoes you seized from the Threadneedles.

I've had a preliminary look at them and so far the small amount of blood I've found on them is consistent with the wearer crouching to touch the body. That's all. I'll give them a more thorough inspection but I doubt if there'll be anything more to tell you.'

'No spray, no splashes?'

'I'm afraid not. Sorry not to be more helpful.'

'Not your fault, Duncan. Thanks for being so prompt.'

I replaced the phone and told Dave the news. 'Bugger,' he said.

'Quite,' I agreed.

CHAPTER EIGHT

Our press office had informed the local agencies of the untimely death of our beloved mayor, which took the load off me. There were people I wanted to see, but having to start by breaking bad news to them doesn't fit in with my interviewing technique. Let them hear it from the telly first. On the way home I collected a *Mumbai machli* with *Peshwari naan* from the Aagrah and had it accompanied by Smetana's *Má Vlast* playing on the CD. No reason. I just looked down the titles and it jumped out at me. It's a great work, about roots, and I hadn't heard it for a while. Just before half past nine I decided the time was right.

'Curzon,' he said after the fourth warble.

'It's DI Priest, Mr Curzon,' I said. 'Sorry to disturb you but I was wondering if you'd heard the news?'

'About Threadneedle? Yes, just now. Bit of a shaker, don't you think?'

'That's right. I was wondering if I could come over for a talk about him. You're one of the few people he could call a friend and I'd appreciate an unbiased opinion.'

'What, now?'

'No. Tomorrow sometime.'

'Of course you can. I'm always here. How did he die?'

'He was shot.'

'Was it murder?'

'It's looking that way. Any particular time?'

'The poor bugger. I wouldn't have wished that on him. No, Inspector, like I said, I'm always here.'

After that it was the one I was looking forward to. 'Miss McArdle?' I said, after her curt 'Hello'.

She'd heard the news, too. You can never be sure how lovers are going to react when they hear about the death of the object of their passion. Some are devastated, as if they'd lost a limb. Others – most – adopt an almost indifferent air, as if fate had stepped in to help them out of a situation that had grown out of control. It was impossible to tell which group she fell into from our telephone conversation. At ten next morning, seated in her office, she still wasn't giving much away.

'How did he die, Inspector?' she asked.

'He was shot in the back of the head. Death would be instantaneous.'

She pulled a face to demonstrate her distaste. 'Ugh! Poor old Arthur. Isn't that the style of a gangland execution, or do I read too much crime fiction?'

She was right, we do regard such killings as executions, but I don't know why. If you want somebody dead the brain is the organ to go for, and if you're going to shoot someone in the head it must be tidier to do it at the back than the front. Shooting someone in the nose or the eye while they were looking up at you imploringly would surely cause loss of sleep in the hardest villain. You didn't need to be in a gang, with a BSc in slaying, to know that.

'I suspect you read too much crime fiction. How well did you know him?'

'Not very well. He interviewed me for this job about a year ago.'

'There's one question I must ask, Miss McArdle. Where were you between eight and eleven yesterday morning?'

'Right here, Inspector, at my desk.'

'Can anybody corroborate that?'

'Oh, about ten people, no problem.'

'That's good enough for me. Tell me, just how does one become manager of a shopping mall and conference centre?'

'I have a degree in business studies and experience as assistant manager at shopping centres in York and Heckley New Mall. I was headhunted when this became available. Is that good enough for you, Inspector?'

She was wearing a skirt and blouse, and curved and bulged in all the right places. Soft and gently rounded, like the ladies on the cover of *Weight Watchers* magazine. It wasn't just Miss McArdle's head that Threadneedle had hunted, that was for sure.

I flapped a hand. 'I just wondered what the career progression was. You seem awfully young for such a responsible job.'

'What are you insinuating?'

'Nothing, nothing at all. What sort of person was Mr Threadneedle?'

'How would I know?'

'You worked for him.'

'No I didn't. I was recruited by a recruitment agency and I work for the shareholders. Arthur had influence with them, that's true, but he wasn't my employer.'

'Was he your lover?'

Colour spread up from under the collar of her blouse like the sun rising out of Bridlington Bay on a bank holiday morning. 'No,' she stated, with just a touch too much defiance.

'You call him Arthur.'

'He told me to. We worked together for six months prior to the opening and...he liked to keep things informal.'

'Last week, after the opening, you took Wednesday and Thursday off. Where did you go?' That shook her. I'd put her in the second category of unrequited lovers: glad it was all over, relieved to be out of a difficult situation. I was thinking that Threadneedle must have used a pneumatic drill to get to her heart, unless it had been strictly a business arrangement right from the start.

'I...I don't know.'

'Of course you know. Look in your diary.'

'I didn't go anywhere. After the previous few hectic days I needed a rest. I stayed at home, read a book. That's all.'

'Ah! A crime book, no doubt.'

'Yes.'

'So are you denying that you spent part of last week at a posh hotel – the Belfry, was it – with the late Mr Threadneedle?'

This time the colour was sucked from her face and she took on the appearance of someone fleeing from the last days of Pompeii. 'Who told you that?' she whispered.

You just did, I thought. 'I put two and two together; it's my job.'

'Does this mean I'm a suspect?'

'It's often the lover who did it. Did you shoot Mr Threadneedle in the head yesterday morning?'

'Of course not.'

'In that case, you're not a suspect.' I leant forward towards her, my arms on her desk, and looked into her face. 'But I need your help. I'm not here to judge or moralise. I want to find the person who killed the mayor of Heckley and I imagine you'd like to see him brought to justice, too.' I explained that our conversation was off the record, but if she said, or was about to say, anything incriminating, I'd suspend the interview and advise her about a solicitor. She nodded to say she understood.

'How long had you been having an affair with Mr Threadneedle?'

'Nearly two years.'

'How did you meet him?'

'I was temping to earn some extra cash while I studied, seven or eight years ago. We met again while I was at York. He was part of a delegation that came on a fact-finding exercise and he recognised me. I asked him to think of me when the positions were being filled and...he did.'

I bet he did, I thought. And no doubt there was a deal of mutual back-scratching in between times. 'Were you married?' I asked.

'Was. My husband left me. He found out...and...we're divorced now.'

'So you're a free agent.'

'Yes, I suppose I am.'

'Had Arthur made you any promises?'

'You mean, did I murder him, or have him murdered, because he let me down? Yes, I thought he was going to leave his wife, but he told me he couldn't. Not for a while, until his year in office was over. Before that there were other excuses. And no, I didn't murder him. I simply recognised that I was another silly woman who'd fallen for the wrong man, a married one, and had been used. That's all. It all came to a head last week, at the Belfry.'

I widened my eyes and said: 'I hope you didn't make a scene at the Belfry, Miss McArdle.'

A hint of a smile flickered across her face. 'A small one, perhaps.'

'So did you revert to your maiden name after the divorce?'

'Yes.'

'What was your married name?'

'I hoped you wouldn't ask. It was Sidebottom.'

'Some would regard that as a fine old Anglo-Saxon name,' I suggested.

'Like my husband did. I wanted to change it, but

he wouldn't, so I never used it. I preferred being Carol McArdle.'

'It's certainly snappier. Have you any children?' I knew the answer, but let her tell me.

'A son. He's called Oscar, nearly twenty years old, studying electrical engineering. What else do you need to know?'

She needed to talk, so I encouraged her. I was an attentive audience. She'd done well, coming from a lowly background to be manager of a multi-million-pound organisation in the public's eye, only to be facing embarrassment and disgrace because of her cheating lover. Her cheating lover who was dead and therefore nicely out of it. It was front-page stuff, and she needed it like Threadneedle had needed a hole in the...hmm, I let the thought hang there.

Oscar was the problem. He'd worshipped his motorcycle-riding, football-playing father, and turned against him when he left without so much as a goodbye. Now the reason for that leaving – his mother's adultery – would be splashed across the tabloids for all to see, and she was fearful that she'd lose her son, too.

Her desk was nearly as untidy as mine. Two huge TFT monitors, wireless keyboard, obligatory photo frame, Pukka Pad and pen, two telephones and piles of correspondence and trade magazines that were poised to slide off the end. Another desk in a corner was equally piled high, awaiting the attention of a secretary who didn't appear to exist. So much for starting with a clean sheet. She had, I noticed, fallen for the spiel of the executive chair salesman.

'Where is your husband now?' I asked.

'I don't know. He had links with a friend in Portugal. I suspect he's working in a bar over there.'

'What's his first name?'

'Barry.'

'And Oscar has no contact with him?'

'No.'

'Can you be sure?'

'Mmm, I don't suppose so. If he has, he's kept it secret from me.'

'Does Oscar work here at all?'

'Yes. He spent a lot of time with the electricians. Now he's in the control room, ironing out the gremlins.'

'Do you have many?'

'A fair few.'

'Tell me about Arthur. Did he ever talk about his enemies?'

'No, not really.'

'In other words, he did.'

'Just, you know, how he'd pulled a fast one on somebody. I never listened. Found it all a bit boring.'

'Any names come to mind?'

'No. None.'

'Did he ever talk about horse racing?'

'A little. He liked to show off about that. And name-drop.'

'What names?'

'The Curzons, who else?'

'Any others?'

'None that meant anything to me.'

I said: 'What about pillow talk, Miss McArdle? He must have let slip some indiscretion when you were together in bed. What did he talk about?'

The colour returned to her cheeks. 'No,' she replied. 'He liked to talk about, you know, what we were doing. That's all.'

Now it was probably my turn to blush. 'And afterwards?' I said. It was Clint Eastwood who said that at his age there was a lot of afterwards.

'He fell asleep.'

I went for a stroll around the mall, checking the positions of the exits and emergency exits. And the price of trainers and hiking gear. And CDs in the HMV shop. Dave and Maggie were in the food court, behind large lattes and doughnuts.

'Anything from the PM?' I asked, slipping into the plastic chair alongside Dave. Three girls who looked too young to have left school were manoeuvring three buggies alongside a nearby table. Maggie pulled a chair out of their way and the prettiest girl thanked her. The children all looked well fed and happy, pleased to meet their little friends in what appeared to be a daily ritual.

'Morning, Chas,' he said, pushing a plate towards me. 'I saved you a doughnut,' but I shook my head to decline it. 'Right then,' he went on, 'the PM. Nothing to add to what we already know, I'm afraid. He was in good shape physically apart from some signs of liver damage. Traumatic gunshot wound... Wait for it...' He pulled out his notebook and flicked it open. 'Here we are...*traumatic wound to posterior parietal bones in the location of the sagittal suture*, if that means anything to you. Otherwise, shot in the back of the head. No other injuries, no exit wound. Partly dressed to go out, no sign of a struggle. Possibly taken by surprise, or restrained at gunpoint, or he knew his assailant. Radio was playing therefore may not have heard his assailant approach.'

'What station?'

'Radio Two.'

'Just checking. Go on.'

'Only item of interest is the bullet. It's soft-nosed and therefore too distorted to be much use, but the prof weighed and measured it and reckons it could be a .32 calibre. Not one you come across every day.'

'Hmm. I believe the target shooters use them. It's not the chosen weapon of your average Yardie. Anything else?'

'Nope.'

Maggie said: 'Are you still going to East Yorkshire or is that line of enquiry abandoned?'

'I want to pick Curzon's brains,' I told her. 'He was a social contact, probably knows about his business dealings. I might find something out. Otherwise, yes, I think it's a waste of time. What are you two on with?'

'We've traced the route taken by the graffiti artist,' Maggie told me. 'Inside and out. Here, I've marked it on one of the store's you-are-here diagrams.' She slid it across the table and spun it round. 'It looks as if he used this fire exit. We were wondering if there was any point in having forensics look at it.'

I was hoping the graffiti incident was dead and buried. Before I could pass judgement we were disturbed by the 'Ride of the Valkyries', with three-part harmonies.

Sparky dived into his pocket to pull out his mobile and

pulled a face when he didn't recognise the pathologist's number. 'Yes, he's here with me. I'll put him on.' He passed it to me, saying: 'It's the professor.'

'Hello, Professor,' I said. 'What can we do for you?'

'How are you getting on with the hunt for Shergar, Charlie?'

I hesitated for a few seconds, then: 'Now, who might have mentioned that to you, I wonder?'

'Ha ha. Don't be too hard on him, he's a good lad. But it did set me thinking, so I rang Huntingdon to check with them and I was right. .32 calibre soft-nosed bullets are used in humane killers, as held by slaughtermen, some farmers and people in the horse racing business. Thought you ought to know.'

'Don't they use fixed-bolt guns?' I asked.

'Apparently not. Fixed bolt are just for stunning, prior to cutting the jugular. For humane killing the gun is modified to fire a single bullet. And as a matter of interest, when used at racecourses the Jockey Club rules require it to be fitted with a silencer. Don't want the poor spectators upset every time a horse is put down, do we?'

'No indeed. So our man could have horse racing connections.'

'It's a possibility.'

'Thanks for that, Professor. You've just changed the direction of the enquiry.'

Dave and Maggie looked mystified. I handed him his phone and said: 'As we were. The East Yorkshire mafia is back in the frame.'

*   *   *

Toby answered the door. 'Charlie!' she exclaimed and for a few worrying seconds I thought she was about to launch herself into my arms. 'Daddy said you were coming so I've been looking out for you.' She was wearing cut-down jeans and a T-shirt covered in paint splashes.

'I drove as fast as I could,' I said. 'How are you?'

'I'm fine. Did you drive here with your blue light flashing?'

'My car doesn't have a blue light. You look as if you've been painting.'

'Only wallpaper. Don't you have one that you can stick on the roof in an emergency, like they do on the television?'

'No. They have lots of things on the television that we don't have in real life.'

'Daddy's in his workshop. C'mon, I'll take you.'

She led the way into the gloomy interior and I felt the temperature drop as we left the sunshine behind. No wonder they all died of consumption, I thought, and that made me think about Toby and her illness.

'Is it true you beat up ten yobs at the hospital?' she was saying.

'An exaggeration,' I replied. 'There were only six of them.'

'Cor! I wish I'd seen it.'

Up a servant-sized staircase, down a corridor lacking windows and carpet, through several doors and we were there. 'Grizzly was impressed,' Toby said as she turned the knob of the final door and bumped it with her hip. 'She said there were bodies flying all over the place.' The door was sticking and I noticed she was breathing heavily from the climb up the stairs, so I reached over her and leant against it until it gave way.

Curzon looked up from what he was doing as if we'd caught him working on some fiendish experiment, but the impression was soon dispelled when I saw the fruits of his labours, lining the walls of his workshop like some exercise in Lilliputian town planning.

'Like 'em?' he said, coming round his bench to shake my hand.

I slowly turned, taking them in. He made dolls' houses. Most were three-storey town houses, Georgian style, with a smattering of country cottages and modern detached dwellings. There was even a corner shop with its fare spilling out onto the pavement, where a delivery boy's bicycle leant against the kerb.

'I'm amazed,' I said. 'Just amazed. They all look terrific.' I stooped to look inside one, and saw a scene from an Edwardian childhood, where a comely woman in a white tunic was reading a bedtime story to a little girl while her parents, dressed to the nines, tiptoed furtively out of the front door to their waiting Rolls-Royce. 'The detail's incredible.'

'We buy the figures in,' Curzon confessed, 'but we make everything else ourselves. They're one-twenty-fourth scale.'

'I do the wallpaper,' Toby announced.

'And a lot of the furniture,' her father added. 'She makes a mean Welsh dresser, don't you, Pumpkin?'

It was a big room with a sloping ceiling, smelling of

wood and glue and equipped with junior versions of every woodworking tool you could think of: bandsaw; jigsaw; circular saw; mitres and routers; planers and sanders; various jigs and templates; all neatly stored but easily reached. Toby showed me her desk in a corner with a high stool, where she painted sheets of lightweight acid-free paper with suitably reduced wallpaper designs from the period of the house her father was working on. An old-fashioned cast iron radiator, like the ones in my infant school, stood next to her workplace, but it obviously wasn't on. An equally ancient pyrene fire extinguisher hung on the wall above it.

Curzon asked Toby if she'd mind leaving us alone, and as she left she said: 'Will I see you before you go, Charlie?'

'Toby, don't be so impolite,' Curzon told her.

I turned to him, saying: 'How about a cuppa in the tea shop when we've finished?' And when he agreed it was a good idea she scampered away.

'Now, how can I help you, Charlie?'

'Tell me about the dolls' houses,' I said. 'Presumably you sell them.'

'Two. I've sold two, but the grand opening of Curzon House Dolls' Houses is in August at the village fete. We hold it on the car park. It all started when Ghislaine was small. We bought her one and when she outgrew it we consigned it to the attic. Toby wasn't interested; she doesn't do dolls. Two years ago I advertised it on eBay and the response was unbelievable. I can make them, I thought, and here we are.'

'What's that you're making?' I asked. 'It doesn't look very dollsy-housey.'

'No, it's not. It's a small display unit to hold a collection of egg cups, for the main house. We do them for thimbles, too.'

I looked at him, puzzled, and he said: 'Don't ask.'

'OK, I won't, but good luck with it. Looks like a winner to me.'

'They pay me for them, and every little helps. Believe it or not, bespoke egg cup racks are difficult to come by. I do it for Toby. She's really involved with them. Do you have children, Charlie?'

'No.'

'You worry about them. Toby doesn't enjoy good health, as you've probably noticed.'

'Yes. She soon starts to puff. Is the atmosphere in here good for her?'

'Not when the saw is in use, but that's only now and then. If necessary she works in her bedroom. Today I'm assembling, so that's OK.'

We fell into an awkward silence until I said: 'Tell me about Threadneedle. How did you meet him?'

Curzon smiled at the memory. 'Ha! He organised a soirée, didn't he. He and his relatively new wife had moved into a house over in Dunkley, near Malton, that had been owned by a racehorse trainer called Jonty Hargrave. You may have heard of him: he trained some good winners. There was a stable block and Threadneedle had ambitions to obtain his trainer's licence and keep the yard going. Unfortunately it's not that easy. You need a lifetime's involvement to get your licence and owners won't risk their horses with anyone. He ended up as just another livery yard, catering for the local hackers and pony club kids.'

'He went downmarket?'

'That's right. It must have been a disappointment to him. Then there was a fire and he lost the lot.'

'Tell me about the fire.'

'Not much to tell. One horse died, I believe, and most of the block was destroyed. Arson was suspected, but nothing ever came of it. Someone may have had a grudge against Threadneedle, or possibly against Jonty Hargrave, not realising he'd moved on. Horse racing is a tough business, as you probably know. Fortunes are at stake.'

'So I've heard. Was there an insurance payout?'

'No idea.'

I skirted round the subject for a few minutes, prompting him here and there, inviting him to tell me again about the time he nearly owned one of racing's aristocrats. I'd heard it all before but he enjoyed telling the tale and I'm a patient listener when it suits me. The punchline hadn't changed, though: owning a horse like that was a fantasy, a daydream, that's all. I said: 'Were there many more soirées with the Threadneedles?'

'Only one, perhaps a couple, if I remember rightly. Janet – Mrs Threadneedle – was a classical-flute player. Listening to her was magical. She was a beautiful woman and a lovely person. She and Laura – my wife – got on so well. I was so sorry when you told me about her problems.'

We collected Toby and strolled to the tearoom, discussing

the weather. Apparently it was about to break in the south, with us following shortly after. Thunderstorms were due. I confessed to being a painter, saying that I'd like to set up my easel in the grounds sometime and see what I could make of the view. They both thought it a great idea, and so did I: it gave me an open invitation to come and visit any time I liked.

I paid the bill – 'my treat' – and left as soon as I could, saying I had a long drive home. Out on the highway I studied the map to see the quickest way to Dunkley, home of Jonty Hargrave, racehorse trainer to the aristocracy. Driving there I ran the day's events through my mind. It had been reasonably fruitful, but it was one of little Toby's comments that was uppermost. She'd said that her sister, the beautiful Grizzly, 'was impressed'. I was grinning so hard I nearly missed the turn-off.

The *Beware Racehorses* road signs reminded me that this was gee-gee country. The hedges and verges were all neatly trimmed and beyond them I could see post-and-rail fences curling off into the distance. A set of traffic lights marked a crossing put there just for the horses, and every cottage and house had a 4X4 and trailer, or a horsebox, standing on the drive.

There was a post office, which simplified things. I signed the petition to save it and asked about Mr Hargrave. He was still alive, a postmistress straight off a packet of wholemeal flour told me, adding, after consulting the clock, that I'd probably catch him 'in the Alice'.

'The Alice?' I queried.

'The Alice Hawthorne. It's the village pub. Can't miss it.'

'Oh, right.'

She was right. He was and you couldn't. Two old-timers were having a game of fives and threes for pennies, with the landlord looking on. Otherwise the pub was empty. One of them was big and prosperous-looking, wearing a jacket and cravat in defiance of the heat; his companion angular and awkward, with misshapen teeth and a laugh like a jackdaw passing a kidney stone. I guessed which was my man.

I seated myself between them as Jackdaw shuffled the dominoes, and said: 'Jonty Hargrave?'

'Might be,' Cravat replied after a moment's hesitation.

I showed him my warrant card. 'DI Priest, Heckley CID. Mind if I interrupt your game and have a word?'

'Looks like I don't have much option.'

The landlord said: 'Hey hey, Jonty. Looks like your past has caught up with you at last.'

Jackdaw held my wrist and studied the card as if it were a thing of wonder until I pulled away. I pointed at their glasses and asked the landlord for refills, with one for himself and an orange juice for me. It was turning into an expensive day.

'You sold your stables to a man called Arthur George Threadneedle,' I began, after we'd all taken a long sip.

'Cheers. Happen I did, happen I didn't.'

The landlord started laughing. 'Maybe he wants his money back, Jonty. You said he was greener than a Sammy Ledgard bus.'

'Cheers. Let's happen you did,' I insisted. 'You might be interested to know that he was murdered yesterday.'

That caught their attention. 'Murdered,' Hargrave echoed. 'How?'

'He was shot in the head. What can you tell me about him?'

'Next to nothing. He was obviously a townie with more brass than brains. As soon as we'd completed I was off to my daughter's in France. Stayed two years but it didn't work out. Came back to Dunkley, didn't I? Never saw him again.' He raised his pint of Black Sheep and took a long draught.

'Was this after the fire?'

He stiffened and the pint glass hit the table hard as he lowered it. 'You know about the fire?'

'I've done my homework.'

'It was just after the fire. I didn't go to look: it would have broken my heart.'

The landlord said: 'There was a lot of bad feeling in the village about the fire. They said a horse died. That's worse than paedophilia in a place like this.'

I looked at Hargrave. 'Would he be insured?'

'I suppose so. He'd be an idiot not to be.'

'Did he take over your insurance when you sold it to him?'

'Come to think of it, yes he did, but I don't think it had long to run.'

'Maybe he renewed it. That would be simplest. Can you remember the company?'

'Aye. They're called Doncaster Equestrian, underwritten by the York & Durham. One of the biggest in the game.'

'Right. Now tell me this: was there a humane killer in the inventory?'

*   *   *

I rang Dave from the pub car park and told him to find out what he could from the insurance company. The distance between Heckley and Ogglethorpe was about seventy-two miles, so I exercised my brain with some mental arithmetic as I drove, and calculated that a return journey would earn me about thirty pounds in expenses. On the other hand, Mrs Smith would only charge me a discounted twenty pounds for B&B. I needed to be back in the village tomorrow, so it would save the firm ten pounds if I stayed overnight. Mr Wood didn't see it that way when I phoned him to explain, but he eventually gave one of his sighs and told me to do whatever I thought was best.

Jonty Hargrave had owned a humane killer but had passed it on when he sold the house and yard. 'Was it fixed bolt?' I'd asked him, and he told me no, it fired a bullet.

'Did you hold a licence for it?'

'It didn't need one.'

'It did if it fired a bullet,' I assured him.

'That's news to me. But it was always kept in a locked box, same as I would with a shotgun.'

'Did you tell Threadneedle it didn't need one?'

'I suppose so.' He was silent for a while, considering just how helpful to be. Or unhelpful. Playing dumb, acting slow, is a Yorkshire characteristic, and I suspected he was an expert.

'You know, Inspector,' he began, leaning forward as if to reveal some great confidentiality, 'here in the country we work to a different set of rules to what you do in the city. But that doesn't make us dishonest. We believe in doing what's right, and that means that sometimes we stray outside the written law, if you understand what I mean.'

I understood all right. Who minded if a gamekeeper poisoned a few birds of prey if it helped the pheasant shoot? Or snared the badgers that might or might not transmit TB? Or if Farmer Giles slaughtered the pig he hadn't registered, in his barn, with an axe?

'I need to know about the two or three years he had the stables,' I said. 'I need names: people who knew him; friends and enemies. Was he involved in any betting scams, or playing fast and loose with somebody's wife? What did the village gossip say? Who did he upset enough for them to want him dead?'

Hargrave shook his head. 'Don't ask me,' he said. 'I was down in the Dordogne, sampling the old *vin rouge*.'

'You know more about him than I do,' I insisted.

'Sorry, but I can't help you.'

The landlord had been standing, leaning on the fireplace, while we talked, listening with a slightly amused expression on his face. But now he looked puzzled. He leant on the table and said: 'What about old Motty? Wouldn't he be able to help?'

'Who?' asked Hargrave, giving the landlord a glare that would have frozen a piranha's heart.

The landlord got the message and fell silent, but they'd reckoned without Jackdaw. 'Tha knows!' he blurted out. 'Old Motty Dermot. He was thy head lad for long enough. Doesn't tha remember?'

Hargrave nodded, as if the knowledge had just come back to him. 'Oh aye,' he said.

'Motty Dermot,' I repeated, looking at Jackdaw. 'Does he live in the village?'

'Aye, but thou'll get no sense from him. He's fell on his head once too often.'

'We'll see.' I turned to Hargrave again, saying: 'Meanwhile, what happened to the humane killer?'

'Nay, don't ask me. I presume you haven't found it.'

'No, but we will.' I decided to take the offensive. 'Tell me: did you make many enemies while you were training horses? Did you have any dissatisfied customers?' Where money is involved, big money, there are always dissatisfied customers.

The self-assured complacency slipped from his face like the duvet sliding off your bed on a winter's morning. 'You mean...?'

I shrugged my shoulders. 'Mistaken identity. Perhaps somebody got the wrong man. It's a possibility we always have to consider.'

'That'll give him something to think about,' I said to myself when I was back in the car, after another visit to the post office. Served him right for calling me a city boy.

Phyllis Smith gave me lasagne and cherry pie with custard, and afterwards joined me for a glass of wine in her front room. I told her about the murder but she'd never met or even heard of Threadneedle, never made it to one of his soirées. Jonty Hargrave was well known, but she hadn't been invited to join his circle of friends, either. I telephoned Jeff Caton and told him I'd probably be in about noon tomorrow.

He'd studied the route taken by the graffiti artist and was organising a fingertip search of the plots of garden that decorated the car parks at the Curzon Centre. West Pennine had complained that we were holding evidence back about the pit bull robberies, but he'd fobbed them off. That was all. I was up to date and sipping good red wine, enjoying a chat with a personable lady who cooked like an angel. What more could I ask for? OK, so I knew the answer, but three out of four isn't bad. When it was dark I announced that I was going for some fresh air and left the house.

My route took me to the Curzon estate, via a bridle path that was a more direct route than the road. The moon hadn't risen and the meadow I crossed was blacker than the inside of a Co-op undertaker's top hat. I didn't trip over any sleeping cows but I could hear them snuffling and grunting in their sleep. Do cows sleep? Eventually I made it to the stile that put me back on the lane right outside the estate. I slipped under the barrier and headed up the driveway, walking flat-footed, like an Indian, to make less noise. The trees on either side were looming black canyon walls, but high above me the strip of sky blazed with the light of the Milky Way. I turned and walked backwards for a few steps, wondering at my shadow, cast by the light of a billion stars.

The car park faced the front of the house, with picnic tables at irregular intervals around the edge. The same two windows were illuminated as before. The full sky was visible now, but the spring and summer constellations are not as familiar as the winter ones. Eventually I identified the Plough, upside down to its winter position, and from it the Pole Star, and that was about it.

I sat on the bench bolted to one of the tables, facing the house with my back against the table. The stars were there every night, I thought, and most of us never took the time to appreciate them. The greatest free show on Earth, and we couldn't be bothered. There was a vociferous movement amongst astronomers to control light pollution, because children were growing up in ignorance of the wonders that were right there on their doorsteps, give or take a few million light years. Maybe I'd join them, write a letter to the *Gazette*.

I didn't know what I was doing there, but looking at the sky was good enough reason. I had, in the past, camped overnight on Blea Fell to watch the meteor showers that were predicted but never materialised. That brought a smile to my face. I was with the girl who was to become my wife for a couple of years, before the pseudo-glamour of being married to a cop faded into a routine of missed meals and late nights. Things were good for a while, though, I remembered, and we'd found ways of compensating for the lack of meteors.

There were others, too, that I'd shared my knowledge of the skies with, some of it true, some of it hastily invented. And one who knew far more than I did, who had gone to her own place up there, in the cosmos, whence we all came.

Perspective. That's what it was all about. Quality time. It was good to be alone sometimes, with your thoughts. Helped you appreciate what you had, and the difference between what you wanted and what you needed. A shooting star, a modest one, fell silently through the sky for a brief moment before slipping away. It had been in at the birth of the solar system, four and a half billion years ago, before burning up in the atmosphere of the insignificant planet we call the Earth.

I was wondering if anyone else in the whole world would have witnessed its demise, its one second of glory, when, away to my left, the unmistakeable sound of an automatic pistol being cocked brought me crashing back to reality.

CHAPTER NINE

My spine became an icicle as I rose to my feet and turned towards the sound. I was, I reminded myself, in the middle of a murder investigation. Someone had killed once, and it was easier the second time, especially if the net was closing in. I had two options: face him or flee. If I fled – the favoured option – it could either be towards the house or into the wood. The wood was the better prospect. I'd easily lose him in there, unless his shooting was lucky. Then the sound of another pistol being cocked, away to my right, caused me to think again. I looked in the directions of the noises. Two dark figures, guns held close and pointing skywards, stepped out of the shadows.

'Inspector Priest, I presume,' one of them said, placing his gun back in its holster.

'Jeesus,' I hissed, sitting down again. 'You scared the living daylights out of me.'

They were the crew of an ARV based in East Yorkshire, detailed to keep an eye out for strange vehicles around the village in response to my tip-off. They'd identified my car outside Phyllis's B&B and linked me to it when the indicators flashed as I used the remote locking. The rest was just for their amusement, at the expense of the hotshot DI from Heckley.

'We come here all the time, don't we, Dave?' one of them was saying.

'Oh, all the time,' his partner agreed.

'See that top window? Well, Ghislaine usually opens the curtains and takes her kit off in it about this time of night. That right, Dave?'

'That's right, Bri.'

'In your dreams,' I said.

They offered me a lift back to the village but the back seats of ARVs are not the healthiest of environments and I'd had enough of their double act, so I declined. They wandered off back to their Volvo and I rested against the table again to give my heart rate chance to settle.

The moon had risen, was playing peek-a-boo over the tops of the trees behind the house when I saw the light. It was in the doorway but hardly visible. After a few seconds a figure emerged from the shadows and headed purposefully towards the gardens, away from me. When it was out of sight I jumped to my feet and raced after it.

She'd turned the flashlight off but was plainly visible in

the middle of the broad path that led between the walled garden and the tea shop and out towards the furthest corner of the grounds. I kept to the shadows, dodging from one patch to the next. Suddenly she did a left turn, through a gate, and was lost in the darkness. I slowed to a standstill and listened. She wasn't making much noise but I could just about hear her. Slowly, picking my footfalls as carefully as possible, I headed in the direction she'd taken and soon found myself on the edge of a clearing. The moon had broken free from the trees and was behind me now, but she wasn't within sight. I counted to a hundred while my eyes adjusted, but I still couldn't see her.

The ground was uneven, criss-crossed with ridges and mounds, picked out by their moon shadows. Here and there bits of stone wall protruded from the earth for a few feet and clumps of thistles grew everywhere. I'd been here before, on my first visit to Curzon House. It was the deserted medieval village of Low Ogglethorp.

'Toby,' I called, very softly. 'It's me, Charlie. Where are you?'

'Charlie?' I heard her reply, almost under my feet. 'What are you doing here?' She was sitting on the ground in a pool of shadow, back against a fallen tree, legs sticking out in front of her. Nestling between them was something I didn't like the look of.

'That looks suspiciously like a shotgun,' I said.

'That's because it is a shotgun.'

'And what were you hoping to shoot?'

'The badger diggers. I think they're coming tonight. There were peanuts scattered all around yesterday. Badgers love peanuts. I think the diggers put them there. It's only a four-ten; it wouldn't kill them. Well, it might not.' She was sobbing as she spoke.

I stooped alongside her and reached for the gun. I broke it and extracted the cartridges. 'You can't shoot people you don't like,' I told her. 'If you did I'd have to arrest you and take you to the station. C'mon, I'll walk you home.'

'Mummy's buried over there,' she announced, pointing into the darkness.

'Is she?' I said, knocked off guard a little.

'Just her ashes. It's called Coneywarren Field because the rabbits have lived there for hundreds of years. Mummy liked to watch them, and so do I.'

'Do you remember your mummy?' I asked.

'No.'

'That's a shame. C'mon, let's go.'

'It's all right. I pretend I remember her, and I have some photographs. Daddy planted a tree.'

We strolled up the lane holding hands, Toby babbling on about the things the diggers did to badgers. I asked about the dolls' houses and the tennis, but she kept returning to the badgers.

'What happened to the people in the lost village?' I wondered.

'They died of plague. And the farmers want to kill all the badgers because they say they spread TB, which isn't true.'

The moon was riding high by now, and the path was bathed in its light, making the shadows on either side even deeper. In another attempt to change the subject

I said: 'How are you tonight? Have you got over the pneumonia?'

'I haven't got pneumonia. Who told you that?'

'Um, I think it was Grizzly.'

'I've got cystic fibrosis.'

'I'm sorry. I didn't know.'

She said: 'I looked it up on Google. It said that my life expectancy is thirty-seven years.'

And that left me speechless. After what felt like about five minutes I thought of saying that I knew someone aged eighty-five who had cystic fibrosis, but I'd lost the moment. I squeezed her hand and pulled her closer.

As we approached the front door she said: 'Will you tell Daddy?'

I'd been wondering about that and the shotgun as we walked. 'Yes, I'll have to,' I replied.

'Oh.'

'Does he keep the gun locked up?'

'Yes, but I know where he keeps the key.'

I made her promise to go straight to bed and stay there, and when she was safely inside I started on the long walk back to High Ogglethorpe and its feather bed, the shotgun hooked over my forearm. As I approached the road a pair of headlights came into view over a crest. They were close together, which meant an elderly Land Rover. No surprise there – this was Land Rover country. It slowed as it approached the turn-off, as if coming to the house. I stepped behind a tree and made myself invisible.

The barrier was down, so it had to stop. The driver climbed out and walked into the headlights' glare as he raised the barrier. He was wearing what looked like an evening suit with a dicky bow, but it wasn't Mr Curzon and it certainly wasn't Kevin. As he drove into the grounds, leaving the barrier raised, I made a note of the registration number. He'd conveniently left the driver's door open as he dealt with the barrier, so I could plainly see his passenger. It was Ghislaine Curzon.

Her driver wasn't invited in for coffee and they didn't talk for long. His reward for his troubles was a perfunctory peck and she let herself into the house. He came past my hiding place again in a spray of gravel and squealed the tyres as he came onto the road, the engine roaring in low gear, the barrier left pointing at the sky.

I crossed the lane, climbed over the stile and turned my back on Curzon House before another act in the late-night melodrama could keep me from my bed. I thought the countryside was supposed to be quiet, but it had been quite a night. I slept like a top for what was left of it, the shotgun propped in the corner for extra reassurance.

The postmistress had told me where Motty Dermot, head lad at Jonty Hargrave's yard, lived, and after one of Phyllis's hearty breakfasts I was back in Dunkley, looking for his house number. It was a brick bungalow in a twee development designed to house a token few of the more elderly villagers, surrounded by a neat communal lawn with borders of pansies and other small flowers giving a modicum of individuality to each plot. The weather was due to change, but it was a bright morning and the man himself was sitting on a bench next to his front door, enjoying the fresh air. A white stick leant against his knee.

'Mr Dermot?' I asked as I approached him. He turned his head and I saw his eyes, milky white through staring into too many sunrises. 'My name's Charlie Priest. I'm a police officer. Do you mind if I sit down?'

He didn't speak but moved slightly to one side in a gesture that I interpreted as an invitation to join him. He was a small man but his head and the hands that rested lightly on the stick were disproportionately large, like Michelangelo's David. His mouth had a slight twist to it, as if he'd had a stroke sometime in the past, and I wondered if there was a pension plan for retired jockeys.

'Can you see me, Mr Dermot?' I asked, twisting on the seat to face him.

He nodded and said: 'See you.'

'My name's Charlie. I'm a police officer. Is it all right if I call you Motty?'

'Motty,' he repeated, nodding again. 'And Charlie.'

'That's right. How well can you see me?'

'Blunt,' he said. 'See you blunt...blunt...not blunt...'

'Blurred,' I suggested.

He seized the word. 'Blurred, see you blurred.'

'Good. Do you have cataracts?' I pointed to my own eyes.

'That's right. Cat...cat...cat'racts.'

'Are you receiving any treatment for them? Are you on the waiting list?'

'Waiting list. Long time. Long time. Put drops in. Nice comes. Not nice...not nice...put drops in.'

'A nurse,' I said. 'A nurse comes and puts drops in for you.'

He nodded his agreement.

'A nice nurse,' I said, and he grinned.

He could have had them fixed privately for about a thousand pounds, which was pocket money to the people who lived all around him. And surely there was a jockey's benevolent fund?

'I believe you were Jonty Hargrave's head lad,' I said, and a smile flickered across his lined and weathered face.

'The boss,' he replied, nodding again. The nod, I decided, was his chief method of communication. It was easier for him to agree than it was for his brain to send signals down pathways that probably were dead ends as they looked for the right words.

'Did you enjoy working for Jonty?'

More nodding, with enthusiasm.

'He trained some good horses, I believe.'

'Tha's right. Good horses. Good man.'

'Any you remember?'

That caused him problems. His face screwed up with concentration and he made noises in his throat until I galloped to his rescue. 'I'm sorry,' I said. 'I shouldn't have asked you that. Did you stay on at the yard after Jonty sold it?'

The nods weren't anything like as enthusiastic now.

'Do you remember who bought it?'

'Thrup... Thrup... Thruppance.' The effort was agonising for him, but the connections in his brain were all wrong and the name wouldn't come.

'Was it Mr Threadneedle?'

His face brightened with recognition. 'Aye. Thread...
Thread...'

'Threadneedle. Arthur George Threadneedle.'

'Aye, him.'

'You didn't get on with him?'

'No. A fool. Not like the *meister*, not like the boss.
Fool.'

'It's about Threadneedle that I've come to see you,' I
said. 'He was murdered on Monday morning. Have you
any idea who might have done such a thing?'

'Dead!' he exclaimed. 'Mur...murdered?'

'That's right. Who do you think I should talk to?'

He shook his head. 'Long time 'go.'

'Nobody comes to mind?'

'No. Long time 'go.'

'We think he was shot with a humane killer. Do you
remember having one at the yard?'

Yes, he told me, after a great deal of hard work, all
yards kept a humane killer to deal with any horse that
broke a leg, but he didn't know what happened to it. He
didn't have it.

I said: 'There was a fire, I believe. Was that while
Threadneedle owned the yard?'

His already dark complexion grew darker than the
clouds that were heaping up in the south as he remembered
one of the less favourable periods in the stable's golden
history. 'Aye. Fire.'

'Were you there at the time?'

He was.

'A horse died, I'm told.'

'Aye. Perki...Perki...' But the name wouldn't come.

'Was that the end of the stable for racing?' I asked.

'Aye.'

'Was the fire an accident?'

No reply. I tried again. 'Do you think the fire was started deliberately?' But I'd lost him. He was at a different time and place, somewhere behind the walls of chalk that defined his horizon. He was at the gallops. Hooves were thundering, shaking the earth, as a gaggle of horses came over the brow and swooped down the hill, the early morning sun glancing off the flanks of the most beautiful creatures in God's vast repertoire. I stood up to leave.

'Thanks for talking to me, Motty,' I said, offering my hand. He took it, clasping my fingers rather than giving a deep handshake. He pulled me closer and for a moment I thought he was going to say something, but the moment passed and he let go of my fingers. 'Look after yourself, and get those eyes fixed,' I told him. 'It's a simple enough operation. I know lots of people who've had it done.'

I'd walked down his little path out onto the pavement when I heard him make a noise behind me. I turned and he was waving his stick, attracting my attention. I walked back to him.

'Peck... Peck...' he was saying. 'Peck... Peck...'

'What is it, Motty?'

'Peck... Peck... Peccadillo.' He flopped back onto the seat as if exhausted by his efforts to speak.

'Peccadillo?' I repeated. 'Is that the name of a horse?'

Enthusiastic nodding.

'Well done, Motty. Was it one of Jonty's horses?'

Head shaking, downcast expression.

'The horse that died in the fire?'

Nodding.

'The horse that died in the fire was called Peccadillo. Is that what you're telling me?'

It was.

'Thanks, Motty,' I said. 'You've been a big help,' but I didn't see how he could have been.

Mad Maggie, with the help of the PNC, informed me that the late-night Land Rover was owned by Martin Chadwick, and further digging by her told me that he was a veterinary surgeon and unmarried. He lived only a mile from Dunkley so I decided to pay him a visit.

His home was a long, low bungalow with a triple garage at one end and an added-on surgery and waiting room at the other. A ranch fence surrounded the entire plot, which was about the size of a football pitch, give or take a penalty area. A sheep and a donkey were quietly grazing at the far end of the paddock, and a man in a country check shirt and pressed jeans was polishing a rather tasty Mercedes 280 outside the middle garage. The Land Rover I'd seen last night was parked immediately by the front door, and the man was about the same height and build as Ghislaine's companion. He straightened up as I approached and dropped a yellow duster into a plastic box that held his car-cleaning stuff.

'Mr Chadwick?' I asked.

'Yes. How can I help you?'

'Nice car. How old is it?'

'1971. Three and a half litres, V8, one lady owner and six boy racers. Want to buy it?'

'No thanks. I had an E-type, once. Nearly put me in the poorhouse.' I showed my ID and introduced myself. 'Can we have a word?' Actually, I sold the Jaguar at a decent profit, but he wasn't to know that.

'Let's go inside,' he suggested. 'What's it about?'

After declining a coffee I told him about Threadneedle's demise and more or less everything I knew about his time in Dunkley. Chadwick nodded his agreement in appropriate places and tut-tutted a few times but didn't add anything of substance.

Eventually I got to the important bit. 'Do you own a humane killer?' I asked.

He didn't. He specialised in small animals and cattle, not horses, and sodium pentobarbitone was much less messy. He was pink and pear-shaped, with thinning fair hair and the sun-damaged capillaries of the countryman. I wondered where he bought jeans to fit him. Did some people have them made to measure?

'Motty Dermot told me about the fire,' I said, 'but he's not easy to talk to. Is there anyone else you can think of who was there?' We were in a *Country Life* kitchen with an oil-fired Aga slumbering against the wall. Chadwick shuffled in his seat, then said: 'Well, I suppose I was.'

I sat up. 'You were present at the fire? I didn't think you'd be old enough.'

'It was back in 1997,' he said. 'I'd be...oh, thirty-fiveish. Yes, thirty-five.'

I did a lightning calculation and made him about twenty years older than Grizzly. 'So you were there in your role of veterinary surgeon.'

'Fairly inexperienced with racehorses – they guard them jealously, won't let just anybody near them – but yes, I was. It was all over by the time I was called. I did a post-mortem of sorts on the horse that died, certified that it had a broken leg for the insurance claim, and that was it.'

'Peccadillo,' I said.

'That's right. Peccadillo. He was a magnificent animal. Only a two-year-old but they had great hopes for him. It was a terrible shame.'

'Who was the owner?'

'Threadneedle was the registered owner but I believe he headed a syndicate.'

'That's interesting,' I said. 'How do I find out who else was in the syndicate?'

'I'm not sure. He'd be the syndicate manager, registered with the BHB, but back in those days I imagine the actual syndicate would be run solely by him. It's much more regulated now.'

'BHB?'

'British Horseracing Board, formerly the Jockey Club.'

'Of course. What happened to the carcass?' I was thinking DNA.

'I'm not sure, it was a long time ago, but the usual thing would be to give it to the hunt, to feed the hounds.' He saw the distaste on my face and said: 'That's the country way, Inspector. There's little room for sentimentality.'

'I suppose not. Tell me, how well did you know Threadneedle?'

'Hardly at all. In those days I did some work with horses and ponies, but not much. He kept a dog. There'll be a file somewhere in my archives. I could probably find it...'

'I don't think that will be necessary. In the days after the fire was there any gossip about how it started? I'll be talking to the fire brigade, but did you hear any suspicion of arson or anything untoward?'

He thought for a while before saying: 'I had a chat with the fire chief, or whatever he's called. He said something about it starting in more than one place. Can't remember the jargon...'

'More than one source of ignition?'

'That's it, or something like it, and something had been used. Petrol, I imagine he meant.'

'An accelerant?'

'That's it. An accelerant.'

'Who discovered the fire?'

'Motty did. He lived in the head lad's cottage adjacent to the stable block. He did his rounds last thing, then went to bed. Saw the flames from his window and called the brigade. He managed to release all the horses except Peccadillo. He'd broken a leg so they had to shoot him to save him from the flames.'

'They?' I queried.

'Um, not sure. Perhaps it was just Motty, but presumably

Threadneedle would be there, too. He lived in the big house, of course, so he'd be soon on the scene.'

'That's very useful, Mr Chadwick,' I said. 'Thank you for your time. Did you ever hear if the insurance company paid out?'

'Word has it that they did for the stable block but not the horse, but it was just talk. You know what it's like in a village.'

I didn't, but I was learning.

CHAPTER TEN

The weatherman on the car radio told me that they were having thunderstorms in the south and localised flooding could be expected. Serves them right for living there, I thought, and hit the button for Classic FM. I made it back in time for lunch, but didn't get the opportunity to have any. Jeff Caton was sitting at my desk with a smug smile on his face and half of one of my Kit Kats clutched in his fist. 'What's new?' I asked, hooking my jacket behind the door and flopping in the spare chair.

He swallowed twenty-five-pence-worth of chocolate biscuit and said: 'We may have had a small breakthrough at the Curzon Centre. Fancy a ride there to test it out? I'll explain on the way.'

'Let's go,' I said, unhooking my jacket again, 'and bring me a bicky, if there's one left.' My mileage was sky-high so we went in Jeff's buzz-box. He was carrying a wire coat hanger as we walked out to his car and I expected him to hang his jacket on it, but he handed it to me.

'What's this for?' I asked.

'It's for hanging a jacket on.'

'Specifically a jacket?' I asked. 'Couldn't you hang, say, a pair of pyjamas on it?'

'I suppose so, but don't most people keep them in a drawer?'

'Do they? I'd have thought they'd get creased that way.'

'And you wouldn't want to go to bed in creased pyjamas, would you?'

'Of course not.'

According to Einstein time passes more slowly the nearer to the speed of light you travel, so we arrived at the Centre several seconds younger than when we set off. According to me, Jeff drives like a lunatic. Whenever I'm in his car I cinch up my seat belt, brace my feet against the bulkhead and pretend it's a fairground ride. He took the coat hanger off me and I staggered to my feet with all the grace of a newborn gnu.

Jeff led the way through part of the shopping centre, past the bare wall where the plaque had been situated and dived suddenly down a passage between the Ellis Brigham outlet and Country Casuals. He'd phoned ahead and Maggie and Serena were waiting for us.

'The security here is not as state of the art as we've been led to believe,' Jeff was explaining. 'The fire doors are supposed to be monitored but there've been so many false alarms most of the audible warnings are switched to the mute position. If a warning flashes up on a VDU the chances of someone noticing it without an audible signal are slim.'

We'd arrived at a pair of emergency fire doors, designated West 14, which led, I presumed, out into the car park. Jeff was saying: 'According to the CCTV these doors are on the route taken by Graffiti Boy on the night before the incident. We found the coat hanger in a flower bed, earlier this morning, and in the next bed we found these.' He pulled a pair of trainer laces, tied end to end, out of his pocket. 'And now my assistant Serena will demonstrate just how easy it is to break into the multimillion-pound Curzon Shopping Mall and Conference Centre.'

Serena leant on one of the panic bars that stretched across each door and half of it swung open. No bells rang; no sprinkler system soaked us with foam; no U-boat klaxon told us to crash-dive. She stepped outside and pushed the door shut behind her.

Jeff knotted one end of the laces around the panic bar and let the rest of it dangle on to the floor. 'Ready when you are,' he shouted.

We stood looking at the bottom of the door. After a few seconds the bent end of the coat hanger worked its way through the gap and moved from side to side. It was a tight fit, but Serena soon hooked the lace and, with a struggle, pulled it under the door at her side. With a good yank the panic bar was disengaged and the heavy fire door swung open again. The glow of Serena's smile rivalled that of the sun.

We called in Thornton's for a coffee and a discussion. The coat hanger and the lace had been swabbed for DNA but the chances were slim. 'They said we'd have to take our turn,' Maggie told me. 'We've used up all our goodwill and now we're at the back of the queue.'

'But they're working over the weekend on our other case,' Serena said. 'They've promised to have something for us Monday morning.'

'The pit bulls?'

'Mmm.'

'Good. So what have we learnt from today's escapade?'

'Not a great deal,' Jeff admitted, 'except how it was done. I'd say it's an inside job, though.'

'Anybody could have left that lace dangling.'

'True, but anybody wouldn't know that most of the alarms are disabled.'

'Or which specific alarms were disabled. That would narrow it down a bit.'

Maggie said: 'You mean, did he make a lucky guess or did he know all the time that emergency exit West 14 wasn't alarmed?'

'Cor...rect.'

I popped the free chocolate truffle that came with the coffee into my mouth and let it melt there, my eyes half closed and a smile playing about my lips. Serena said: 'So how was your visit to Curzon House?'

I swallowed and cleared my mouth for a few seconds, before telling her that my visit had gone well.

'Did you see her?'

'Who?'

'You know who!'

'I saw lots of people.'

'*Her!* Did you see *her*?'

'Are you referring to Miss Curzon?'

'Yes!'

'Oh. Right. Well I don't expect you to believe this, but at about one o'clock this morning I was enjoying a moonlit stroll through the grounds of Curzon House, hand in hand with a certain Miss Curzon.'

'I don't believe you.'

I gave a rough approximation of the Boy Scouts' salute and said: 'Cross my heart and hope to die.'

Jeff said: 'Ah, so that's why you were worried about the creases in your pyjamas.'

'Eggsackley,' I replied.

Serena shook her head and Jeff never noticed Maggie pinching his chocolate.

Back at the nick I called in the ground floor toilets for a pee. I was just finishing when I heard the door go and a few seconds later the shadow of big Geordie Farrell, one of the traffic cops, fell across me. He took a quick peek over the porcelain barrier that separated the stalls we were using and said: 'Flippin' 'eck, Mr Priest, for a minute I thought you were being attacked by a one-eyed albino boa constrictor.'

For the second time in a few hours I was lost for words. I could have said: 'An easy mistake to make, George,' but I was halfway up the stairs by then.

Mr Wood had left me a note. It said he'd asked for some help for me and the ACC had suggested that a certain Superintendent Kent might be gainfully employed taking an overview of the murder enquiry. 'Great!' I hissed as I crumpled the sheet of paper and hurled it into the basket. Karen Kent looking over my shoulder was just what I didn't need.

I brought the crime diary and logbook up to date and wrote the mileage in my personal diary. The report reader's summary was there for me. Identifying the spectators at the Curzon Centre opening was progressing and a good few had been interviewed. I took the report and left it in Jeff Caton's in tray. He could deal with that. We now had a list of Threadneedle's cronies that he played golf and drank with and there was a note saying the inquest had been opened and adjourned. I found the number for Janet Theadneedle's sister and picked up the phone.

They lived in a big pre-war semi with bay windows, on the Knaresborough road out of Harrogate. I parked in a side street near the football ground and walked back to the house. Sister June made us tea and introduced me to her husband, Mike. He'd taken early retirement from a managerial post with the NHS after a heart bypass operation and was now looking for a part-time job with no responsibilities.

'Lollipop man,' I suggested. 'That's what I'm going to do. Helping all the young mothers across the road.'

'That might aggravate my condition,' he said, earning a 'Huh!' from his wife.

I tactfully asked if I could talk to Janet in private and they took their teas into another room. We made small talk about the inquest and the investigation until I told her about the humane killer and steered the conversation back to when they lived in East Yorkshire and owned the stables.

'Mr Curzon asked how you were and sends his condolences,' I told her. 'I said you were being remarkably strong.'

'That was kind of him. Tell him "thank you" if you see him again.'

'He spoke very warmly of you and your playing. "Magical" was the word he used. He also told me about the fire. Do you remember it?'

'Of course I do. It was something you'd never forget.'

'I have to ask: where were you and your husband at the time?'

She was wearing a fine woollen cardigan the colour of tinned peaches and was fiddling so much with one of the buttons that I expected it to come off in her hand. 'I was in bed.'

'And your husband?'

'He told me he'd gone to a club in York. A nightclub.'

'You don't sound too sure.'

'I know. He said none of his pals were there so he just sat by himself, having a drink, watching the dancer. Next morning, while the fire brigade were clearing up and the police were asking questions, he said it might be better if I said he'd stayed in all evening. He said it could look suspicious when he made an insurance claim if he had no witnesses.'

'And did you?'

'Say he'd stayed in?'

'Hmm.'

'No. Nobody asked me.'

'Did he make an insurance claim?'

'Yes, but I'm not sure if it was successful. All I know is that he was like a bear with a sore head for months afterwards. We had to tighten our belts for the first time in our marriage and eventually moved to a smaller property in Heckley. That's when...' She stopped in mid sentence.

'Sorry. That's when...?'

'That's when I started enjoying a drink. Or two.'

'How are you coping now?'

'Just about.'

'Well, stick at it. It can't be easy.'

I asked about the gun but she'd never seen it, neither at the stables nor in Heckley. Our forensic people were still looking over the house, I told her, and asked if we could stay there until the following Tuesday. I didn't mention that we'd be doing a reconstruction of her final supermarket trip on the Monday, round all the counters she'd bought from, to the same checkout she'd used and out to a Day-Glo orange Focus just like the one outside her house.

The husband, Mike, walked me to the door after I'd expressed my thanks, and I gestured for him to come outside. He pulled the door closed behind him and stood close to me like a fellow conspirator.

'How did you get on with your brother-in-law?' I asked.

'Not very well,' he admitted. 'He thought I was a bit of a failure because I opted for security and a steady income while he was a gambler. He claimed that his father left him a run-down business with lots of debts, but I suspect he was OK. Arthur played his cards close to his chest where money was concerned. He's done well, though. I have to give him that.'

'Did he ever talk to you about his horse racing exploits?'

Mike grinned at the memory. 'Oh yes. He certainly did.'

'Go on.'

'Ha ha! The Shergar conspiracy. June and I have had some good laughs over that one.'

'I'm listening.'

'Well, it was a horse he bought. We went over to see it at his stables, at Arthur's invitation, and it certainly was a magnificent animal. He showed us some photos of a horse just like it winning various races and parading in the winner's enclosure with lots of posh people hanging on to it. Women in big hats, the men in toppers, that sort of thing. It looked exactly like Arthur's horse, quite distinctive, with a white stripe down its nose and four white socks on its feet. Turns out the horse in the photos is Shergar, the Derby winner kidnapped by the IRA, and the implication – nudge nudge, wink wink – is that Arthur owns one of its pups. And guess what? For the trivial sum of fifteen grand I could be a joint owner, with a dozen other suckers. We politely declined and the invitations to visit ceased after that, which upset June but not me. Is that what it's all about?'

'Probably. How did he pitch the sale? Did he try to impress you with his successes so far? I'm trying to find any members of the syndicate, but nobody's admitting it.'

'Well you wouldn't, would you? Family and friends; that's who snake oil salesmen approach first. He did tell me one name – thought it would impress me.'

'Which was?'

'Hmm, I've forgotten. Owned a stately home over that way. The faded gentry, down on his uppers like the rest of them.'

'Try Curzon for size.'

'That's him: Lord Curzon.'

We spun Threadneedle's house without finding anything incriminating. Unless you call a wad of calling cards for young ladies who taught French while dressed as maids incriminating. There was an office and we found lists of names and numbers but our fraud people couldn't make any sense of them. He had secrets, but he kept them well buried. His company offices were in Halifax and we turned them, too. He had a small staff but they were the legitimate front of his activities. The general picture was that he could do quite nicely within the accepted business practices of palm greasing and 'entertainment' without overtly breaking the law. I gave the cards to Maggie and told her to look one or two of them up, see what they could tell us. I wasn't hopeful: you don't bite the hand that fondles you.

Janet Threadneedle was our *numero uno* suspect, much

as it pained me to admit it. She had motive aplenty and might even sail a manslaughter rap if she confessed. She had opportunity and she may have had a gun. Trouble was, what did she do with it? And with her clothes? The boffins assured me that they'd be spattered with bits of Arthur George, but where were they?

We drew routes from the house to the supermarket and back, and searched every dumpster, litter bin and hedge bottom within shouting distance. We had the mounties on the towpath, the underwater search unit frolicking in the canal and the task force on their knees in the park, all to no avail. We found enough used condoms to rubberise an airship, several dead animals, a Honda C90 and the statue of Buddha that vanished from outside the Bamboo Curtain in about 1995. No gun, no bloodstained shoes, no outer clothing. I began to think about other suspects.

Friday morning it rained, and the shorts and tees that had predominated gave way to umbrellas and rain hats. Office girls who'd had a week of clacking about in flip-flops with exposed midriffs were suddenly clad in oilskins and sou'westers, like Whitby lifeboat crew. I sat in the car at the traffic lights, wipers slapping to and fro, and wondered how they did it.

Most of the team were in the office, doing reports to leave the weekend clear. I hung my wet jacket up and joined them, after checking the kettle. It was empty, as usual.

'I'll get it,' Serena said, rising to her feet.

'It's OK,' I told her, and went to fill it.

We had tea, regular coffee, decaffeinated coffee and a

couple of sachets of hot chocolate. I made myself a hot chocolate, because I deserved it, and tipped a spoonful of creamer into it, purely for the vitamins and trace elements it contained. I watched the clouds it made swirl and fold for a few seconds, wishing I could capture the moment on canvas, then carried it to the chair Dave had shoved my way.

'So what have we got?' I asked, sitting down.

'You're invited to Frankie & Benny's tomorrow afternoon,' Dave told me. 'It's Dan's birthday. We were hoping to have a barbecue but the forecast's terrible, so we asked him where he wanted to go and he said Frankie & Benny's.'

Dan is Dave's teenage son and a pal of mine. 'Who are Frankie and Benny?' I asked.

'No idea. Just two blokes who started a restaurant, I suppose. In America, of course.'

Brendan said: 'Maybe they were a couple of celebrities, like the film stars who started Planet Hollywood.'

'You mean, like, it could be Frank Sinatra and Benny Goodman?'

'Exactly.'

Jeff said: 'Sammy Davis Junior and Ella Fitzgerald were the first to open a celebrity restaurant.'

'Gerraway.'

'Yeah. It didn't do very well, though, but what did they expect with a name like Sam 'n' Ella's?'

We tried not to laugh but it was difficult. The ringing of the phone saved me. Dave picked it up and caught my eye as he listened.

'I'll put him on. James Curzon, for DI Priest,' he said, proffering the handset.

'Hello, James,' I said. 'How can I help you?'

'Hello, Charlie. I'm sorry to ring you at work but I'm trying to find out about restorative justice. Do you know if there's a scheme in East Yorkshire?'

'Umm, I'm not sure. The probation service is the place to ask. Can you tell me about it?'

'Yes. It's Toby. She's been arrested for stealing.'

CHAPTER ELEVEN

I sometimes see myself as a salesman. Or a sales manager. Make that an *executive*. I fly about all over the country, taking orders, finding new markets, spreading goodwill. Then I call in the troops to do the dirty work, stack the shelves, take the flak. I wasn't sure where keeping a precocious thirteen-year-old out of the juvenile court fitted into the template, but there was some leverage in it, that was for sure. I told Curzon that I'd be over about ten the next day, which was Saturday.

He'd filled me in over the phone. The Country Homes Association ran the commercial side of Curzon House and now owned most of the furniture and stately home trappings that went with it, including a collection of egg cups.

'Egg cups?' I'd queried, before remembering that he'd

been making a display unit for them when I saw him in his workshop. He told me that the history of the decorated egg cup was the history of the nation. In the days before satirical television the subversives in our fair land resorted to any means available to promote their views, of which the humble egg cup was just one avenue.

'It's still going on,' Curzon told me. 'Even today,' he said, 'a certain sector of the population like to start the day by bashing in the prime minister's skull.'

'I'll believe you,' I'd said. 'Go on.'

'Well, perhaps I am overselling them a little,' he'd replied. 'But when we handed over to the CHA there was a modest collection, which they have built up to be one of the biggest in the country. We didn't have Chippendales in every room, or a Harrison clock – had to make do with what we had.'

An antiques dealer in Scarborough had bought five egg cups over the previous weeks from a youth who'd called in his shop with them. Recently, the dealer had paid a visit to Curzon House, seen the collection and guessed that it was the origin of his egg cups. He'd reported to the security staff and the police were informed. CCTV was rigged up and yesterday Toby was filmed palming one from the collection.

'What does she say?' I asked.

'She's upset and shamefaced, but defiant. Hasn't said anything. She can be a proper little madam when it suits her. I'll be grateful for any help you can offer, Charlie. She looks up to you. I'm just her stupid old dad; you're a figure of authority. I'm not asking you to pull any strings. I could do that myself but she'll have to have what's coming to her. I was hoping you might have a word with her, point her in the right direction... Oh, I don't know what I wanted. I'm sorry, Charlie. I'm wasting your time.'

'What does Grizzly think you should do?'

'She's down at Sandringham again, doesn't know about it.'

'How old is Toby?'

'Thirteen. She's older than she looks.'

'OK. The worst scenario is that she'll be given a reprimand. If she's contrite, and considering that it was once her own home, we'd probably prefer to forget the whole thing. A reprimand is not a criminal record, but it might stay on the file until she's about eighteen. It's a while since I was in uniform and dealt cautions out, and they keep changing the rules.'

'I don't want her to think she's got away with it, and what about the youth who she stole them for?'

'She won't say who he is?'

'No.'

Which was why, lunchtime Saturday, I was parking as near as I could get to my usual place in front of Curzon House. The overnight downpour had slowed to a steady drizzle and the blossom that had laden the trees for the previous few days was now drifting across the roads, clogging the gutters and lying in sodden, swirled heaps where the streams of water had deposited it. What had been a source of beauty was now an eyesore.

'Is that Ghislaine's car outside?' I asked Curzon as we

clumped up a wooden staircase, its threadbare carpet held in place with brass stair rods.

'That's right.'

'What happened to Sandringham?'

'Cancelled at short notice. His royal nibs has been called to an exercise on Salisbury Plain, playing cowboys and Indians in tanks and helicopters. I think she's a bit disappointed, but she knows that's one of the prices she has to pay.'

We were there. Curzon knocked on her bedroom door and pushed it open. 'Inspector Priest to see you,' he announced.

Toby was sitting in a rocking chair near the window, polishing her spectacles, the latest *Harry Potter* on her knee. Her father was carrying a tray that held two mugs of coffee and a plate of sandwiches. Toby had been grounded since the offence, sentenced to eat in her room, but had not touched any of her meals.

'It's "Inspector" today, Toby,' I told her. 'I'm on duty.'

'Oh.'

Her father placed the tray on a low table and backed out of the room. 'I'll leave you to it,' he said, reluctantly, unsure if he was doing the right thing.

I looked around the room before sitting near the table, across the window from Toby. Apart from being the size of a small country's airport terminal it was much like any other child's room that I'd been in, and that was quite a few. Posters on the walls that contrasted oddly with each other: a sweaty Rafael Nadal facing Winnie the Pooh; a boy band – McFly – next to Munch's *The Scream*; the inevitable teddy bears and good ol' Bart Simpson on his skateboard. Not many bears; just enough to remind you that it was the room of a young person at the crossroads. A painting of a seabird with sheer white cliffs in the background hung on the wall behind her bed. I thought about the owners of those other rooms I'd been in. Most of them were never seen alive again. I chose a sandwich and bit into it. Smoked salmon and cream cheese, very nice.

'So what would you like to tell me?' I asked between mouthfuls, waving the uneaten portion at her.

'Just that I'm very sorry for what I did and won't let it happen again.'

'Is that all?'

'I...I... They used to belong to us. It's not fair. I only took what I thought was ours. Daddy used to own all this, once. I did it for the badgers. It costs money to look after them. I didn't keep any money for myself.'

'What did you do with the egg cups?' I took another sandwich. Chicken and mayonnaise this time.

Long silence, then: 'I gave them away.'

I told her that technically it was thieving and wrong: the egg cups belonged to someone else. A few nights ago I'd caught her with a shotgun, threatening to shoot someone, and now she'd been caught stealing. If she went to court she'd be branded a criminal and that would stay with her for the rest of her life. I was upset, I told her, because I thought we were friends, but I was a cop and had to be careful about my friends. And what about her daddy? He loved her but was worried stiff that she'd get into serious trouble. He wanted to be proud of her, not ashamed. We all did. It was good that she cared about the badgers, and there were some cruel people about, but the law should be left to deal with them.

I don't know how much she took in. When your life expectancy is thirty-seven it probably colours your outlook. The next sandwich was rather tasty beef, sliced very thinly, with horseradish.

'They break their jaws,' she protested, 'then set the dogs on them. Or they pull their claws out and chain their legs so they can't fight properly. They don't stand a chance.'

'I know,' I said. 'There are some wicked people out there, but there are laws to deal with them. You've got to decide which side of the law you want to be on: inside or outside. You can't take them on all by yourself, Toby. Tell what you know to the professionals and leave it to them.'

She sat back in her chair and rocked it to and fro, the light from the window reflecting off her spectacles so I couldn't see her eyes. 'Did you do the painting?' I asked, nodding towards it.

'Yes.'

'It's very good. A puffin, isn't it?'

'Thank you. Yes, they're my favourites. Daddy was going to take me to see them at Bempton, but I don't suppose he will, now.'

'Oh, I don't know. I've a feeling you can twist him round your little finger.' That was why he'd called me in: to represent the stern face of the law, but I was failing miserably. I tried again: 'Whose idea was it for you to steal the egg cups?' I asked, through a mouthful of sarnie.

'It was mine,' she replied, head down, hardly audible.

'But someone encouraged you?'

'They were only stupid egg cups.'

'They belonged to someone else.'

'We needed the money.'

'The badger protection group?'

'Mmm.'

'What's the group called?'

'We don't have a name. Newt...our leader...says names only make it easy for people to label us.'

'Do individuals have names?'

'No, not proper ones.'

'How do you address each other?'

'We have *noms de guerre*.'

'War names. Is that how you see it, as a war?'

'I don't know.'

'So what's your leader's war name?' She didn't answer, sat looking down at the carpet. 'It's decision time, Toby,' I said. 'What's his name? I need to know that you've broken away from the group, that you are sincere when you say you're sorry.'

'He's called Newt.'

'As in Newton?'

'No. As in *Triturus vulgaris*, the common newt.'

'Latin,' I said. 'I only know one Latin name for anything.'

'What's that?'

'*Turdus*...something or other. Can't remember what it was, though.'

She gave a little laugh and I had a glimpse of the Toby of old. 'That's a thrush,' she told me.

'I'll believe you. What's your war name?'

'I don't have one, yet. I'm not important enough.'

'But you'd like to be?'

'I suppose so.'

'How old is Newt?'

'He's nearly twenty. It's his birthday next week.'

'Where does he live?'

'I think he has a flat in York.'

'How do you keep in touch?'

'By our mobiles.'

I think she told me all she could. Newt claimed he was a pal of Swampy, the legendary protestor who made his name by digging tunnels under the new runway at Manchester airport. Democracy was fine, Newt told them, but if you wanted to change things, direct action was the only way. I remember reading Chairman Mao's 'Little Red Book' when I was a student, and it all sounded frighteningly familiar. What goes around comes around.

I said: 'The antiques dealer who bought the egg cups gave Newt five pounds each for them. How do you feel about buying them back for the collection, at, say, seven pounds each? Do you have thirty-five pounds?'

'I'll save it out of my pocket money.'

'Good girl,' I said. 'So how about if I arrange for you and I to be taken out in a traffic car, if they're not too busy?'

'What's a traffic car?'

'A police Volvo, with luminous stripes and flashing blue lights.'

'Seriously!'

'If they're not too busy.'

'Wow! That's great. But it should be *you and me*.'

'Of course, my apologies. Anything you want to ask me?'

'Umm.' She looked at the plate and its meagre contents. 'Could I have a sandwich, please?'

I drove down to Driffield and spent an hour at a borrowed desk in the police station, making phone calls. The local collator said she'd ring me back and while I was waiting I sweet-talked the traffic chief inspector into sanctioning a ride for a certain Miss Curzon.

There was a local file on the badger protection activists, the collator reported when she called me, with a character known as Newt listed as the leader. I didn't ask if a Toby Curzon was in there because if I had the collator would have pencilled her in. The civil disobedience and anti-terrorism squads didn't have anything on them, nor did MI5. That made them very small beer. These days a letter to *Saga Magazine* can earn you a file at MI5.

Dave and Bri were on duty and they gave me sideways grins when I introduced them to Miss Toby Curzon, but she won them over within seconds and they would have let her drive if she'd asked. We sat in the back, Toby in the middle seat so she could see as Bri explained all the technical stuff to her.

'This is the ANPR,' he said. 'That's the automatic number plate recognition. If a car goes by that isn't registered or insured, or is reported stolen, the ANPR lets us know.'

'Wow!' Toby exclaimed. 'And what's that?'

'That's the video recorder. It films whoever we might be following and records their speed.'

'Wow! And what's that?'

'It's a system known as Lantern. We can take a suspect's fingerprints on it and check them against the seven million we have on record, in about five minutes.'

'Wow! And what's that?'

'That's called Tracker. It gives a signal if we're within about twenty yards of a stolen car that's fitted with it.'

'Wow! And what's that?'

'What?'

'That.'

'It's a cup holder.'

'Wow!'

We did a short burst at one hundred and twenty-five miles per hour on the M62 with the lights and siren on before they took us back to Curzon House. 'Thanks, Dave, thanks, Bri,' Toby said as she climbed out. 'It's been smashing. Do you want a cup of tea?'

'No, we'd better get back to catching criminals. Nice to meet you, Toby.'

I thanked them and walked to the house with her. 'That was great. Thanks, Charlie,' she said; then, after a pause: 'Do you know how fast a Chinook goes?'

'A bit faster, I'd say.'

It didn't matter, though. Big sister Grizzly might have flown in a Chinook but she'd never ridden in a cop Volvo.

*   *   *

I'd justified the trip east by thinking a talk with the vet, Martin Chadwick, was overdue, but Mr Wood was on holiday and the lure of a triple-decker beefburger with Dave's family was stronger than the pull of instant coffee in Chadwick's showcase kitchen. I put my foot down and made it back to Heckley before they'd placed their orders.

'They're doing the tests,' Dave told me after I'd wished Dan a happy birthday, 'and it's looking good. Serena's left a message on your ansaphone.'

'We're talking pit bulls?'

'That's right. All the samples are viable and they've promised a report by Tuesday morning. Jeff's told them to be in the nick with their briefs by ten o'clock.'

'Tuesday?' I queried. 'What's wrong with Monday?'

'It's a bank holiday, and they're civilians. They're allowed a day off, now and again.'

'Great. But they'll have something for us on Tuesday?'

'That's right. Now, are you ready for the bad news?'

'Go on.'

'Superintendent Kent wants to be in on it.'

'You're kidding.'

'Cross my heart and hope to die. She wanted to know where you were.'

'Sugar! What did you tell her?'

'That you were grouse shooting with your friend the chief constable. She was impressed.'

I hoped he was joking, but with Dave you never can be sure. The burgers came. Dave's wife, Shirley, said: 'That's enough shop talk. Eat your burgers,' so we did.

Sunday morning dawned bright and dry, so nine a.m. found me strimming the garden, annoying the neighbours. Served them right for complaining to the council. I fell asleep in front of the television, waiting for the Formula One to start, woke up in the middle of the champagne-spraying ceremony.

Tuesday we set up interview room one with a video link to next door, so we could watch the procedure. I'd decided that Jeff and Serena would do the interview and I'd observe from next door, with Ms Kent, if she made it. Gareth Adey, my uniformed counterpart, volunteered to sit in with us, for which I was grateful. He's better at cop-speak than I am. Carl and Sean Pickles were using the same solicitor, so he was in for a busy morning. Carl was the alpha gorilla, so Jeff decided to interview him first, with Sean in the cell furthermost away, well out of earshot. The long-awaited lab report arrived, rushed over by a traffic motorcyclist, and we had six copies made.

Carl was wearing his best shell suit and hadn't bothered to bring an overnight bag. I wondered if Terry Bratt had nipped round to comfort their mutual relative but decided there was no hurry – he'd have her all to himself in an hour or so. We'd had words with him and he'd made a statement about loaning his dog to the brothers. He thought they were just taking it for walkies and we'd agreed to go along with that. Poor Serena was dwarfed by the men, but the Manila envelope on the table in front of her would give her an edge when the time came.

Jeff made the introductions and was officially cautioning

Carl when the door behind me opened and Karen Kent appeared. 'Sorry I'm late,' she said in a hushed voice. 'Heads of agreement meeting.' Superintendent Karen Kent is the acceptable face of the force for the twenty-first century. Six feet tall; double first in law and psychology; black belt in kick-boxing; fast-tracked through the ranks; looks good in uniform; engaged to an EU human rights lawyer.

Never made an arrest single-handed. Never kick-boxed anyone more belligerent than her instructor; never investigated the flashing lights on a trading estate at two in the morning, without backup. I introduced her to Gareth and turned back to the video monitor.

Jeff said· 'This interview is being recorded by sound and video. It concerns a series of aggravated burglaries that took place on the following times and dates at the following addresses.' He read them out and the brief took notes. 'Can you tell me where you were at those times?'

'Round and about. Nowhere special,' Carl replied.

'You'll have to do better than that.'

'Can I phone a friend?'

'Do you deny you were anywhere near those locations at those times?'

'Never been anywhere near them.'

Jeff went into a series of questions about specific events in the robberies, all of which Carl denied. He'd never visited a cash machine with one of the victims; never threatened the husband; never terrorised the children. He became cockier by the minute, convinced that we had nothing to link him to the crimes. At one point the brief warned him about his answers but he ignored the advice. He was enjoying himself, and Jeff was content to keep on paying out his rope. Alongside me, Ms Kent made the occasional tutting noise to indicate her disapproval of Jeff's technique.

'Have you done a psychological profile of the suspects?' she whispered to me.

'No.'

'Or taken any advice on how the interview should be handled?'

'No.'

Jeff was asking about the dog. 'Are you acquainted with the pit bull cross known as Bruno?'

'Yeah. It belongs to my nephew, dunnit.'

'Does your nephew have a name?'

'Terry Bratt. The dog's his.'

'Do you ever borrow it?'

'We take it for a walk sometimes.'

'Did you take it for a walk on the dates I mentioned earlier?'

'No. Haven't taken it for weeks.'

'Do you often take other people's dogs for walks?'

'Not often. We was thinking of buying it off him, wasn't we?'

'But you didn't?'

'No. We ordered a pup, though, if it ever fathered any, didn't we? Pick of the litter, like me.' Big grin.

Jeff sat in silence for a while, ran his fingers through his hair. The video camera was high on the wall, so we were seeing a distorted, wide-angle view of the room. Jeff and

Serena were under the camera with their backs to it, so they suffered the most distortion. Carl and the brief were full-frontal. The interview rooms were designed with a pair of CCTV cameras each. One fixed and one that could be manipulated. We quickly learnt that the moveable camera was intrusive, while the fixed one was quickly forgotten by the suspect in the heat of an interview. We were using only the fixed one today.

'Have you ever heard of SmartWater?' Jeff asked, aiming the question at the brief as well as the suspect. Heads were shaken, blank looks exchanged.

'No? In that case, I have a few leaflets here which may enlighten you.' He delved into his briefcase and produced the leaflets and a SmartWater kit. The solicitor took his copy and fumbled for his spectacles.

'As you will see,' Jeff continued, 'SmartWater is a clear, proprietary liquid that is used in crime prevention. When painted on an article it will remain *in situ* for years. Anyone who comes into contact with it will pick up a small amount, which can then be easily detected by UV light.'

The brief tossed the kit onto the table to emphasise his disdain for it and said: 'If you are wanting to subject my client to a UV test, the answer is no. There are dozens of substances that react to UV light.'

And we'd be accused of exposing him to carcinogenic radiation, I thought.

Jeff said: 'We don't want to subject anyone to UV. I was going to say that each SmartWater kit carries a unique DNA signature, which is recorded at the local police station. This enables stolen property to be linked to its rightful owner and also linked to whoever stole it. Any questions?'

Carl was starting to fidget. It was above his head and he had an attention span comparable with a cheap firework. His brief waved an arm and said: 'Are you telling us that the property stolen in the course of the unfortunate burglaries you mentioned earlier is all marked with this SmartWater fluid?'

'No,' Jeff replied. 'None of it is marked with SmartWater. West Pennine haven't received their quota, yet, and ours came only last week and hasn't been distributed.'

'I'm sorry, officer, but you've lost me.'

'And me,' Ms Kent hissed.

The brief went on: 'In the absence of anything remotely resembling evidence I must insist on my client being released forthwith.'

'Not SmartWater,' Jeff said, 'but something considerably cheaper and equally effective. We call it DogPiss.'

CHAPTER TWELVE

Serena was next on. She explained how she and a SOCO and a uniformed PC had visited the scenes of the robberies and taken swabs of all the places where a dog might mark its territory by peeing up against lamp posts, drainpipes and door jambs. These had been taken to the lab at Weatherton and tested for DNA. A small quantity of DNA, Serena told us, was flushed out during the act of passing urine – more so in a bitch than a dog but still a significant amount from a dog.

I'd worried about letting Serena conduct part of the interview but my concern was misplaced: the girl was doing good. Had she known that our new whiz-kid super was watching she'd probably have gone to pieces, but then again, perhaps not.

'DNA was also obtained from hairs collected from the

male pit bull cross known as Bruno, owned by Terence Bratt,' Serena told us, 'and this was compared with that obtained from the sites of the robberies. Bruno is a dog and dogs, unlike bitches, like to mark their territories. Four of the samples are perfect matches...'

And then she stopped. Go on, I thought. Tell them the odds. Tell them that the chances of the DNA coming from a different animal were billions to one against. That always impresses briefs. Tell them they were down the toilet without an Andrex, but she didn't. Serena stared at the two-page report from Weatherton, shuffled the pages, turned them over to see if anything was printed on their backs, looked in the envelope to see if she'd missed anything. When she couldn't find whatever she was looking for she stood up and said: 'I'd like to take a ten-minute break.'

I tried to leave it to Jeff and Serena to sort out, but Superintendent Kent insisted on being in on the action so I ushered everybody upstairs to Mr Wood's office. 'What's the problem, Serena?' I asked.

'This,' she replied, handing me the report. 'It only arrived ten minutes before the meeting. I'd only briefly looked at it, concentrating on the summary sheet. We'd given the samples serial numbers, with Bruno's being the last one. But the lab has shuffled them around to make it a blind test, which means that Bruno is now number three, not number five, as I'd assumed. Four samples match, but Bruno isn't one of them. All we've proved is that the same dog visited the crime scenes but it wasn't Bruno.'

Jeff said it was his fault, he'd done a quick read of the report and come to the same conclusion as DC Gupta. I said I'd have to carry the can as department head. Gareth Adey said the blame lay with the demand to meet quotas. Serena said she was sorry. Karen Kent said that the importance of quotas mustn't deflect us from our core aim of providing justice for all, and some emphasis would be given to providing us with the skills required to eliminate incompetence and engage with the new wave of criminals that we were coming across. I glanced up at the portrait of the Queen on the wall behind Gilbert's desk, and I swear she winked at me.

'There'll be no talk of incompetence,' I said. 'Some good detective work has been done on this, and DC Gupta led the way. A mistake was made, for which I take full responsibility, due to lack of staff out there on the ground. What we need to do now is find the right dog. We have to hand their briefs copies of the report, and they'll soon discover what our problem is. So let's get out there and find that dog before they do. We need twenty-four-hour surveillance on their acquaintances for the next day or two.' I turned to Karen Kent. 'Can you help us with that, ma'am?' I asked, and was rewarded with a look that would have etched tungsten.

'We need to talk,' she said through gritted but whitened teeth, and somehow I didn't think it would be about Yorkshire's chances in the Roses game.

Our case was severely weakened but we decided to run with it. Jeff and Serena went back into the playpen and Jeff explained to them that there was an error in the report and handed copies to the brief. He didn't tell him where the error was, but he'd find it soon enough.

Carl jumped up and tried to give his solicitor a high five. The brief was more restrained but he was inflating visibly and his expression moved a notch up the smugness scale as he stuffed papers into his Louis Vuitton briefcase. 'So are my clients free to go?' he asked.

'No,' Jeff told him. 'Terence Bratt has made a statement saying they borrowed Bruno on several occasions. I have copies for you. And witnesses from three of the premises burgled are more than glad to face your clients in a line-up.'

Serena said: 'So we'll be charging them with aggravated burglary, robbery and kidnapping and opposing bail. Any questions?'

'Fuckin' Paki cow,' Carl spat at her.

'Actually,' she began, turning to face him across the table, 'I was born in Heckley, like you. Unlike you, my parents were married.'

We were back in the observation room, watching and listening. Gareth let out a 'Yeah!' under his breath after Serena's response but Karen Kent just glared at the TV monitor.

She suddenly spun on her heels to face me. 'Could you run me back to HQ, Mr Priest? I have an asset planning meeting to prepare for.'

'I'll get one of the pandas to take you,' I suggested.

'If I'd wanted a panda car I'd have asked for one. I want you to take me so we can synchronise our diaries. I've instigated a committee about best practices, and I think we can learn lessons from this morning's fiasco, don't you agree?'

'Yes, ma'am,' I replied, but I knew my lessons would be different to hers.

I pulled out into the traffic and switched on my brand-new Airwave digital radio system, with the volume way down low. Gone were the days when you could park up in a bad reception area and sleep off your hangover. Nowadays we could be plotted to the nearest five metres. I'd never synchronised a diary before, so I waited, expectantly. The chatter on the radio was the usual post-bank holiday stuff: people coming home from a long weekend in the caravan to find their block paving had been removed; stolen barbecues; an old lady trying to climb the slip road on her battery scooter; traffic building up through Huddersfield.

Ms Kent took a deep breath and I braced myself, but the radio saved me. 'Attention, all units. Silent alarm activated at Royal Bank of Dubai, High Street, Heckley.' I leant over to turn up the volume and my passenger exhaled. 'Come in, all units. ARVs, confirm positions.'

The radio fell silent for a moment, then buzzed with noise as someone made a connection. 'Hotel Yankee 1 to control. We're on the M62, just passing Scammonden reservoir, heading west. We'll do our best.' They were miles away, going in the wrong direction. Even with blues and twos it would be fifteen minutes before they'd be on the scene.

'Hotel Yankee 4 to control. We're at a possible code blue RTA near Cleckheaton; can't really leave it.'

A couple of panda units radioed in to say they were on their way, and an ARV from West Pennine and one from Leeds offered to help, but again, they were miles away. And pandas don't carry firearms but bank robbers usually do. I slowed almost to a standstill, studying the scene behind through my rear-view mirrors. We'd just driven down Heckley High Street.

'Are we anywhere near?' Superintendent Kent asked.

'We've just driven by,' I replied, pulling towards the kerb and braking as I studied my mirrors. I couldn't see any alarms flashing but an elderly Ford Fiesta was parked on double yellows where I thought the bank was situated. Banks like the RBD don't go in for big signs. Discretion is all part of the service. At a price, of course. 'Hello, control,' I said, 'this is Charlie Puma. I've just passed the scene. Will turn back. Suspect a red Ford Fiesta is involved; reg mark coming up.'

I held my headlight flasher on and made a U-turn across two lanes of traffic. We were now behind the Fiesta, crawling towards it.

'Hi, Chas,' came the response. 'Right man in the right place, as usual.'

'Luck of the Irish, Arthur. I have Superintendent Kent with me. She's in charge.'

'OK. Standing by.'

'Charlie Puma to control,' she chanted into the RT. 'This is Superintendent Kent. We are on the scene in Heckley High Street. Will observe only. No unarmed units to become involved. That's an order. Repeat, nobody to approach the bank until we have firearms support.'

But I just kept rolling, quite slowly, towards the Fiesta. 'Radio in the number,' I said.

She twisted in her seat. 'What the fuck are you playing at, Priest?'

Cops and robbers, I thought, *it's what they pay us for*, but kept it to myself. The driver's window was down, even though a slight rain was falling, and his arm was dangling outside. A cigarette was held between his fingers and a puff of smoke blossomed for a second before being torn away by the breeze. I cruised gently to a standstill behind him and saw the fear in his eyes as he considered his options. Should he sound his horn, just drive off, or stick it out? Black smoke from the exhaust showed that the engine was running and badly needed an overhaul. I held my arm out across in front of the super, who was generating enough radiation to defrost a turkey. 'Take it easy,' I said. 'No sudden movements,' as I popped the lock on the boot lid.

I climbed leisurely out of the car, strolled round to the back of it, felt for the catch and raised the lid. Toby Curzon's shotgun was laid across the boot, hard up against the seats, wrapped in the tartan rug I keep in there. I'd forgotten to return it to her father when I last saw him. I slid my fingers inside the bundle and lifted it out.

The youth in the getaway car was more relaxed now that we hadn't made a drama of things. We were just a couple of wealthy citizens checking on our investments, with enough clout to flaunt the parking regulations for a couple of minutes. When I was alongside his door I let the rug slip to the ground and swung the gun barrels through the open window.

'This is a four-ten Magnum shotgun,' I told him. 'Probably the most powerful shotgun ever made, and at this range would blow your head clean off, so don't move a muscle.' Actually, it would just about kill a rabbit at twenty feet, but with both barrels jammed under his ear it probably would have blown his head off. I could feel his fear being transmitted down the gun as he tried to speak, choking on his words, his body wracked with terror.

'Now, put your hands behind your head.' He did as he was told, shivering like a condemned man on the scaffold, and I pulled the key from the ignition. When he was face down on the pavement I turned to the super, who was standing behind me, and told her to cuff him.

'I don't carry any,' she hissed.

'In the boot,' I told her, over my shoulder.

I met the other two in the doorway. One was carrying what I imagine were money bags and his pal, the black one, was holding what looked like a 9mm semi-automatic.

Oops, I thought.

If I'd gone for the gun he'd have pulled the trigger as a reaction, and that would have been Goodnight Vienna, so I stuffed the twin barrels of the four-ten into the stomach of the other one so hard that he gasped in pain and swung him round to put him between me and the nine-mil. I shouted: 'Armed police! Licensed to kill! Drop the gun!'

'Fuck, man. Fuck, man,' the black one said. He was wearing an Adidas hooded top with a baseball cap under the hood, the peak at precisely ninety degrees to his direction of travel. He might be robbing a bank, but looking cool is all.

'Drop the gun!' I shouted, 'or he dies.'

'Fuck, man. Fuck, man.'

'Drop the gun or he'll kill me!'

'Fuck, man. Fuck, man.'

'Drop the gun!'

'Drop the gun!'

His options were as exhausted as his vocabulary. He dropped the gun. I flicked it with the toe of my shoe, sending it spinning across the pavement to drop harmlessly into the gutter, as if it was something I'd practised for years. Superintendent Kent appeared alongside me, pink-cheeked, bright-eyed and breathing heavily. We marched the Sundance Kids out onto the pavement and ordered them to lie down on the wet flags. Ms Kent fetched two more plastic cuffs from my boot and when we'd made them comfortable I gave her the shotgun.

'If one of them moves, shoot him,' I said, for their benefit, not hers, 'while I round up the witnesses.' Her jaw dropped but she took the gun.

The cavalry arrived and gradually the nervous tension subsided, giving way to smiles, outright laughter and the camaraderie of a shared, but thwarted, danger. I was in the banking hall, listening to a lady who'd defied the Mau Mau in Kenya and wasn't going to be intimidated by home-grown villains, when I felt a hand on my arm. It was the photographer from the *Gazette*, Heckley's answer to CNN, wanting a story.

I excused myself from the colonial lady and said: 'Hiya, Flashbang. You took your time, seeing as you're next door.'

'What's the story, Charlie?'

'What you see is what you get. Attempted armed robbery; nearly made it with four million in used hundred-pound notes; silent alarm in the nick; Bob's your uncle.'

'Who's the lady outside with the gun?'

'Ah! That's Superintendent Karen Kent, seconded to Heckley for a short while to bring us up to speed with the latest advances. She's widely regarded as chief constable material. Did you get a picture of her?'

'A couple of good ones. Want a look?'

'Ooh, yes please.'

The yobs were carted away and Ms Kent came looking for me. 'I need to get back,' she said, 'or I'll be late for my meeting. Can we go, please?' Her breathing had settled down but her cheeks were still pink and a lock of dark hair was falling across her eyes, causing her problems. I tried to remember if she'd been wearing a hat. I felt certain she had been when she came into the office, earlier in the day.

'No problem,' I said. 'They don't need us here. Let's go.'

We were both feeling manic, the adrenaline rush hardly abated. 'Three good collars,' I said as I swung another U-turn across the High Street.

'Do you know them?'

'No, they're strangers to me.'

'From out of town?'

'Probably.'

'Does a bank like the RBD keep much money on the premises?'

'No idea.' We drove in silence the rest of the way to HQ, where I swung into the ACC's vacant parking space, nose up against the brick wall. I could have murdered a coffee but she didn't offer and didn't make an attempt to get out. We sat there, looking at the wall, not speaking, like an old married couple. The bricks were slimmer than standard size, in two shades of ochre arranged in a herringbone pattern. I was about to start counting them when she said: 'I'll have to make a report. You understand that, don't you?'

'Well,' I began, 'you were instrumental in collaring a gang of armed robbers and preventing a bank robbery. Of course you'll have to make a report. The CPS can only act on what we tell them.'

'I'm not referring to the robbery. I'll come to that. I'm talking about the shotgun that was in your car boot. The press will have a field day if they learn that one of our senior officers is in the habit of driving about with an unauthorised loaded shotgun in his car. And then there's a little matter of sloppy radio procedure. And the rubbish DNA evidence. They'll already be laughing at that in chambers, believe me.'

I looked across at her. 'What do you mean, loaded?' I demanded. 'Who said it was loaded?'

'Wasn't it?'

I pointed to the glovebox in front of her. She fumbled with the catch until the lid fell open, revealing the two cartridges I'd removed from the gun the night I took it from Toby.

'Oh my God!' she said, lifting them out. 'Oh my God!

We could've been killed. We could've been killed.' Her hands were shaking so much that the cartridges dropped to the floor.

I sweet-talked Janet Threadneedle into staying a little longer with her sister, so we were able to hold the reconstruction of her shopping trip on both the Monday, which was a bank holiday, and Tuesday, which wasn't. We have specialists we can draw on for tasks like that, so I'd no need to be involved. Wednesday morning their results and a copy of *The Sun* were on my desk, awaiting my scrutiny.

The Sun headline shouted *Atta Girl!* over a full-page photo of Superintendent Kent astride the three would-be bank robbers, shotgun held across her chest, their faces pixellated out but hers aglow with triumph. The brief text underneath proclaimed that this was exactly the type of policing we needed in the lawless Noughties. I turned to page three to see what I was missing (Emily-Mae, who is studying architecture. *Her front balcony looks good enough to us!*) and turned the page again to find the football, but it wasn't the beautiful game that caught my eye.

It was a photo of the royal princes, William and Harry, skulking out of a club called Chinawhite in the early hours, each with the obligatory blonde giving support. The photographer had struck gold, catching 'Kevin' in mid-blink, his eyes half closed as if surrendering to the effects of an evening's imbibing. Presumably the Sioux uprising on Salisbury Plain had been quelled, I thought, and the thought saddened me.

The reconstructions of Janet Threadneedle's last ride had produced five probable sightings, and the person who called out to Ghislaine at the ceremony had been identified as a youth who lived in Elland. I sent Maggie to interview him, and Serena and Dave to talk to the five possible witnesses. I didn't know how Superintendent Kent organised her mornings but I was on the road east before she could include me in her itinerary. Diary synchronising would have to wait awhile.

Outside Dunkley I telephoned ahead and was sipping coffee in Martin Chadwick's front room before ten o'clock. I'd expected hunting prints and the odd Stubbs, but the walls were adorned with cinema posters from the Fifties. Brando, brooding in *A Streetcar Named Desire*; hapless Jimmy Stewart in *Vertigo*; *Shane*; *The African Queen*. Memories came flooding back, the very names triggering off whatever it is that controls our happiness and that feeling of well-being we call nostalgia.

'You're a cinema buff,' I deduced.

'You've noticed.'

'I'm trained to pick up things like that.'

'Fifties cinema. I reckon it was the golden age.'

'I'd probably agree with you.'

'How's the coffee?'

'Fine. Just fine. I hope I'm not keeping you from your work.'

'No. I've a surgery later, that's all. So, how can I help you, Inspector?'

He was wearing jeans again, with a white shirt and a

quilted body warmer, even though it was a mild day. The rain had stopped and the cloud cover broken up. Shafts of sunlight shone on the low table between us, illuminating the steam that rose from our coffees, and a ginger cat purred comfortingly in the fireplace, dreaming of past conquests. 'I was hoping you could tell me something about the horse racing industry,' I said. 'As you know, I'm looking into the murder of Arthur George Threadneedle. We have our suspects among his business interests, but these days that's not good enough. We apply as much effort and credence to eliminating all other possibilities as we do to chasing the favourite candidate. I'll be grateful for anything you can tell me about Threadneedle and about the horse called Peccadillo.'

He smiled. 'Does this mean I'm a suspect? Did I ought to have my solicitor?'

I didn't smile back. 'I'm not regarding you as a suspect, Mr Chadwick, but if you are about to say anything that might be incriminating, let me know and we'll consider the need for a solicitor then. At the moment I'm asking you for general information, that's all. Let's say you're my local expert witness.' What I really wanted from him was the dirt on his fellow villagers, but first I needed him talking.

'Right. Fire away.'

'How well did you know Threadneedle?'

'Not very. He kept animals and I'm a vet. That's about it.'

'He and his wife held musical soirées. Were you invited?'

'No. They were couples only, I'm told.'

'Are you implying that there's some significance in that?'

He shook his head. 'Nah. Just malicious talk by small-minded people. You can't scratch your balls in a place like this without word getting out that you have crabs. I suppose I ought to tell you about the drugs.'

'I'm all ears,' I told him.

'It won't have escaped your notice that although I live in a horse racing centre I don't have much business with the horses.'

'You're right; it hasn't.'

'That's because I won't play their game. I don't like the way they treat them so the trainers retaliate by taking their business elsewhere. And it's a lucrative business.'

'What drugs are we talking about?'

'Phenylbutazone and Ketamine hydrochloride, better known as Bute and Special K. As a veterinary surgeon I'm authorised to prescribe them, but not in the quantities they'd like.'

'Are we talking about human consumption or equine?'

'Both, Inspector. Bute is a tranquilliser, used mainly to treat arthritis, and Ketamine is an anaesthetic with hallucinogenic properties. It's class C, only available under the Medicines Act. I'm told that it's more predictable than LSD, but I wouldn't know.'

'What's the objection to Bute?' I asked.

'Overuse. They stuff the poor animal full of it, just in case. Or they use it to prolong its competitive life long after it should have retired. It has side effects, including kidney damage.'

'And Threadneedle asked you to supply him?'

'That's right.'

'You refused?'

'Not at first, but he only had about ten horses in training. Then he started asking for ridiculous quantities. He made noises about making it worth my while...' Chadwick rubbed his finger and thumb together in the universal gesture for bribery '...and I was tempted for about ten seconds. Having a bent vet in your pocket could be highly profitable for somebody unscrupulous, but the risks were too high for me. He was sounding me out, but I suggested he take his business elsewhere. I think he'd overstretched himself financially, and peddling a few drugs was one possible way of improving his cash flow.'

'Presumably this was before the fire.'

'Oh yes. A few months before. He'd asked me to sign a markings certificate for him, which I did. That confirms that the horse they are hoping to race is the same one that was born to that particular thoroughbred stallion and dam, which it was. They were nondescripts, never likely to be more than selling platers, but Peccadillo was a fine-looker; had potential, he thought.'

'Did you sign?'

'Of course. No reason not to.'

'Were you aware that Threadneedle was telling people that Peccadillo was an offspring of Shergar?'

'Ha ha! You've heard about that, have you? It was village gossip. People around here might be cabbage-looking but they're not green. Threadneedle hinted that Shergar was the genuine sire to drum up interest in his syndicate. It certainly looked the part but I doubt if anybody fell for it, apart from him.'

'Does who your parents are make any difference?' I asked. 'Presumably the laws of genetics are the same for humans as for horses, but I don't recall hearing of Roger Bannister's children running the mile any faster than he did.'

'You're dead right, but don't tell the breeders that. To them, ancestry is everything. And racing improves the breed.'

'You sound sceptical.'

'Just a little. You mentioned Roger Bannister. He ran the mile in three minutes fifty-nine seconds, back in 1952. The record at the moment is sixteen seconds faster. *Sixteen* seconds. That's four seconds a lap quicker. The record for the Derby is two minutes thirty-two seconds, set by Lammtarra in 1995, knocking a whole second off the previous record, set back in 1936. *One second* in nearly sixty years. So much for racing improving the breed. Shergar won four, or was it five, races. He was retired to stud, where he sired about forty foals at, oh, think of a number, fifty thousand pounds a time. Then he was stolen. None of them has won anything significant. A horse called Northern Dancer is in the record books as siring over a hundred stud stallions that went on to produce over a thousand offspring. Storm Cat himself sired over a thousand foals.'

'What happens to them all?' I asked. 'They can't all be racing against each other.'

'Good question,' he replied. 'It's a bit like blue tits.'

'Blue tits?'

'Mmm. Blue tits need only produce two offspring to maintain numbers, but they lay about eighteen eggs. If it wasn't for predators – magpies, sparrowhawks and cats – we'd be up to our elbows in blue tits in five years. It's the same with thoroughbreds. Some of them have successful careers; some don't but the owners cash in by breeding from them; a significant number become steeplechasers. The lucky ones get away with it, but generally speaking they're not built for the jumps, not robust enough, so they break a leg and have to be put down. Nine in a single day at Cheltenham recently.'

I sipped my coffee and looked beyond him, out of the window, thinking about what he'd told me. The clouds had cleared and beyond his paddock a flock of rooks was soaring high above the chestnut trees in some spring ritual that would ultimately help perpetuate the species. I wondered if blue tits were part of their diet and decided to change the subject.

I said: 'When I was a kid there was a man down our street who kept racing pigeons. He let me help him clean out their boxes. I loved sitting there, surrounded by them as they fed and bowed and curtsied to each other. It was like being in a different world. Then, one day, he didn't see me approaching. He picked up this bird and wrung its neck. It was dead, just like that. He loved his pigeons, but he didn't carry passengers.'

'I know what you mean,' Chadwick replied. 'People who race greyhounds are the same. They make super pets, but if they can't race they're surplus to requirements and have to go.'

'How well do you know Ghislaine Curzon?' I asked in a conversational tone, adding, so I couldn't be accused of trickery: 'You were seen with her a week ago.'

He gave a little snort of pleasure at the memory and wrapped his coffee mug in his fingers, holding it close. His fingernails were bitten down to pink stumps. He looked me in the eyes and smiled but didn't blush. 'I've known her all her life, Inspector,' he said. 'It was the RCVS spring ball last Tuesday. Local branch, that is. I invite Ghislaine every year and she does me the honour of accompanying me when she can.' The smile slipped from his face as he went on: 'I suspect it's because she feels safe with me. It does my kudos with the group good, and I'm grateful for the few crumbs that fall from the table. That's all.'

'I know the feeling,' I told him, rising to my feet. Oh yes, I certainly knew the feeling. I thanked him for his time, told him I'd no doubt have some more questions, and picked up my coffee mug. We walked through into his kitchen, towards the outer door, and I rinsed the mug under the tap, leaving it upside down on the draining board. He pulled the door open for me but I paused, one leg outside, one in, and said: 'You told me that a significant number of racehorses that were bred every year went into steeplechasing.'

'That's right.'

'So what happens to the rest of them?'

'The rest of them? Well, a few are adopted as pets. Lawn ornaments, we call them, and the others, most of them, are exported to Belgium. The Belgians put them in pies and eat them.'

CHAPTER THIRTEEN

The landlord of the Alice Hawthorne was watering his hanging baskets as I drove by, so I swung into his car park. It was early, but I stopped and we wished each other a good morning and commented on the weather.

'Need a drink?' he asked as he tipped the last few drops of water onto the cobbles.

'Any chance of a coffee?'

'Oh, I think we might manage one.'

I followed him into the gloom of the bar and he led me to the end where the Douwe Egberts dispenser stood. It was hot and strong and loaded with enough caffeine to dull an amputation.

'Cor! That's good stuff,' I said, lowering my cup.

'So have you caught him?' the landlord asked.

'The murderer? No, but we will. Did Threadneedle

come in here when he lived nearby?'

'All the time. Thought he owned the place.'

'Did you know about the syndicate he was running?'

'For that fancy horse he'd bought? We heard about it.'

'Were you invited to join?'

'We were *offered the opportunity.* Unfortunately, due to prior commitments, we had to reluctantly decline the offer.'

'Did he have any takers?'

'Not that anybody's admitted to.'

'Did he push the Shergar angle?'

'Just enough to appeal to the greedy and the gullible.'

'Who are usually the same people.'

'Exactly. He'd fallen for it, over in Ireland. Some pinhooker had kidded him on that it was a classic contender when all it was good for was pulling a milk float. It looked good, but it had no heart. You can't see heart, but that's what wins races.'

'So it had a race?'

'No. But we watched it on the gallops. Drew quite a crowd did young Peccadillo. We thought maybe the jockey was holding him back, but he said he wasn't. Threadneedle chewed him off a strip and sacked him, but it didn't help – the horse was a waste of a good skin.'

'What's a pinhooker?'

'Oh, a dealer who finds cheap flashy horses and sells them on.'

'I see. Some of them make a living from it, do they?'

'More than you'd believe.'

'Did *anyone* buy into the syndicate?'

'Word has it that Curzon bought a share. Serves him right if he did. Couldn't have happened to anyone better.'

I slid my cup across the counter for a refill. 'You said that with feeling,' I told him. He replenished it and placed two sachets of sugar in the saucer even though I hadn't touched the first two.

'Aye, well,' he said. 'It goes back a long time.' I didn't comment. If he wanted me to know he'd tell me in his own way. A woman came in, asked him for 'the key' and went through into the private quarters. I thought the spell was broken but he came back to my end of the bar and started to tell me.

'My great-grandfather was head gardener at the estate,' he said. 'Lived in a tied cottage. On the day he died Lady Muck Curzon paid his wife a visit and handed over a ten-pound note to pay for the funeral. It was the first ten-pound note great-grandma had ever seen. The day after the funeral the estate manager came a-calling and gave her a week's notice to be out of the cottage. That's the Curzons for you. That's why I say it couldn't have happened to anyone nicer.'

A couple of houses in Dunkley had B&B signs hanging outside, with sliding boards indicating that they had vacancies. I made a mental note of where they were and wrote a phone number down in case I was staying over and felt like a change from Phyllis Smith's place, although I couldn't see that happening. Driffield said I could have the desk in the corner, with a telephone, and I spent an hour catching up with the troops.

Maggie had seen the youth who called out to Ghislaine

at the ceremony, and her heart had skipped a beat when he allowed her into his living room. Hanging over the mantelpiece was a full-page photograph of Princess Diana, cut from one of the tabloids. It was framed, with glass, and dominated the room. Standing on the television was another framed photo. This time it was of Ghislaine, taken by him at the ceremony, moments before she opened the curtains.

But it was all downhill from there. He was a pleasant lad, Maggie said, with a legitimate interest in beautiful girls due to being a hairdresser. Thursday to Saturday he hired a chair at one of the more expensive salons in town, and the rest of the time he went mobile, visiting his clients at home. He'd allowed her a quick look round and there wasn't a shrine to Lady Di, complete with electric candles and Elton John whining in the background, in any of the other rooms. Maggie had thanked him for his cooperation and booked an appointment for a trim.

Dave and Serena had interviewed five people who'd come forward after the reconstructions of Janet Threadneedle's last ride and it looked good. They'd seen her loading her distinctive car assisted by a tall youth parked in an adjacent space. When showed printouts of the hoody making his furtive way through the Curzon Centre two weeks earlier they'd all said, with varying degrees of confidence, that it could have been him. I asked Dave to track young Mister Sidebottom down and arrange an interview for in the morning.

We saw him in the incident room we were still using at the Centre, although now the murder had replaced the graffiti job in our affections and had its own incident room back at the nick. The two may or may not be linked, we thought, but for the moment we were hunting a murderer.

Oscar Sidebottom was not to know that. 'Where were you on the fourteenth of May at ten o'clock in the morning?' Dave asked. 'That was the Monday morning Miss Curzon came to officially open the Curzon Centre.'

Young Oscar was a gangling, fresh-faced youth with a diffident manner that came across as barely suppressed arrogance. He'd declined our suggestion that he consider having a solicitor present, and positively recoiled at my offer to allow his mother to sit in on the interview. We pointed out that he wasn't under arrest and he could walk out any time he wanted. He said he understood. In other words, he was just how we like them.

'I was at home,' he replied.

'Which is where?'

'Student quarters at York. Do you want the address?'

'Yes please.'

Dave wrote it down. The interview wasn't being taped but Dave was taking notes. His shorthand speed is in single figures, so I spoke slowly. 'You don't live with your mother?'

'I have a room in her apartment. I stay there sometimes.'

'You didn't want to be at the opening? Didn't want to enjoy your mother's little moment of glory?'

'Is that what you call it: her *moment of glory*?'

'What would you call it?'

'I'd call it pandering to the Establishment; encouraging

them by perpetuating their influence over the working classes. I had no desire to be a part of it.'

Dave said: 'Where were you a few hours earlier? Say about one a.m.'

'I was drinking with friends in the uni bar until nearly midnight, then I went home to bed.'

'Can anybody verify that?'

'Yes, but I can't give you a name.'

'Out of old-fashioned chivalry? Highly commendable.'

'No. Out of not remembering it.'

I took the A4 CCTV hard copies that Maggie had done for me out of my briefcase and slid them across the table. 'Does he remind you of anybody?' I asked.

He studied them for a long while, staring at each before placing it underneath the others, then placing them side by side on the desk. 'No,' he said, eventually.

'You don't sound too sure.'

'Well I am. But I can see where you're coming from. It's not me, though.'

'Do you have a hooded top?'

'Yeah, like everybody I know.'

'And a baseball cap?'

'Likewise.'

'You've spent a lot of time at the Centre, Oscar, behind the scenes, and we're convinced that it was an inside job, to coin a phrase. Does the figure in the photos remind you of anybody?'

'No.'

'How do you think he got in and out without meeting anybody or triggering an alarm?'

'No idea.'

'You must have given it some thought, Oscar. From what I'm told you're the expert on security at the Centre. So how did he do it?'

'I don't know.'

Dave said: 'Would you tell us if you did?'

'Probably not,' Oscar replied. 'We need another shopping mall like we need a dose of clap. If I could do anything to put the mockers on it, I'd be in there. I hope whoever did it gets away.'

'But you've no objection to working here, taking the man's money,' I said.

'It's to pay off my student loan, and there's an irony to using their own money to work against them.'

I saw a way to run the interview and I'm sure Dave saw it, too. Get him on his hobby horse, well away from the enquiries, and eventually he'd let slip whatever it was that made young Oscar Sidebottom tick.

'So it's all about green issues, is it?' I asked, closing my notebook and sliding the photos back in their envelope, as if we were concluding the meeting, but I was too late: his training kicked in and he came out with response number seventeen, chapter five, of the anarchists' handbook:

'No comment,' he said. 'I think I've answered enough of your questions.'

'You've been very patient with us,' I told him. 'Where will you be staying the rest of the week, in case we need to talk to you again?'

'No comment.'

'Have they taken the plaque down?'

'No comment.'

'Are all the alarms on the fire doors and emergency exits activated?'

'No comment.'

'OK, you can go.' I flapped an arm to dismiss him and looked across at Dave. He pulled his *don't look at me* expression and pushed his chair away from the table.

Young Sidebottom stood up and headed for the door. As he reached it Dave called after him: 'Oscar.'

He stopped, one hand on the handle and looked at us.

'Come and sit down,' Dave said, and he did as he was told, his self-assurance crumbling as he realised we hadn't finished with him yet.

There was a water cooler in the corner, half full, and I walked over to it and filled two beakers. Oscar declined when I asked him. I took a long sip and it tasted good. I told him that, as before, he still wasn't under caution and could terminate the meeting any time. 'Where were you on the morning of Monday the twenty-first?' I asked. 'That was a week last Monday.'

'No comment.'

'In case you haven't realised it, that was the morning Arthur George Threadneedle was shot.'

'No comment.'

'Did you know him?'

'No comment.'

'Had you ever met him?'

'No comment.'

I said: 'Your allegiance to the cause, whatever it might be, is commendable, Oscar, but murder is a serious offence and the advice given to you by whatever tame lawyer your group uses is, believe me, bad advice. If you continue to be uncooperative I shall be forced to arrest you and interview you under caution. The least that could happen then is that you'd spend two nights in the cells with a bunch of drunkards. So, did you know Arthur George Threadneedle?'

'No comment.'

'Did you know his wife, Janet?'

'No comment.'

'Somebody answering your description was seen helping her with her shopping on the morning in question. Was it you? If it was, believe me, we'll find out.'

'No comment.'

'OK,' I said. 'We get the message. You can go. Bugger off.'

He looked mystified, raised himself from his chair but paused half stooped over the little table. 'I can go?' he asked, as if he hadn't heard properly.

'That's right. We haven't time to play games with tosspots – we've a murderer to catch. Don't leave the country.' He was out of the door before you could whistle the overture to *Iolanthe*.

Miss McArdle hadn't been answering her phone, but it seemed a shame not to give her a visit while we were in the building. Much to my surprise Dave's knock was answered by her shouted invitation to enter. She still hadn't found herself a secretary.

Miss McArdle was standing behind her desk and a middle-aged man was standing opposite her. From the expressions on their faces it looked as if we'd interrupted some form of disagreement and saved them from scratching each other's eyes out. 'Ah!' Miss McArdle exclaimed. 'We were expecting someone else.' She turned to the man. 'Very well, Turner, I'll arrange for your pay to be docked. That will be all.'

Turner, ashen-faced, stormed past us and slammed the door in his wake. I winced and Dave pulled a face. Miss McArdle invited us to sit down. 'Apologies for the unpleasantness,' she said. 'We thought you were his Usdaw rep. How can I help you?'

'We were in the building,' I told her. 'We've just had a talk with your son, Oscar, about his whereabouts when the graffiti was done, and we showed him the photographs. We advised him to invite a solicitor along, which he declined, and suggested as an alternative that you sit in on the interview, which he again declined. He answered all our questions with a "No comment". He's not doing himself any favours by refusing to cooperate.'

'I thought we'd dropped the enquiry, Inspector. Are you saying that Oscar is a suspect?'

'Everybody is a suspect until someone leaps into the frame. Oscar might be completely innocent, but he knows the people who work here, may even be able to point a finger at the culprit. The fact that he refuses to, or even denies being able to, casts suspicion on him. You know what the official caution says, Miss McArdle: *it may harm your defence*, and all that.' I turned to Dave and explained that Miss McArdle was an avid reader of crime fiction.

'In that case, *help*!' he retorted, and immediately jumped up as his mobile phone started to vibrate in his pocket. 'Excuse me,' he said, glancing at the display, and stepped outside the office, closing the door behind him.

'What did we do without them?' I wondered out loud, rather lamely.

'I'd be lost without mine,' Miss McArdle confessed.

'Tell me...' I began, then hesitated, not sure about the diplomacy of my words. 'Tell me, did you know the Curzons at all?'

'No. I knew of them, but never met them.'

'But you lived in that neck of the woods, didn't you, when you were working in York?'

'Yes. We lived in Malton, which is not far away from them. I was born there; moved away when I went to university.'

'What about Oscar? He's a bit young for Ghislaine and too old for Toby, but he may have had...oh, I don't know...a holiday job at the house; or used it in a school project; or played tennis there. Anything like that?'

'He's my son, Inspector, and I'm not happy answering these questions. I suggest you ask him.'

'OK, I'm sorry,' I said. 'You're quite right.' Except, of course, that sweet baby Oscar wouldn't answer our questions and was as forthcoming as a dead clam. I decided on one more try. 'Tell me this, though,' I said. 'Did your son ever meet Mr Threadneedle? Or his wife?

We need to know for elimination purposes.' I like saying that: *for elimination purposes*. It's always assumed that we're talking about eliminating the person in question, but it could equally mean every other person in the world *except* him.

She puffed herself up with a deep breath and blew it out slowly, her mind racing, deciding which avenue to take. She'd read the books, and if her beloved son had left his prints or DNA anywhere incriminating it would help his case if she disclosed that he regularly frequented that place. Her hair had changed since our previous meeting. It was jet black, close cut in an asymmetrical shape, like a helmet, and nearly obscured her left eye. It probably cost a fortune but it looked good. No doubt about it: Miss Carol McArdle was back in the race. So when she answered my question I'd forgotten what I'd asked.

'Yes,' she said.

'I'm sorry...'

'Yes, he did.'

'Right. Good.' I hadn't a clue what she meant, but had faith that the patron saint of detectives would come to my rescue, and there she was, right on cue.

'Oscar is quite a musician. He plays the guitar, like so many young people, but wanted to take it more seriously. I mentioned it to Arthur and he suggested his wife, Janet, could give him lessons. Her principal instrument was the flute, but she was a respectable pianist and knew all the theory, of course, so he went to their house for lessons.'

Phew! Hallelujah! I said: 'Wasn't that...you know...a bit dangerous?'

'That's what I said, but he just laughed, thought it added something to our relationship. He told her that Oscar was the son of one of his employees and she believed him.'

Psychiatrists say that the risk of being caught adds a certain something to illicit sex. They also say that psychopaths build castles in the air, schizophrenics live in them and psychiatrists collect the rent. Dave knocked and came back in, mumbling an apology.

Walking back to the car he told me about the phone call. 'Three messages for you,' he said. 'A Miss Toby Curzon wants to speak to you. Said nobody else would do. Then Special Branch returned your call. Have you been chasing them?'

' 'Yep. And the third...?'

'Ah! This is the one you'll love. Superintendent Krypton Knickers herself would like an audience, if it's not too much trouble.'

'Karen Kent? Jeez! What does she want?'

'Well, she *is* the boss. What shall I tell control?'

'Huh! Tell them we're in East Yorkshire, doing follow-ups. It's about time you were familiarised with the locality.' We'd reached the car. I zapped the door locks and we climbed in.

Dave is the nearest I have to family. We go back a long way, have shared a few scrapes, covered each other's back on more than one occasion. We even played in the same football team for a while. I'm his daughter's godfather. As we pulled onto the motorway I said: 'So Sophie didn't make it to Dan's birthday?'

'No, she sent him a card with a cheque in it.' He made it

sound as if they'd laced the money with the anthrax virus.

'I suppose they have their own lives to live,' I said.

Sophie went to Cambridge University and was Dave's golden girl. Mine too. She got pregnant and married during her second year, and now Dave and Shirley never see her or the baby.

'They manage to see *his* parents often enough,' Dave told me. 'Young Courtney's growing up and Shirl's missing his best years. She's pretty upset about it. We didn't even see him for his first birthday. They sent us a photograph and that was that.'

A sixteen-wheeler came steaming by and I pulled out into his wake. It's not often we get the chance to gossip on a personal level. In the car, with the radio turned off, is the best we can do. The overtaking lane was clear so I moved over and put my foot down. We talked about holidays and young Dan's job prospects. He'd walk a decent university, but his sole ambition is to play for Manchester United.

'I'm a bit concerned about Karen Kent taking over the enquiry,' I admitted.

'Whatever for?' Dave asked. 'You could eat her for breakfast.'

'Hmm. On the whole, I think I'd rather have a full English. It's just that, you know, you can always find something that you should have done, or could have done better. She's never led a murder enquiry, but it would look good on her CV, so she'll be anxious to put her stamp on the job. Hindsight, and all that.'

'Such as?'

'Well, for a start, if it was young Oscar helping Mrs Threadneedle with her groceries in the supermarket car park...'

'Which it almost certainly was,' Dave asserted.

'...which it probably was,' I concurred, 'his prints would have been all over the bags. But we didn't check for them.'

'There was no reason to,' he said. 'She'd been to the supermarket and done some shopping. Big deal. You can't dust everywhere for prints.'

'Will you explain that to KK or shall I?'

'OK, so the bags will probably have gone to the dump but all the stuff she bought will be in her fridge and larder. He'll have left his mark on something that will prove he was there.'

'Too late,' I said. 'While you were answering the phone outside her office Carol McDoodle told me that Janet Threadneedle was giving young Oscar piano lessons. His prints could be anywhere in the house.'

'Oh, right. Back to the drawing board.' He sat silently for a while, then turned to face me. 'Would that be piano lessons or "*piano lessons*"?' he asked, making that quotation marks gesture with his fingers.

'Surely not,' I said. 'She's old enough to be his mum.'

'Charlie, where have you been for the last hundred years?'

I was doing ninety-five in the fast lane and a BMW was tailgating me. I pulled to the left and he accelerated away.

'What did you want Special Branch for?' Dave asked.

Special Branch are not some super-special, hi-tech cloak-and-dagger outfit, dedicated to protecting citizens of our fair country at considerable danger to themselves. For a start, they rarely make arrests. Every force has its own Special Branch, whose members spend most of their working day loafing around airport arrival lounges, looking at faces, checking passenger lists. They gather intelligence. Once, they were concerned with normal, routine, cross-border crime; then drug smuggling became flavour of the month; now it's international terrorism that keeps them awake at night. The jobs they used to be involved with, like organised crime and VIP protection, have been offloaded onto specially trained firearms officers, under the watchful eye of CID, which means me.

'Barry Sidebottom,' I said. 'The aggrieved husband. He's supposed to be in Portugal but I'd like to know his recent whereabouts. It'll be interesting to learn if SB have anything on him.'

We'd had a cold, cloudless night, courtesy of high pressure off North Utsire, wherever that is, and now the fields were steaming as the sun burnt off the early-morning dew. But the rivers – the Wharfe and the Ouse – clung to their smoking blankets and at Stamford Bridge we plunged into gloom as we crossed the narrow humpback over the Derwent, where, nearly a thousand years earlier, history had reached a tipping point. Here, one September morning in 1066, the final page in the *Anglo-Saxon Chronicle* was begun. The Vikings were routed but the Normans were mustering in the South, and nothing would ever be the same again.

There's a steep hill leaving the town, which has been the scourge of generations of caravan-pullers, but the engine revved like a turbine, taking us charging up out of the valley and in seconds we were bursting out into the sunshine again. The birds were singing, the sky was straight out of a holiday brochure and we were doing what we do best.

'Look!' I said, thumping a dozing Sparky on the arm.

'W-What?'

'Buzzard.' It had showed itself briefly above the trees, soaring on the updraught, and been lost behind us.

'Oh, right.'

I said: 'Do you think the Curzons came over with Bill the Conqueror?'

'Probably.'

'I bet they did. I bet they were given a few thousand acres for services to William.'

'So they were the enemy, back then.'

'Most likely.'

'Are we nearly there yet?'

CHAPTER FOURTEEN

I drove to Dunkley first, pointing out the Alice Hawthorne, which had that desolate look reserved for pubs that are closed, and the little housing project where old Motty Dermott lived. I parked outside his house and rang the bell, just once, but he didn't appear. A neighbour came out and told me it was Springfield House day. I chatted to her for a while and learnt that the old-timers went there twice a week for a hot meal and game of bingo. Otherwise, she didn't want to talk. This was a small village, and I looked like a policeman, and curtains were already twitching.

At Curzon House I stopped in my usual spot, bang in the middle of the park. About ten visitors' cars were parked sensibly near the entrance, and a minibus with *Barbara Castle Comprehensive* emblazoned along its length was in the shadows at the end of the house. As I stretched myself upright I heard the chatter of children coming from that direction. The tennis court was down there, so they were probably having a tennis lesson.

'Where's the old deserted village?' Dave asked.

I pointed. 'That way. About quarter of a mile, that's all. It's called Low Ogglethorp, without an 'e' on the end. High Ogglethorpe has acquired the 'e'. It's probably a Victorian affectation.'

'And you're hot on Victorian affectations.'

'They're my speciality subject. What's the interest?'

'Sophie did her thesis on lost villages. There are hundreds of them, all over the place. I took her round a few. Not this one, though. Became a bit of an expert, though I say it myself.'

Sophie read history at Cambridge. First one in the family, and all that. Dave plays the disappointed father but underneath he's as proud as Punch of her, and quite rightly. Me? I'm merely a neutral observer. It must be something in her perfume that makes my hormone levels go haywire every time I see her. I pulled myself together and said: 'Let's go look at it, then.'

'It'll do later,' he said. 'We're supposed to be on an investigation.'

'We are,' I replied. 'You do your measurements, or whatever, and I'll sit on a stone and cogitate. It's that way.'

We strode off along the lane I'd followed Toby down, nine nights earlier. The freshness of the morning was turning into a warm day, and the burbling of a distant lawnmower explained the smell of cut grass that followed us.

'It was the Enclosures Act did it,' Dave informed me.

'Did what?'

'Got rid of the people. Back in the sixteenth century all the peasants had their own little allotments and got on as merry as pigs in muck, give or take the odd plague or Black Death. They grew wheat and had home-made bread every day. Delicious.'

'For every meal,' I suggested.

'Well, yes, but they got by. Then Mr Brutal Landowner worked out that he'd make a lot more money out of keeping sheep, without all the unpleasantness of collecting taxes from the common people. So he drove them off the land and bulldozed their cottages.'

'They had bulldozers, back then?'

'Very primitive ones.'

'Of course. Left behind by the Romans, perhaps.'

'Could be. So now only a couple of families were kept on, to work as shepherds, with no land of their own, and the landowner was freed of all the hassle he'd had before. And nobody was snaffling his deer and pheasants every night.'

'They had pheasants?'

'Hmm, possibly not. Rabbits, though.'

'They definitely had rabbits. If we meet Mr Curzon you'll try not to bring up the depopulation of the countryside, won't you, please? It could be a touchy subject.'

'I'll try not to.'

'Good. Turn left, through that gate.' It looked benign in the sunshine; had lost the air of spookiness that enveloped it on my last visit. 'This is it,' I said.

Dave was impressed. Most of the ones he'd seen were simply grid references on a map, with little to show that a community had once lived, played, argued and dreamt there. They'd been moved on and then the very stones they'd owned were taken away to build a bigger house for the master, and stables for his horses and cattle. When he'd cast his expert eye over the place I said: 'The rabbits are through there. It's called Coneywarren Field.'

'This way?' He pointed to a narrow path that cut through the overgrown strip of wood that separated the two fields.

'Yep.' I stepped after him, dragging through the brambles that covered the track, dodging the odd branch that he let fly back. Suddenly he stopped and raised an arm. 'What?' I asked.

'I can hear voices.'

I could hear them too. Or perhaps one voice, muttering something unintelligible, over and over again. I gestured for him to move on, and in a few seconds we were on the edge of the clearing known as Coneywarren Field.

Toby was wearing cut-off dungarees and a T-shirt that made her look like a hillbilly. Her back was towards us and she was attacking the ground with a garden rake. After a while she dropped the rake and gathered up a bundle of rubbish that she'd produced, and all the time she was muttering to herself: 'Bastards, bastards' – word I didn't catch – 'bastards.' She shoved the rubbish into a bin liner and picked up the rake again.

'Toby,' I said, but she didn't hear me. 'Toby!' Louder this time, and she spun round, her empty expression turning to shock as she recognised me. I walked over to her, Dave following, and put my hands on her sparrow-boned shoulders. Her face was distorted with hatred and betrayal, her bottom lip trembling, and she'd aged thirty years in the few days since I'd last seen her.

'What is it, Toby?' I asked. 'What's upsetting you?'

'Look,' she replied. 'They've trashed it. Look at all the rubbish. And they've pulled Mummy's tree over. What will I tell Daddy? He mustn't see it like this. He mustn't.' She started to cough, and we both gave her tissues, but there was little else I could do for her except watch, helplessly, willing her to pull through it, paralysed by my inadequacies.

Dave did better. He enveloped her in his arms and told her she'd be all right. 'Take it easy,' he whispered. 'You'll be OK. Everything is fine. Breathe through your mouth. That's the way. Big breaths...in...and out...in...and out.' After a few minutes the convulsions subsided and Toby looked more like her old self. Dave relaxed his grip on her.

I cast a glance over the place and saw what she meant. Someone had held a party, complete with bonfire, takeaway pizzas, and copious quantities of Foster's and alcopop. The evidence was spread about for all to see. Not content with having a good time, they'd pulled over the substantial silver birch tree that had been growing in the middle of the clearing. As I looked I realised we were standing in the middle of a stone circle, a miniature version of Avebury. The tree, I remembered, was planted over Toby's mother's final resting place. No wonder she had murder in her heart; I was feeling the same.

'Let's sit down,' I said, and led her over to the same log

we leant against before. 'Don't worry about your daddy,' I
told her. 'He'll be more upset to see you like this. He'll be
OK, I promise you. Don't worry about him.'

Dave had followed us. 'This is Mr Sparkington,' I said.
'He's a detective, too.'

Toby held out a solemn hand and big Dave shook it.
'Are you Charlie's boss?' she asked.

'Only on a Thursday,' he told her.

'That's today.'

'I know. That's why he's so grumpy.'

'Ah! You're having me on.' There was just a flash of
the old Toby as she jousted with him. 'Have you ever done
a hundred and twenty-five in a cop Volvo?'

'No. That's too fast for me.'

They were getting on well, so I drifted off out of earshot
and dialled Curzon's mobile. He was in the greenhouse,
planting up hanging baskets, and thought Toby was in her
room.

'What days does she go to school?' I asked, after I'd
filled him in with the morning's bad news.

'She tries to go Monday, Tuesday and possibly Wednesday,
but doesn't always make it. Apart from anything else she
can't run about like the other kids, and it frustrates her.
Thursdays, Fridays and Saturdays she has a tutor for an
hour or two. It's maths for her this afternoon. She's doing
well, keeping up, no bother. Toby's a competitive little
devil, doesn't like being beaten.'

'I need to talk to her, with your permission and in your
presence, if that's OK. We'll keep it light, won't put her
on the spot.'

'That's fine, Charlie. When were you thinking of?'

'In about twenty minutes? In your kitchen?'

'Oh, as soon as that. Right, we'll see you there. Um, can I have a word with her first, just to reassure her?'

'Of course.'

Grizzly joined us in the kitchen, which was a pleasant surprise. Toby had gone to fetch her father and we sat in silence for a while, after I'd described what we'd found and told her how upset Toby had been, and how worried she was that her father would see the clearing in its trashed state. I sipped my coffee and wished I had a big comfortable kitchen like this one, with a rocking chair and top-notch hi-fi system, and an American fridge filled with cheap white wine and frozen curries. I could get used to this, I thought.

I said: 'Are you working at the hospital today, Miss Curzon?'

She gave me a sideways look that I interpreted as: 'What's with this "Miss Curzon"?' What she actually said was: 'Yes, Inspector Priest. I'm on the mid-afternoon shift all week.'

I told her about Dave's interest in vanished villages, courtesy of Sophie, and she suggested he bring her along sometime, to see what she could tell them about it. The local history society wanted to excavate the site but their expertise was questionable and a competent job couldn't be guaranteed. James Curzon came in, with Toby, and we made room for them at the end of the refectory table. Dave jumped up and introduced himself.

When our coffees were replenished, with orange juice for Toby, I said, looking at Curzon: 'We were discussing the medieval village but I couldn't help noticing that there's a stone circle in Coneywarren Field that could be much older. Is it genuine Neolithic?'

'Ah!' he exclaimed. 'I'm sorry, Charlie, but you've been duped. It's early Victorian, probably built to provide some work during a bad time. Soldiers returning from the Napoleonic wars, something like that.'

'Or to ease the landowner's conscience,' Ghislaine suggested, 'after they'd turfed all the peasants off the land.'

Toby told us it was a folly, and the twelve stones represented the twelve Apostles, or the numbers on a clock face, or they just happened to have available twelve stones of the right size, depending on your beliefs.

'We turfed nobody off the land,' Curzon told us, 'although you'd have difficulty convincing some of the villagers of that. The house came into Curzon hands in about 1890, at the market price.'

I turned to his younger daughter. 'How are you feeling now, Toby?' I asked. 'You had us really worried, back there.'

'I'm all right. Thank you for looking after me.'

'That was my trusty assistant.'

'Did you have your medication with you?' Ghislaine asked.

'No. I haven't needed it for ages. It was only because of...because of...'

I said: 'Because you were upset by what you found.'

'Yes.'

Which brought us neatly round to where we wanted to be. I said: 'It looked as if there'd been a party. Were you invited?'

She shook her head. 'No.'

'Was it your friends who held it?'

'Mmm.'

'The badger protection people?'

'Mmm.'

'But they didn't invite you?'

'No.'

'So how did you learn about it?'

'Aspen told me.'

'Aspen?' I queried.

'Aspen lives in the village,' Ghislaine told us. 'She's a school friend of Toby's, although she's a couple of years older.'

'She's fifteen,' Toby confirmed.

'So when did she tell you about the party?' I asked.

'Last night. After I was in bed. She texted me wondering why I wasn't there. Then she phoned and said she was coming home because a load of Newt's uni friends had arrived and they were drunk. They were messing about and she was scared. And she had to be in by eleven.'

'Was Newt there?'

'Yes. She used to fancy him, but she said he was drunk and she's gone off him. It was supposed to be his birthday party so she'd bought him a present, but he just laughed at it and wasn't nice to her. She was frightened so she came home.'

'It looks to me as if it all got out of hand,' I said, and Toby nodded, staring down into her glass of orange juice.

After a silence I said: 'Aspen sounds as if she's a good friend.'

'Mmm,' Toby agreed.

'We like her,' Curzon added.

'Did she tell you anything else?' I asked.

Toby was still gazing intently into her glass, pretending she was on another planet and if she concentrated hard enough we'd all go away. Ghislaine put her arm around her sister's shoulders, pulling her closer, and whispered something in her ear. Toby took a sip of her drink and placed the glass back on the table with studied care, as if it were a phial of some exotic brew that could burn its way to the centre of the Earth if spilt.

'I phoned her just now,' she informed us, 'and asked if she knows Newt's proper name.'

'And does she?'

'Yes.'

'And did she tell you it?'

'Yes.'

'Go on.'

'He's called Oscar. Oscar Sidebottom. Stupid, *stupid* name.'

We didn't bother writing it down.

Dave and I stuffed some evidence bags in our pockets and went back to have a more professional look at the crime scene. Curzon came with us. He very politely asked if he could and we couldn't really refuse. He owned the place, after all, and he was interesting to talk to.

We put on a show, just for his benefit, crouching over discarded lager cans, lifting them carefully between fingertip and thumb, looking for footprints leading into the bushes. Dave felt the temperature of the ashes, where they'd had a fire, which I thought a bit over the top.

We gave most attention to the silver birch tree. It had been pulled over until the roots came out of the ground and it was lying almost horizontal. We decided that it might recover if it were pulled upright again and held by three or four substantial stakes. Curzon told us that the silver birch had been his wife Laura's favourite tree and her ashes were buried somewhere under it. I wondered if Newt and his gang hadn't known the full story and had been after her skeleton. In their drunken states it would have sounded like a merry jape to them, no doubt, but I didn't mention it to her husband.

As we set off back to the car Dave hung back, to have a pee in the bushes, he said, but really to leave me alone with Curzon. He caught up with us at the house and we shook hands and said our farewells. The tennis players could still be heard in the distance.

'Learn anything, Tonto?' I asked.

'Yeah. It was a bit of an orgy. No wonder Aspen left early. I found a used condom near the path, and a needle. We'd better inform Curzon about the risk of needles before they do a clean-up. Did he tell you anything new, *Kemo Sabe*?'

'Only that those tennis players we can hear are the

sixth-form girls from the comprehensive.'

'Really?'

'Honest injun.'

'In that case, do you think we should check that there are no undesirable middle-aged men paying them too much attention?'

'Definitely.'

They were a bit older than Toby, almost swinging themselves off their feet with rackets that were too big for them. Four were on the court, with a tracksuited gym mistress, and four more were standing outside the cage, watching the action. I didn't notice Toby for a while. She was standing a little way away from the other spectators, with her back to us, her face against the wire and her fingers hooked into it as she watched them play. I remembered what her father had said: *She can't run about like the other kids*, and felt as if I'd been run through with a bayonet.

We had a swift half and a sandwich in the Alice, but a busload of tourists arrived before we could have a chat with the landlord and we left him pulling pints of Speckled Hen as fast as his arms would go. Down the road the vet, Martin Chadwick, was riding on his big lawnmower, cutting the grass around his immaculate ranch-style house. I parked off the road and we went to meet him. Chadwick killed the engine, removed his ear defenders and climbed off the fearsome machine.

'That looks fun,' I said, and introduced him to DC Sparkington.

'My favourite job, chopping the daffodils down. How can I help you, Inspector, or is it a social call?'

'A bit of both. We've just been to Curzon House and while we were in the district we thought we'd see if you wanted to apprise us of any sparkling insights you've had.'

'Ha! I'm a bit low on sparkling insights, lately, but I make a decent instant coffee.'

We declined a coffee but I told him about the trashing of Coneywarren Field and he was horrified. 'Poor James,' he kept saying. 'Poor James.'

'I believe you said you'd known the Curzons all your life,' I reminded him.

'That's right. My parents were good friends with them. They were very kind to me. I was a promising tennis player but I had to go to York to practise, so James had the bright idea of building a tennis court adjoining the house.'

'So it's really the Martin Chadwick Court,' I suggested.

'I wouldn't go that far. I played in the Wimbledon Juniors qualifying rounds a couple of times, but never got past the first round. There to make the numbers up, like most of us. Then, when I was fifteen, I started putting on weight and lost interest.'

Dave said: 'But you'll be able to tell your grandchildren that you played at Wimbledon.'

'Unfortunately not. The qualifying rounds are at Roehampton.'

'Oh. In which case, forget I said that.'

'It's in good use at the moment,' I told him. 'The

comprehensive school are practising there. Maybe your influence will trickle down and produce us a champion, one day.'

'One day,' he echoed, 'and I'll be making a fortune treating pigs injured in flying accidents.'

We had a chuckle and bade him goodbye. In the car Dave said: 'Sounds as if he was about as good at tennis as we were at football.'

'Don't remind me. What time do schools finish these days?'

'All over the place. Why?'

'We need Oscar's phone number, then you can check the records, see if he's had any contact with his father in Portugal. If that's where he is. There's a pecking order in the badger group: Toby's on the bottom rung; her contact is Aspen. Aspen may have a number for Oscar. There can't be that many rungs.' I hit the brakes and dived into a lay-by. James Curzon answered the phone straight away. I didn't go into details; just told him I'd like a talk with Aspen and was wondering if he knew her surname.

'She's called Smethick,' he said. 'Aspen Smethick. They live in the village, on Main Street, but I don't know the number.'

Ten minutes later we were entering High Ogglethorpe, driving slowly past the Boar's Head, or the Whore's Bed as it was known locally. You might not know the number, I thought, but I do. Number 22. Who'd live in a small village?

Phoenix Smethick was bare-legged and bare-footed, wearing voluminous layers of silken kaftan held together by beads and bangles. Her hair was black and unkempt, falling loosely about her shoulders and a twisted strand of plaited wool sliced off the top of her head. She was a big woman, and the riot of colour added to her impact.

'Mrs Smethick?' I asked, wondering why she'd stayed with such a mundane surname.

After the formalities and reassurance that her daughter was in no trouble she invited us in and the interior of the house was a surprise. It was *normal*. There was a three-piece suite with a traditional Chesterfield, a unit holding glassware, a bookcase and coffee tables. No widescreen television. Only the cloying odour of potpourri and perhaps something more exotic gave a clue to the tastes of the householder. The pictures on the wall were 3D collages constructed from natural objects and flotsam, made, I guessed, by her ladyship herself. And they were good.

Dave explained about the party and told her about the desecration of the grave, saying that this had probably happened after Aspen had left. Mrs Smethick was shocked. She was a spiritual person, and the dead were to be revered, not mocked.

The outside door opened and closed and a voice shouted: 'I'm home, what's for tea?' to anybody in earshot. Then the room door opened and we saw Aspen for the first time and she saw us, likewise. Her mouth fell open and her gaze flicked from me to Dave and back again. Ours remained resolutely on her.

She was wearing the school uniform of grey pleated skirt, white blouse, maroon jacket and school tie. With dyed black frizzy hair, white make-up, black lipstick and Moto-X boots, Aspen was a Goth, and this was as near normal as she ever conceded.

Her mother broke the impasse. 'I know what you're thinking,' she said, 'and the answer's "no". If she wants a tattoo or piercing job she can wait until she's eighteen or I'm in my cardboard coffin, whichever comes first.'

I jumped up, grinning, and held my hand out. 'I'm Charlie Priest,' I told her. 'I'm a friend of Toby's.'

She'd heard about me, but I didn't dwell on what Toby might have told her. Her immediate contact in the badger group was called Peter by his parents, Slug by his comrades, and he had direct contact with Newt, or Oscar as we now knew him. After a discussion Aspen rang Peter and said she was resigning from the group and wanted Newt's mobile number so she could tell him personally and tear him off a strip about the party. Peter said he was upset about it, too, and gave her the number.

The party had started about nine, she told us, but some of the older ones had been drinking from much earlier. It was OK to start with and they made a bonfire, which was cool, she said. I remembered the fun we had with fires when I was a kid, and realised that it was probably a novel experience for most of them.

But then they started playing silly games and some of the girls went off into the bushes with the boys. She'd bought Newt a present – a jester's hat with bells on the horns – which he started playing football with until it went on the fire. 'It cost me eight pounds,' she told us. That's when she sent Toby a text, asking why she wasn't there.

'I heard you come home,' her mother said. 'It was about half past ten. Wasn't expecting you for another half-hour.'

'Were you there when the tree was uprooted?' Dave asked.

'No. Which tree?'

'The silver birch in the middle of the circle.'

'Oh no! That's terrible. Toby will be heartbroken. And her dad. That was over her mother's grave. Have they seen it?'

'Yes, but they're OK, now. Toby would probably appreciate a call from you. She regards you as a good friend.'

'We are good friends.' We sat in silence for a while until Aspen opened her mouth to speak, then closed it again.

'Go on, Aspen,' I prompted.

'I...I'm not sure. It might have been a toy. What are they called – replicas? – it might have been a replica.'

I felt my heart stop and heard Dave adjust his position, leaning forward. 'What might have been a replica, Aspen?' I asked.

'The gun. Newt had a gun, but it didn't look like a proper gun. Everybody laughed at him, saying it was a toy. He said it was real, but it wasn't loaded. He kept playing Russian roulette with it, putting it against his head and pulling the trigger. One of the girls was screaming, telling him to stop, but he only did it more. I was scared stiff. We all were. That's when I came home.'

How does it go? *Hell hath no fury*, and all that. Especially when she's fifteen years old and wearing Moto-X boots.

CHAPTER FIFTEEN

'You drive,' I said, dangling the keys under Dave's nose when we were back at the car. 'I'll try to raise Special Branch.'

'What do you reckon?' he asked.

'I reckon we could have found the gun,' I said.

'Shall we spin his flat and car?'

'And what about his room at his mother's?'

'That too.'

'I dunno. We'd look pretty stupid if we found nothing.'

'Not as stupid as if someone else was shot.'

'That's true. I wonder how many bullets were with it. Not many. Two or three, I'd guess.' I dialled the number I had for Special Branch at the Met. One of the advantages of being the longest-serving inspector in Yorkshire is that

I know everybody who's anybody and they all know me. Many of them have graduated through the Charlie Priest Detective Academy; some will do me a favour, if I ask; one or two wouldn't dare refuse.

'Shagnasty!' I was greeted, after I'd identified myself and been put through. 'How are things up in the sticks?'

'Oh, you know: a bomb factory in every cellar; a skunk farm in every attic. We keep busy. What have you got for me?'

'I hope you're keeping your friendly neighbourhood SB officer informed.'

'Of course. In fact she said exactly the same thing to me last night, in bed.'

'Aha! OK, so what have we got? For a start, Barry Sidebottom is on our books. That in itself doesn't mean much. The Archbishop of Canterbury is in there, too. We have a green tag on his file. That means that the man himself hasn't transgressed, to our knowledge, but he has some dodgy associates.'

'Um, I assume you mean Sidebottom?'

'Yeah, sorry. Not the archbishop.'

'What sort of dodgy associates?'

'The usual crew. First they sought sanctuary in the Spanish Costas, but when the Spanish government put the heat on them they moved to Portugal. Unfortunately for them there are language difficulties there and it's not as anglicised as Spain. And, of course, they're our oldest ally. We go back a long way. The villains like to be within driving distance of the Old Country, not dependent on airlines, so now they're moving to the Eastern bloc countries. I'm told Bulgaria is highly desirable.'

'The Russians will have something to say about that, I imagine.'

'You're dead right. Cross one of the old London gangs and they'll break your legs as a warning. Offend the Ruskies and you're toast, no messing.'

'Anything else?'

'I've hardly started. You say his ex-wife's lover was shot dead on Monday, twenty-first of this month. Barry Sidebottom came into this country one week earlier, on Tuesday the fifteenth, via the Santander-to-Plymouth ferry. He was driving a leased Peugot 407 estate filled with cigs and booze, strictly for his personal use, of course. As far as we know he's still here.'

'Was he stopped?'

'No. He was borderline, so they let him through. He's done the trip before and Customs and Excise are watching him, but they're after bigger fish. Someone bent but clean is useful to the underworld for setting up bank accounts, laundering money, hiring cars – that sort of everyday stuff that can be a pain if you have a record.'

'Dare I ask for an address?'

'No problem. He's drawing disability allowance, so it was easy.'

'You're kidding?'

'Nope.'

'Is he at home?'

'No idea. We thought we'd better leave something for you to do.'

'You done good, boy. I'm grateful.'

'Don't come too often, Chas. How's big Sparky keeping?'

'He's here next to me. We're in the car. Want a word?'

'No, my other phone's ringing. Give him my regards. Bye.'

'Bye.' I switched the phone off and placed it in the glovebox: 'He sends his regards.'

'Thanks. Where are we going?'

'Home. I've had enough.'

Friday morning we had a big meeting in the Heckley incident room. Enquiries were ongoing, as we like to say, into Threadneedle's business activities but nothing incriminating was coming to light. Jeff Caton was handling that side of the case, assisted by the fraud boys and girls, and I was happy to leave it with them. I told them that the graffiti was almost certainly done by Oscar Sidebottom, who had links with the Curzons through Toby and with Mrs Threadneedle through the piano lessons.

'Is that "*piano lessons*" in quotation marks?' Jeff asked.

'That's what Dave wanted to know,' I replied. I'd been sceptical at first until I recalled my second meeting with Mrs T, after her husband had left for the Belfry. 'I'll bear it in mind when we talk to him. Or her.' I turned to a uniformed sergeant who was sitting patiently, waiting to inform us of his contribution. 'Yes, George,' I said. 'What have you got for us?'

George was from the task force, and his men were scouring every roadside ditch, fly-tipping site, lay-by, dustbin and roadside litter bin within two miles of Heckley, with renewed emphasis on the road towards York and the students' quarters there. 'Not much,' was the answer to my question, but I asked him to keep trying.

'It's been eleven days since the murder,' I said, 'so any dumpsters along the route will have been emptied at least once, possibly twice. But keep looking. We're desperate for a forensic link. The murderer will have been sprayed with blood, so we need those clothes. Serena!'

'Yes, boss.'

'Do me a chart plotting the possible ownership of the humane killer, starting with Jonty Hargrave. From him it went to Threadneedle, we believe. And so on. Do you follow me?'

'Yes, I think so.'

'Talk to the manufacturer. They probably have records going back a hundred years. Ask how many bullets it came with.'

'Will do.'

'Maggie!'

'Yessir!'

'Any luck with the photos?'

'Sorry, but no. It's a bit of a wild goose chase. We've identified most of the people there, but they're all straightforward punters, out to ogle Miss Curzon.'

'OK, but it's got to be done.' I was rushing through things because I knew that a few miles away a certain Superintendent Kent would be winding up her working breakfast, acclimatising her schedule, practising her Pilates and power breathing while sitting at the desk, and rehearsing what she'd say to her number one detective inspector if she should ever make contact with him again. 'Go to it, my fine young Turks,' I urged, lifting my jacket off the back of the chair and nodding to Dave.

Barry Sidebottom's address was a three-bedroomed detached house in a respectable estate on the edge of Leeds, north of the river. The garden was block-paved to cut down maintenance and a substantial fence gave a modicum of privacy. The Peugeot stood on the drive in front of the integral garage's open door, with an elderly Focus alongside it. I parked across his gateway and we reached for our warrant cards. We found him round the back, fiddling with a gas-fired barbecue, watched by a brittle blonde in platform sandals and a cut-down toga, like an extra for *Carry On Cleo*. He looked up from the barbecue and his expression changed, as if he'd found a dead cicada in his pina colada.

'A word,' I said, and indicated for him to join us. He was wearing baggy Bermuda shorts with flip-flops, and a pale-blue Adidas singlet that showed off his perma-tanned biceps. Sun-bleached hair spilt out of his singlet and the gold chain and matching bracelet that graced his neck and wrist would have put a deposit on a modest yacht. He'd have walked an audition to play a Great Train Robber, no sweat. He took us into the kitchen and we sat on high stools around a breakfast bar.

'What's it about, gentlemen?' he asked.

'We're investigating the murder of Arthur George

Threadneedle,' Dave told him. 'Had you heard about his death?'

'Yeah. It sounds a nasty business, but I'd never met the man.'

'How did you learn about it?'

'My son told me about it, didn't he?'

'Oscar?'

'That's right.'

'You're in contact with him?'

'No, not really. He was confused, needed someone to talk to, so he rang me.' Sidebottom paused, wondering how much false concern to inject into the conversation, then said: 'I...I suppose you know about my ex-wife and what's-his-name... Threadneedle.'

'That they were having an affair? Yes we do.'

'Well, Oscar had only just found out, hadn't he? Up to then he thought I'd walked out on them; that I was the guilty party. I let him think that way because he was better off with his mum, I thought. I wanted him to get an education, and besides, I'm not really a family man. Playing happy families isn't my style.'

'How did he find out that you were the innocent party?'

'I don't know.'

I said: 'Where were you on the morning of Monday the twenty-first?'

'Down at the gym, wasn't I, working out. I try to go Monday, Wednesday and Friday, about nine o'clock.'

'Can anybody verify that?'

'I suppose so: they have a signing-in book.'

'Are you here to stay or is it just a visit?'

'This is my home.'

'I thought your home was in Portugal.'

'Then you were misinformed. My bolt-hole is in Portugal. I have a pal who has a bar there. He's trying to talk me into becoming a partner, isn't he, so he can expand. I came home to try and raise some money.'

Dave said: 'Are you acquainted in any way with James Curzon, who lives in Curzon House, East Yorkshire?'

'No.'

'How about Jonty Hargrave, a racehorse trainer?'

'No.'

'Did you know Threadneedle at all, before your marriage broke up?'

'No.'

'Do you own a gun?'

'No.'

'Did anyone ever try to sell you shares in a racehorse syndicate?'

'Sorry, Sergeant, but the answer's "no" again.'

'When are you going back to Portugal?'

'I'm not sure. Can I ask you a question?'

I said: 'Of course.'

'How did you know I was in England?'

I had to be careful how I answered. Special Branch have no more authority than the humblest constable on the beat. Data protection, human rights, race relations, freedom of information. They've all to be followed to the letter. 'Your satnav,' I said. The sucker marks on the inside of his windscreen showed he had one. 'The lady up in the sky told us you were home. She has to know where you are before she can give you directions.' It wasn't true, but we're working on it, and it would give him something to think about.

The phone records didn't show that Oscar had been in contact with his father in Portugal. It wasn't definitive but it was the best we could do. Back at the nick I emailed SB and spent some time filling the crime log and studying the summary that the report reader had prepared for me. Nothing sprang off the page and grabbed me by the throat. Dave brought sandwiches from over the road and we ate them in the incident room, our backs to the photos of Arthur George Threadneedle's spilt brains, hoping Superintendent Kent was safely in a meeting somewhere. When the phone did ring it was Jeff Caton, and he was overflowing with excitement.

I waved for Dave to join us on a party line and told Jeff to calm down. 'Dave's listening,' I said. 'Tell us again.'

'Big dumpsters,' he said. 'Industrial-sized ones, at the university campus. They're normally emptied on a Monday, but last Monday was a bank holiday, so they weren't emptied. They're full to overflowing. Task force have been going through them and have found a bin liner with some clothes inside. There's like a jogging suit, made of some velvety material. Two-piece with a zip down the front. You wouldn't go jogging in it. It's a woman's, I'd say, more for wearing inside. And there's some socks in there and some cotton gloves.

'What colour's the suit?' I asked, remembering the pea-pod outfit she'd worn that first day, with its wayward zip down the front.

'Bright green.'

'Any bloodstains?'

'It's a bit messy but can't tell if it's blood. I tried picking some up on a cotton bud and it's the right colour.'

'Any sign of a gun?'

'No, sorry, but they're still looking.'

'Have you bagged it all?'

'In paper bags, as per instructions. Shall I get them straight to the lab?'

'Yes please, but tell them to keep it away from all the other Threadneedle stuff.'

'Will do. Are you coming over?'

'Try to stop us.'

There was a disused filling station down the road from the dumpsters, which was just right for our purposes. It was a big, concreted area with a roof high enough to clear a sixteen-wheeler. We had the dumpsters brought there and the task force boys and girls started to methodically work their way through them.

It was a smelly, nauseating job. Some of the stuff had been in there for nearly two weeks, and the weather was warm. As the level of garbage lowered rats were seen, unable to climb out, and a confiscated airgun was appropriated and put to good use, popping them off. I collected a crate of lager and one of mineral water from the nearest supermarket and distributed them amongst the sweating bodies. I was in for a roasting over my mileage expenses, so a bit more wouldn't hurt. It took them the rest of Friday and most of Saturday before we could confidently conclude that there wasn't a gun in there.

Mrs Threadneedle had been back in her home for a week, so I decided a visit was overdue. I didn't ring first; just turned up on her doorstep like a Jehovah's Witness who happened to be passing. She made me welcome and invited me in.

'Had we left the place in a mess?' I asked when I was seated behind the compulsory coffee. She'd managed to keep it within the confines of the china cup and there was no sign of the gin bottle.

'You had, a bit,' she replied. 'There was this...dull bloom...on everything, but I've given it all a good polish and I think we've topped it.'

'Blame the fingerprint boys,' I told her. 'They brush everywhere with aluminium powder. They've probably identified some prints as being yours, from, say, your dressing table, but they may come back and ask you to do what they call a tenprint form, just to verify they are yours. They'll have taken DNA samples, too, probably from your hairbrush. I'm afraid it's all rather intrusive, but necessary if we're to find your husband's killer. Will you stay here, have you decided, or will you move away?'

'I'm not sure. I suppose moving to somewhere smaller would make sense. Do you know when we'll be able to have a funeral, Inspector?'

'I can't see a problem. I'll have a word with the coroner's office. I have to say, Janet, you're bearing up remarkably well.' She was smartly dressed in skirt and crisp blouse, and looked as if she'd visited her hairdresser again.

'And I haven't touched a drop,' she said, with a triumphant smile.

I asked her if it was difficult and she told me that the alcoholism was largely an act to annoy her husband. She could take it or leave it, but he hated people who couldn't handle their liquor, probably due to his family background. I wasn't sure if I believed her, but she looked just dandy on this particular morning. I thought about confessing that I'd hit the bottle rather hard when my marriage broke up, just to go for the empathy vote, but decided not to.

'Do you mind if I ask you a few questions?' I asked. 'You're under no obligation to answer and not under caution or anything. In fact, if I were a solicitor I'd advise you to keep silent, but I only want to clarify a few things. Does that make sense?' It didn't to me, but she nodded her consent.

'When did you first learn that your husband was having an affair?'

'Oh, it would be some time last summer. May or June. It was a hot day, I remember, and we didn't have too many of them.'

'How did you find out?'

' I had my suspicions. Leaving the birthday card in his golf bag more or less proved it. There were other things. I made a few phone calls and it all made sense.'

'How did you discover it was with Carol McArdle?'

'I found a phone number, rang it a few times and it all fell into place.'

I didn't say anything; left her room to volunteer. She picked up her cup and saucer and took a long, delicate sip. I picked up my cup and downed half its contents.

'There's this boy...' she went on. 'Arthur said he was the son of one of his employees. He wanted music lessons and Arthur suggested I become his teacher. One of Arthur's more considered ideas, I thought. I hadn't taught for years and I enjoyed it. Turned out that he was her son. They shared a phone number.' A hint of a smile flickered across her face, as if the memory amused her.

'That would be young Oscar,' I said.

'That's right. Oscar Sidebottom, which was why I didn't realise sooner. He said his mother had gone off with her boyfriend, meaning Arthur. Naive must be my middle name.'

'I'd say that was to your credit. We, on the other hand, are trained to be suspicious of everyone.' I remembered Jeff's and Dave's comment and said: 'Would that be music lessons in inverted commas?'

'You're very astute, Inspector.' I didn't reply, just waited for her to tell me whatever she wanted me to know, in her own time. She looked into her coffee cup, then replaced it on the low table. 'I was heartbroken,' she began, 'and felt a fool. Revenge was uppermost in my mind. I decided I'd leave Arthur, then realised that I'd only be making it easy for them and I wanted to hurt them both. Humiliate them. I wanted retribution. I had a good cry, thought my world had ended, until I remembered that Oscar was coming for a lesson that afternoon. Two can play at your game, I thought. What's sauce for the goose will do for the gander.

And besides, Arthur had been neglecting me and he was a good-looking boy...'

She stood up and walked over to the window. With her back to me she said: 'It was a warm day. I had a shower, used a little make-up and dressed to suit the weather: T-shirt and shorts. I put on the expensive perfume Arthur bought me for my birthday. Oscar was similarly dressed. I'd made some lemonade and set the table outside. I put a generous measure of gin in my drink to give me courage, and a smaller measure in Oscar's. When we went into the music room it was quite cool in there. It's at the back of the house. I told Oscar to play Hoagy Carmichael's "Heart and Soul", to warm up his fingers. Do you know it?'

I shook my head. 'No.'

'It's a simple piece, a bit like "Chopsticks".'

'I know "Chopsticks".'

'Everybody knows "Chopsticks". After he'd played it I sat alongside him and told him to play the right hand while I played the left. We raced through it a few times, had a laugh. It was fun. I put my right arm round him to stop myself falling off the stool and told him to try the same with Beethoven's "Bagatelle in A minor", more commonly known as "Für Elise". I was shivering so he put his arm around me. It's a slow, romantic piece and we played it right through. As it finished I...I turned to him. I thought he'd be shy and inexperienced, but I was wrong. After I'd – how shall I put it? – given him permission, he took control of things. He led me upstairs. We made love on my bed, with the curtains open and the sun streaming in. After that we stepped up the lessons, but his piano playing didn't improve.

I decided not to say anything to Arthur and...her.'

She turned to face me again. 'I didn't find that easy,' she said.

'I know you didn't.' I wasn't sure if she was making fun of me, letting me know what I'd turned down, but I gave her the benefit of the doubt. 'When was this?' I asked.

'A few weeks later, after I'd learnt about Arthur and her. Probably in July. It will be in my diary...'

'That's OK, Janet. Did you terminate the lessons?'

She stood silently for a while, one arm hanging loose, the other across her chest, clasping it, thinking. Outside, a supermarket delivery van turned round and drove away. A horse plodded by, ridden by a girl in jeans and a T-shirt, not wearing a hard hat. Janet's back was to the window now, and the sun had found a way between the clouds again. Because of the brightness behind her I couldn't read the expression on her face.

She said: 'This is the point, Inspector, where I'll take the advice of my imaginary solicitor and decide not to answer any more questions.'

'That's fine,' I said. 'You've been very frank.' I rose to my feet and picked up my cup and saucer, but Janet took it from me.

I had half a plan to hit her with a sidewinder as I was leaving by telling her that we'd found the bloodstained jogging suit and were awaiting DNA comparison results from the lab, but the sun was shining, the bees were fumbling the flowers and her little cul-de-sac was a haven of peace in a world of turmoil. It would all come crashing down soon enough, without any prompting from me. I said: 'Thank you for the coffee,' and left it at that.

The best way to deal with trouble is to meet it head-on. There was a game on at Heckley Cricket Club and a couple of the lads were in the team, so I parked up and found myself a seat. We were eighty-seven for three, which didn't sound very good to me. I pulled out my mobile, dialled HQ and asked for Superintendent Kent. Her voicemail told me that she wasn't available. She's probably at home, I thought, reconfiguring her undies drawer. 'It's DI Priest,' I said, 'returning your call. I'll catch you tomorrow or Monday. Have a nice weekend.' I switched the phone off just as a ripple of applause ran round the ground. 'Thank you,' I said, because I deserved it. 'Thank you, thank you.'

Mad Maggie Madison rang me at home, to say that Oscar had vanished. He wasn't at his flat or at his mother's apartment.

'He has girlfriends,' I told her. 'He's probably shacked up with one of them.' I hoped he hadn't been hiding upstairs at Janet's, but didn't voice my fears. Sometime in the next few days the results from the lab would land on my desk and they might change everything. Meanwhile, we wouldn't sit on our heels and wait, but a certain amount of urgency was removed from our enquiries. We could afford to ease up a little, back off with the routine stuff that came with every murder enquiry, providing Lady Kent kept her distance. 'Leave it until Monday, Maggie,' I said. 'Then we'll spin his premises. Get some warrants, please, for his flat, his room at his mother's, his locker at work, if he has one, his car, wherever it is, and anywhere else you can think of. Make everyone aware that he might have a gun, but one that only holds a single bullet.'

'That's all it takes, Chas.'

'I know, I know.'

CHAPTER SIXTEEN

Serena did a simple chart showing who might own the gun. It wasn't very helpful. Jonty Hargrave had passed it on to Threadneedle, he said, but we hadn't found it when we searched Threadneedle's house. It could have been stolen; borrowed and not returned; sold to someone else in the animal-killing business or simply lost. I decided to have a drive east for a word with Jonty.

He was in the Alice, clutching a hand of dominoes, opposite Jackdaw, his eternal rival, like the chess players in Bergman's *The Seventh Seal*. He'd enjoyed two years in the South of France, imbibing the local flavours, but given it up to spend the remainder of his days beating a candidate for the title of Village Idiot at a game of chance. I imagined a snapshot of him sitting in the sunshine on a tiled patio, still in his hacking jacket and cravat. A buxom gypsy lady leant over his shoulder to replenish his glass and the bougainvillea was in full blossom.

'The gun,' I said, twisting a chair round from the adjacent table and sitting down. 'I need to know where it went.'

He downed the remainder of his pint with much smacking of the lips and plonked the empty glass on the table with a show of approval. I ignored the invitation to buy him another. 'Are you sure it went to Threadneedle, with the house?' I asked.

''Appen it did.'

'That's not good enough. Either it did or it didn't.'

'Right. As far as I can remember, it did. I remember showing him it, telling him about it.'

'Had you bought it new?'

'No. I inherited it.'

'Was it in a box?'

'Aye. A proper one, designed for it, with a lock and a carrying handle. Made of mahogany, I'd say.'

'What about bullets?'

'There were some slots for them inside the box and they were held in place when the lid was closed.'

'How many?'

'You've got me there. About four. Six, maybe. Call it five originally but two had been used, so there'd be three left.'

'You don't sound certain.'

'I'm not.'

I turned to his domino opponent, Jackdaw, and asked him if he remembered the fire. He did and I invited him to tell me what he knew.

'Not much,' he replied. 'Old Motty looked out his

window as he went to bed and saw flames and reek
coming from t'stables. He phoned the brigade, I reckon,
and phoned the boss. Then he went to let the horses out.
'Cept one of 'em had brocken its leg, hadn't it? He had
to shoot that one.'

Hargrave listened, his expression impassive, though I
was sure he disapproved of Jackdaw's cooperation.

'Who do you mean by "the boss"?' I asked.

'Threadneedle,' I was told.

I turned back to Hargrave. 'You said two bullets had
been used. Who used them? Was it you?'

'We'd used it once to kill a horse, that's what. Broke its
leg when it stepped in a rabbit hole.'

'And the other one?'

'I'd had a practice, that's all, when we acquired the
gun. Didn't want to look an amateur if I ever had to use
it.'

'Was it easy to do? Did you need some help?'

'It was lying down, so it was no problem.'

I couldn't get the car out onto the road because a string of
horses were picking their way back to their stables. Six of
them, steaming and glowing; some walking purposefully, a
couple skittering sideways, jumping at shadows to invite a
slap from the rider's whip. They were giants, towering over
my car, their jockeys dwarfed by charges that were barely
under control. I remembered reading somewhere that these
days the stable boys were just as likely to be female, and
from Eastern bloc countries. They didn't mind shovelling
shit at five in the morning for minimum wage. The string

turned right onto a bridle path and the impatient convoy of cars that had built up behind them accelerated away on the clear road. I fell in behind.

It wasn't Motty's day for fleecing the old ladies at whist or bingo, so he answered my knock after a while and invited me in. He'd been outdoors all his life and hated being cooped up, so when I suggested we sit outside he readily agreed.

We exchanged pleasantries about the weather and he called me Charlie and appeared genuinely pleased to be with someone who made an effort to communicate with him. It was hard work, though, and I took short cuts, jumped to conclusions that I paid for later. I suggested he let me take him to the Alice for a snifter, but he was content to sit in the sunshine. I studied him and noted that he was below average height, about five foot three at a guess, even before the curvature of his spine became permanent.

'I've been talking to Jonty in the Alice,' I said, 'about the fire. He says it was a bad business. He was living in France at the time, but his dominoes pal knew about it. He told me that you phoned the fire brigade.'

'Aye. Phoned brig...brig...brigadeer.'

'Brigade,' I told him. 'The fire brigade.'

'Aye. Them.'

'And the boss?' I suggested.

'Aye. Phone boss.'

'Did the boss come quickly?'

'No, not quick. Long time...long time coming. After brig...brig...'

'The fire brigade. He came after the fire brigade? I was

told that you let all the horses out except Peccadillo, which had broken its leg. Is that right, Motty?'

'Aye. Pecc'dillo. Leg bad.' He rubbed his own shin to illustrate the point.

'Did the boss come before Peccadillo was shot?'

'No. Not before.'

'So you had the humane killer?'

'Aye. Kept in house. Motty kept it.'

'Who took it away?'

'Not sure. Boss. Think boss.'

'You think the boss took it away. Mr Threadneedle. You think Mr Threadneedle took the gun away.'

'Aye. Him.'

'But you shot the horse?'

I thought I'd lost him again as he remembered a bad time that he believed was forgotten but which could come back to overwhelm all the good times he'd experienced. He shook himself back into the present and said: 'Aye. Motty,' making a gun barrel with his forefinger and firing an imaginary bullet into the lawn.

'Just you.'

'Aye. Just Motty.'

Twenty minutes later I was sitting in the waiting room of Martin Chadwick's veterinary practice, wondering what was wrong with the evil-looking Persian cat that the lady opposite me was coo-cooing to through the bars of its carrying box. Ten minutes later she came out of the surgery carrying the box, which was now empty. Chadwick said goodbye to her and ushered me in to his inner sanctum.

'What was wrong with the cat?' I asked, assuming that the rules on medical confidentiality didn't include cats, even if they were aristocratic.

'She's through there,' he replied, 'having her nails clipped,' and a feline shriek of disapproval confirmed what he'd said.

'Oh. I assumed she'd had her put down.'

'Her husband, possibly, but Fatima, never. What can I do for you, Inspector?'

I told him about my talk with Motty, about how he'd said he was the person who'd pulled the trigger. I confessed that I didn't know much about horses but that I'd noticed, in the last few days, that they were big – very big – and bad-tempered. 'Tell me,' I said, 'could you determine from the way Peccadillo had fallen whether it had been standing or lying down when it was shot?'

'It had been standing; no doubt about it. Its legs were folded under it.'

'Where exactly would you put the gun if you were killing a horse?'

Chadwick unhooked a calendar advertising foodstuffs from the wall and turned the months over until he reached October. The picture showed a horse in full gallop towards the camera, the jockey perfectly balanced as he urged his mount onward, his extended whip arm capturing the tension of the moment. 'There,' he said, indicating with the tip of his ballpoint. 'Draw two diagonals between its eyes and its ears and place the muzzle of the gun about five centimetres higher than where they cross. Lift the back of the gun until it's pointing in line with the horse's neck, come back another five centimetres or so and pull the trigger. Bingo! One dead horse.'

He made it sound simple. An actual killing would be different. The horse would be in agony and scared; tension and tempers would be high. Where was the humane killer? Who was licensed to use it? Had anybody done it before? Was it the right thing to do? What would the owner think? How much was the horse worth?

'Right,' I said. 'I couldn't help noticing that Mr Dermot is not very tall. He says he killed Peccadillo before anybody else came. Could he have done it by himself, even if he'd stood on a box?'

'Good question. On one side, Motty can handle horses. If anybody was capable of doing it, it would be Motty. On the other side, Peccadillo was a thoroughbred, which, roughly translated, means neurotic. He was also only a two-year-old. Most thoroughbreds of that age are as mad as snakes. And if that wasn't enough, the stables were burning down around them. In other words, Inspector, my opinion now, in the light of what you've told me, is that he couldn't have done it by himself, box or no box.'

'So who is he protecting, and why?'

'Loyalty, Inspector. Motty is a simple man with old-fashioned virtues. Perhaps he's saying he killed the horse because he was licensed to do the job, as per the Welfare of Animals, Slaughter or Killing Regulations. Maybe somebody who wasn't licensed helped him do the deed then left the scene.'

'Somebody like Threadneedle?'

'You said that, not me.'

'No, but you were thinking it and you've been thinking about it for ten years. I'm an informal sort of bloke; can I call you Martin?'

'Of course. It's Charlie, isn't it?'

'That's right. Truth is, Martin, I'm not too concerned about the fire and who killed Peccadillo. My remit is to apprehend whoever it was who murdered Threadneedle, and one route to his killer is via the gun. We can't be sure, but it looks as if the same gun killed them both. It appears to have vanished after Motty used it. You didn't happen to put it in your bag, did you?'

'Sorry, Charlie. Not guilty this time.'

Superintendent Wood answered the phone when I rang the office. 'What are you doing there?' I asked. 'I thought you were off for another week?'

'You know how it is, Charlie,' he replied. 'Difficult case like this one, constantly on your mind, gnawing away. It was bothering me and I thought you'd appreciate some help, someone to take a bit of the responsibility off your shoulders.'

'The fish weren't biting.'

'Um, now you mention it, things were a bit slack. Too much colour in the water after all the rain.'

'Does this mean that the multi-talented Miss Kent is off the case?'

'That's right. She's been relieved of her duties in the field and pulled back to the Reichstag.'

'Yippee! You're a toff, Gilbert. So what's happening?'

'Well, in your absence, Maggie and Dave have filled me

in and Maggie's been collecting search warrants. Finding the missing son is today's problem, it would appear. The lab has told Serena that they might have something for her tomorrow. What are you up to?'

I told him about my talk with Motty, said we'd had a slight breakthrough in that Motty must have had some assistance to shoot the horse and was covering for someone, probably the recently deceased Arthur George Threadneedle. It was looking as if they'd planned an insurance scam that went wrong and faithful old Motty had been left to carry the can.

'Are you coming back or are you staying in East Yorkshire?' Gilbert asked.

'I'll come back.'

I needn't have bothered. His flat in students' quarters was a one-roomed stinking pit with galley kitchen that wasn't much more desirable than the dumpsters nearby that we'd emptied over the weekend. The assistant residence manager let us in, so we were denied the pleasure of kicking his door down. The man himself was nowhere to be found and there wasn't a gun under the mattress. We grade houses on a scale of one to five on how much the carpets stick to your soles as you walk across them. This was a two with patches of four where he'd spilt his beer. The manager person expressed his disgust and said Oscar was a candidate for eviction. Dave nodded towards the Greenpeace poster on the wall and said: 'But his heart's in the right place.'

'His arse'll be in the right place – on the end of my

toe,' the manager person assured us. 'What do you want him for?'

'Murder,' I said, 'so watch how you go.'

Things were different at his mother's sixth-floor riverside apartment. First of all, we had to arrange to meet her there and I had the pleasant duty of telling her about her son's alfresco birthday party and the trashing of Laura Curzon's grave. She believed us, which made a change. Mothers usually defend their detestable offspring to the death, even in the face of twenty-seven reliable witnesses and four hours of CCTV footage. Carol McArdle turned grey when she learnt about the gun and quivered with rage.

But it didn't help us. There was a crispy clean duvet on his bed and two Peter Scott prints on the walls, but no gun under his pillow or beneath the Calvin Klein underpants in his shreddies drawer. We had to be thorough, so I took Miss McArdle to one side and suggested she make herself a coffee. She nodded and blew her nose. I almost felt sorry for her.

Barry Sidebottom had conveniently gone to the wine shop when we visited him, so we had a chat with his lady friend while we waited. She smoked incessantly, and had a voice like a milkman's van crossing a cattle grid. The ashtray was at my side of the coffee table that stood between us, but she preferred reaching over rather than pulling it closer, so every three inhalations I was treated to a view through the gates of paradise.

'Are you Mr Sidebottom's partner?' Dave asked.

'I suppose so. We're not married.'

'Do you live with him in Portugal?'

'Yes.'

I didn't want to hear about her complicated domestic life, so I said: 'Have you ever met Oscar, Mr Sidebottom's son?'

'No, poor little sod, saddled with a name like that. No wonder he left home.'

We were prevented from asking any more questions by the arrival of the Peugeot. I was treated to one more glimpse of boiling dumplings as she stubbed out her cigarette before Barry Sidebottom burst into the room with his indignant head on. We stood up and showed him the warrant, explaining that we wanted to get to his son before he blew off his own or somebody else's head. He put on a show for his girlfriend then calmed down.

It didn't do us any good. Oscar hadn't visited and hadn't contacted his father again. We had a debriefing at the nick which confirmed that we'd had an unprofitable day and all went home. With luck, we'd have some DNA results tomorrow. I'd had cottage pie with broccoli and carrots and was putting out my M&S bread-and-butter pudding when the phone rang.

'It's me: Superintendent Kent,' she said.

'Well...' I began, knocked slightly off guard and speaking through clenched teeth, 'this is a surprise. How can I help you, Miss Kent?'

'The Threadneedle case,' she said. 'Have the DNA results come back yet? I'd like to follow it through.'

'No, not yet,' I told her, 'but possibly tomorrow.'

'Would you like me to have a word with them; jolly them along?'

Like hell, I thought. Her jollying along would put at least another three days on the job. 'Oh, that's helpful of you,' I said, 'but can we leave things as they are? If they don't come up trumps tomorrow I'll let you know.'

'Right. Can I hear music playing?'

'Um, yeah, it's a CD.'

'What is it?'

'I'm not sure.'

'Right. Perhaps I'll hear from you tomorrow.'

Not if I can help it, I thought as she rang off, and skipped the CD back to the beginning of the track. It was Leonard Cohen, *Alexandra Leaving*, and I didn't want to share it with her.

A motorcyclist brought the news, late the following morning. It was what we expected. Whether it was what I wanted I didn't know. I read the report six times, propped it against my telephone and went for a sandwich. I had a feeling it was going to be a long afternoon. I listened to the midday news, my feet on the desk, and had a snooze until my head fell forward and woke me with a start. The weather pattern had settled again and some warm days were promised. I unhooked my jacket and trudged out to the car.

Janet Threadneedle answered the door, a look of welcome on her face until she saw my expression and realised I was bad news. 'Can we sit down, please?' I said.

'Shall I make some coffee?'

'Not just yet.' I stepped round the low table we'd sat at three days earlier so that this time the sun would be on my back but on Janet's face. God's spotlight, I thought, and slid the report from its envelope. 'This is a report from our lab at Weatherton,' I began, when she was seated opposite me. 'Last Friday certain items of clothing were found in a dumpster in the York university campus, near some students' accommodation. They were sent to the lab for forensic examination and analysis, and this is a statement of the lab's findings. I won't read you the technical stuff, but what it says is that analysis of fibres found inside a green velour jogging suit are a DNA match with hairs from a hairbrush on your dressing table, assumed to be your hair. We'll be asking you for definitive samples, either of hair or mouth swabs, but I imagine you know what the result will be.'

Mrs Threadneedle sat quietly, leaning forward, her feet together and her hands in her lap. I noticed they were trembling and she'd stopped wearing her wedding ring.

'Bloodstains were also found on the suit,' I continued, 'distributed in a way consistent with it being in close proximity to a gunshot wound. DNA tests show this blood to be a match with DNA obtained from your late husband. Chances of these DNA tests being false matches are a billion to one.' I didn't tell her about the bloodstained shoes and socks, the gloves and the scarf. She'd wrapped herself well before doing the deed, all of which indicated a big measure of premeditation.

'Oscar hasn't been seen since last Thursday,' I told her. 'He was at a party for his birthday. He got quite drunk and started flashing a handgun around. We haven't found the gun that killed Arthur, but it seems reasonable to believe it's the same one. We're worried that he'll shoot someone else. Do you know where he might be?'

She said no. After some prompting she suggested the places where we'd already looked, then admitted that Oscar had found a new girlfriend recently – someone 'nearer his own age'.

After a long, burning silence I said: 'Do you want to tell me about it?' I told her that I wasn't taking notes but would have to arrest her and take her to the station, where she'd be interviewed officially and a decision taken whether to charge her or not. She didn't reply, so I said: 'Let's have that coffee, eh?'

I followed her to the kitchen and leant on the door jamb as she rattled the cups and struggled with spoon and coffee jar. 'No milk,' she remembered.

'That's right.'

I carried the tray into the other room and set it down on the table. Before I took my seat again I looked out of the window and saw the hardwood table and chairs where she and Oscar had sipped their lemonades in the sunshine before rutting each other brainless, nearly a year earlier. She hung back, then followed me with a plate of biscuits. I shook my head when she showed me them.

'Oscar was upset about the Curzon Centre,' she told me, 'and was mad about Arthur's involvement with it. He decided that ridicule was the best weapon against Arthur, and came up with the graffiti idea. It worked a treat, but unfortunately didn't produce the desired effect. Ghislaine

Curzon was too popular with the press and they united to save her from embarrassment. The plan fell flat.' She took a sip of coffee and went on: 'In fact, it backfired completely on Oscar. He became more and more annoyed about the whole thing. He used to ring me, late at night, saying what he'd like to do to the man who'd built the Centre and also driven his father away. One night he said he'd shoot him if he had a gun. I said: "I have a gun."'

CHAPTER SEVENTEEN

'I was in the garage, looking for his golf clubs, when I found this wooden box that I'd never seen before. It was locked and it intrigued me. We have a biscuit tin containing all the keys we've accumulated over the years: spare door keys; spare car keys; spares for suitcases; the windows; the garage. You know how it is.'

'I recognise the picture,' I said.

'Well, I found the key to the box and opened it. There was this funny-looking gun inside, and some bullets.'

'How many bullets?'

'Three, I think.'

'Go on, please.'

'I thought about it for a day or two and decided to do nothing at first, but I'd keep it, just in case. When it all came to light about Arthur and his girlfriend I decided I'd shoot him. I thought about it a lot, decided that was what I wanted to do, but I couldn't find the courage. Then I told Oscar about it.'

'Oscar came straight round,' she continued. 'He was intrigued by the gun, couldn't stop playing with it.'

'Guns are like that,' I told her. 'They affect some people like a drug. Give them confidence, feelings of power. Most people recognise it for what it is and enjoy the moment, others start to believe it, think they're God's messenger. They go to a shopping mall or a school and loose off at the crowd. What did you do next?'

'We planned and plotted. Oscar knew all about forensic science. He said the problem was getting rid of the weapon and the other evidence. We came up with a plan. I'd shoot Arthur then completely change my clothes. Oscar said that if I had no blood on me, I couldn't have done it.'

It was a simple plan. Mrs T would do the deed, then go to the supermarket. They'd park next to each other at the quiet end of the car park, away from the CCTV, and Oscar would help her transfer her shopping into the boot of her Day-Glo Ford Focus. They couldn't do anything about the distinctive paint job, but that was a risk they'd have to take. Oscar would drive a long way away and dump the bloodstained clothing and the gun; she would go home to find her husband dead on the bedroom floor. Except that Oscar had taken a liking to the gun, and decided to hold onto it.

'What will happen to me?' she asked, after she'd finished relating her story.

'You'll be charged and remanded,' I told her. I recited

the caution and told her to make up an overnight bag. We drove to the nick in silence, the sky an impossible blue, the colours of the clothes on the pedestrians brighter than I remembered them, other drivers courteous and obliging. The bakery opposite the nick had just taken a batch out of the oven and the smell wafted across the car park.

Sitting in the car, I said: 'I've done my bit, Janet. I'll let one of my colleagues do the interview. You need the best defence lawyer money can buy. You can afford it. Mental cruelty is a powerful defence. If you say you'll live at your sister's, and promise to behave, we might not oppose bail.'

'Thank you, Inspector,' she said, 'and can I apologise for all the trouble I've caused you?'

'C'mon.' I said. 'Let's go.'

We were having our debriefing meeting and on a high when the shout came. The lab had run some more tests on the dog pee and now were telling us that although the guilty dog wasn't Bruno, there was a definite relationship between the two of them, probably siblings. All we had to do was find the second dog.

'Lean on young Bratty,' I said. 'Use his dog as leverage. Lead him to believe that Bruno could be put down but might be saved if we found the true culprit.' I was about to tell them that in my opinion Terence Bratt hadn't been totally forthcoming with us, and wondering how much meaner I could get, when an internal phone started beeping.

Brendan picked it up and after a few seconds raised a

hand to silence the babble that always breaks out when there's an interruption. 'He's here,' he told the caller, making eye contact with me. 'I'll put him on.' He passed the handset my way, saying: 'It's control. Young Sidebottom has been sighted.'

He was on the move and a mobile had spotted his Mini heading west between York and Leeds. Within minutes he was being followed and units ahead of him were waiting to take over. I brought the ARVs off the motorway and told them to stand by.

We guessed that he was heading either to Leeds or Heckley. He had contacts with animal rights activists in Leeds who would no doubt give him a smelly mattress for a night or two, or he could be heading to his mother's and an Egyptian cotton, down-filled duvet. On the other hand, there wouldn't be a nubile media studies student at his mother's to take the chill off the sheets and his mind off his recent troubles. My money was on Leeds.

'Lima Sierra 3 to Heckley control. Target vehicle on A64 approaching A1M turn-off. He's signalling left. Now he's on the slip road. Can confirm he's heading south on the A1M. Can someone take over from me, please?'

I was wrong. He was coming home. We told the chopper pilot to warm it up and issued firearms to a couple of panda crews who were authorised to carry them. Twenty minutes later it was obvious he was coming to Heckley and we deployed all available units around the snazzy converted mill that housed his mother's apartment. The adjacent streets became filled with cars that cruised silently to a standstill and waited, lights off, burly occupants not speaking. The reformed smokers felt for the Polo mints they always carried, took one and offered the tube to their partner. Declined with a shake of the head; mints returned to the foetid gloom of trouser pockets.

Hotel Yankee 2 radioed in to say that a light had gone out on the fifth floor, below where Miss McArdle's apartment was believed to be, and a few minutes later a Toyota RAV4 had left, driven by a woman. I leant across in front of the controller and pressed the *Transmit* key. 'Did you get the number?' I asked.

'Hi, boss, that you?' came the reply, irreverent as always. 'Course we got the number. We remembered our training. Always get the number, we were taught. And besides, it's the most excitement we've had since the shout came.'

Excitement. That's what most of us joined the force for, although we didn't admit it at the interview. Then it was all about putting something back into society; making communities that were safe for women and children; helping any brother who'd strayed off the straight and narrow to repair his ways. We didn't mention the pension scheme or the housing allowance, either. Or the decent football and cricket teams. Or the like-minded female officers, some of whom looked sensational in or out of uniform. What was it that Confucius said? *May you live in exciting times.* Except he meant it as a curse. He was right, though. I've had enough excitement to last me to the end of my days. Sometimes, on a winter's morning, a little piece of metal wedged against my spinal column reminds me what excitement feels like, and I can do without it. A decent penalty shoot-out on *Match of the Day* satiates my adrenalin craving on any day of the week.

So why was I in the back office, grovelling under the counter, looking for a stab-proof vest that still had its Velcro tabs attached and didn't have a family of mice nesting in it? Because of Hotel Yankee 2, that's why. The crew might be irreverent but at any minute they could be asked to outface a nutter with a gun, and I'd put them there.

I'm a trained hostage negotiator. There's a note in my HR file that says so. I remember doing the course but don't think I've ever been formally notified that I'd passed. Once in a blue moon I'm on standby, and I've been called upon just once, otherwise it's one of those skills that we take for granted in all police officers, like traffic point duty or delivering a baby, neither of which had I ever been asked to perform. I couldn't do any negotiating from Heckley nick so I threw the stab-proof over my shoulder and drove to where I hoped the action was.

As I rolled to a standstill behind the firearms unit's Transit, two streets away from the address, somebody broke radio silence with: 'Charlie's here, look busy,' in a stage whisper.

The sergeant in the Transit was more respectful. Firearms officers usually are. I explained about the humane killer and emphasised that I wanted young Sidebottom in custody, alive and kicking. He gave me the spiel about shooting to kill, but only if an innocent life was at risk. In that case, I told him, I wanted to talk to Sidebottom before any of his men had him in their sights.

It was about then that it started to go pear-shaped. The

mill had been converted into what is known as a 'gated community', designed to insulate the inhabitants from the grubby realities that surrounded them. There were two gates: a wide one for vehicle access, controlled by a keypad on a post but overridden by a built-in vehicle recognition system; and a small, unlocked gate for pedestrians.

Oscar's car was tracked by mobile units, the helicopter and CCTV all the way from the motorway to Heckley town centre. Right on cue, Hotel Yankee 2 reported that headlights were approaching, then turning into the little precinct where his mother lived. Straps were tightened, breathing regulated, the desire for banter suppressed.

'False alarm, false alarm,' they reported. 'It's the woman in the Toyota.' They informed us that the gate was trundling open automatically, and the RAV4 was moving slowly forward, anticipating the widening gap.

We all relaxed, resumed breathing, then came: 'As you were. Second set of headlights approaching. Coming fast. Recommend moving in.'

'Can you make a positive ID?' I shouted into the microphone.

'Sorry, boss. It's a new-style Mini, that's all. When he turns in will get a visual of his reg mark. Wait for it... Wait for it... Yes, it's him. Move in, move in.'

But fate was on the side of youth, for the moment. Or perhaps his spatial timing and judgement were more finely tuned than that of the ageing policemen who were pursuing him. Either way, tyres squealing, he made it through the gap with millimetres to spare, Hotel Yankee 2 didn't. The Rover 25 panda tore the gate off its wheels and demolished the post holding the keypad, which jammed under the car, and came to rest behind the pedestrian gate, rendering it permanently closed. Fourteen highly trained cops, bristling with weapons, jogged on the spot in a disorderly queue as they tried to pursue their quarry.

Earlier, two firearms officers had concealed themselves in the shrubbery inside the precinct, and now they jumped out, shouting the warning about being armed, but to no avail. The woman thought they were car thieves, after her top-of-the-range Toyota, and fled as fast as her fake Jimmy Choos would allow, towards the door of the apartment block, closely followed by young Sidebottom, who caught her as she held her electronic key against the sensor. Once again, his timing was faultless. The door slammed shut behind them and quarry and pursuers exchanged brief glances through reinforced glass until Sidebottom roughly grabbed the woman by the arm and pulled her towards the stairway and out of sight.

She'd been for a takeaway and had left a trail of prawn crackers, bean sprouts and fried rice from her car to the security doors of the apartment block. She lost her appetite when the door shut behind her and she realised she'd backed the wrong side. Sidebottom unwrapped the humane killer and ordered her into the lift.

I was out of my depth so I sent for help and a superintendent from Leeds was called in. Before he arrived I'd evacuated all the residents, who promptly notified the media and organised a street party. The locals heard about it and came to enjoy the fun, so I cordoned off the whole area before a balloon artist and a stilt-walking juggler could make their contribution to the carnival atmosphere. The superintendent, who'd arrived in full evening regalia right up to cummerbund and dicky bow, organised listening posts on either side of Miss McArdle's apartment and the woman herself was found in her office at the Curzon Centre. At fifteen minutes past ten, after full coverage on local TV, Sidebottom could contain himself no longer. The news item told him that 'the police hunting the killer of a local businessman have arrested a forty-eight-year-old woman, believed to reside at the same address.' He appeared in the Juliet balcony that graced the window of the master bedroom, fifty feet up, and ordered us to leave the building. I'd always wondered what they were for, and now I knew: hostage negotiation.

As I'd met him before, I was appointed chief spokesman for law and order and given the megaphone. In our initial conversation I suggested we talk on his mother's telephone, and he agreed. Two minutes later I was thanking him for his cooperation and reminding him who I was, without the rest of Heckley listening. I didn't tell him that every word was being recorded and would be pored over by students and academics, criminologists and psychologists for as long as mankind existed.

'First of all, how's the young lady you kidnapped?' I asked, reminding him how serious the offence was.

'She's fine.'

'How are you holding her?'

'She's tied to a chair.'

'That's not good,' I told him. 'It would be in your favour if you let her go.'

'Then you'd shoot me.'

I explained the law and how we applied it; told him about when we would shoot to kill; suggested he come to the front door and put the gun down. 'What are you hoping to achieve by all this?' I asked.

'I want to see her.'

'Who?'

'You know who.'

'Remind me.'

'Janet. Mrs Threadneedle.'

I turned to the super who gave an almost imperceptible shake of the head. We were in the Transit, hastily set up as a communications centre and now parked just outside the damaged gates.

'You can't,' I told him. 'She's applied for bail, which she will be given, but under condition that she does not attempt to contact, or communicate in any way with, possible witnesses to the case. If you spoke to her she'd have to stay inside, and you wouldn't want that, would you?'

'No.'

'So are you coming out?'

'No.'

'You'll have to, sometime.'

'I have to see Janet.'

'Janet's OK. She's telling us her side of the story, and if it stands up in court, and she gets an all-female jury, she could walk free on a manslaughter charge.'

He didn't come back to me after that. I'd tried to sow some doubt in his mind; made him think that perhaps Janet was selling her young lover down the river. She'd pulled the trigger but he'd supplied the weapon and been the chief motivator.

I said: 'Are you still there, Oscar?'

'I...I'm thinking.'

'What's the young woman called?'

He asked her; came back with: 'Maxine.' That fitted in with the car registration.

'I think you should let Maxine go. She's nothing to do with all this. It wouldn't change the situation at all.' He didn't reply, so I went on: 'We've notified your mother and she's on her way home. She was working late.'

I heard his snort come down the line. 'Working late with one of her boyfriends,' he said. 'She started all this. It's her fault. If she comes in here I'll kill her. That's a promise.' The line went dead and he wouldn't pick it up when we dialled.

'Give him half an hour to rethink his strategy,' our resident expert told us, 'then try again. He might be more compliant when reality grabs hold of him. Can we get a cuppa round here?'

We had another session of pointless talk, during which his demands switched from seeing Mrs Threadneedle to being given a Subaru Impreza with a full tank, then escalated to having the helicopter put at his disposal. We compromised by filling his Mini with petrol and fitting it with a couple of tracking transmitters. Only the Home Secretary had the power to release Janet, we told him, and she was in Iraq, and he wasn't insured for the Subaru or the chopper, but we couldn't stop him from using his own car. The more outlandish the deceit, the more likely you are to be believed by someone as deranged as he was. I had to keep reminding myself that he was armed and capable of murder.

The damaged gates were hauled out of the way and Oscar's Mini, complete with racing stripes, moved to a position in front of the complex's door. The driver abandoned it as ordered in the middle of the driveway and hotfooted it to safety. I strolled across the weed-free block paving until I was in a triangle with the doorway and the car. Our plan was that he'd release Maxine and be allowed to drive away. Somewhere outside he'd be boxed in by traffic cars and brought to a standstill. As plans go, it wasn't much. 'Will this do?' I asked into my mobile, glancing up at his figure in the Juliet window.

'Yeah, stay there. We're coming out. Don't try anything or I'll shoot her.'

A minute later he appeared inside the door, holding a bewildered and terrified Maxine by the collar of her coat. I took off the flak jacket, as agreed, and tossed it a few feet away. I was wearing a short-sleeved shirt and jeans and had nowhere to conceal a gun. I turned slowly on the spot, like a dog settling into its basket, to show I was unarmed. He came out through the sliding door, dragging Maxine by the collar, and I had my first sight of the gun that probably killed Arthur George Threadneedle. All around me, fingers caressed triggers and tongues sought out moisture in the recesses of mouths.

He was supposed to let her go and I would become the hostage. That was the concession he'd had to agree to for a tank of petrol, which made me worth about thirty pounds. I'd convinced the expert super that I had a rapport with Oscar, which wasn't quite true, but I wanted him alive, and he'd given me my way. It was the president's ball at his rotary club that evening, which helped him come round to my way of thinking. Long, drawn-out sieges are good news for journalists on expenses, but the short, sharp result plays less havoc with one's social life.

'OK, Charlie,' he'd said, 'but it's on your head.'

It usually is, I thought. It usually is.

Unfortunately the plucky Maxine hadn't been a party to our plans, so when she took a swing at Oscar, knocking his gun hand upwards and giving him a modest split lip, they went clean out of the window.

She ran, straight at me, as if I were some sort of demilitarised zone where she would be given sanctuary. I caught her and spun round so my back was to Sidebottom. A gun went off and I tensed myself, but it wasn't meant for me – this time.

Officers were running and shouting, but it was all over. Sidebottom was on the ground, writhing in convulsions that ran up his body from his feet to the top of his head. I told Maxine she was safe, used her name, and handed her over to a policewoman who wore a suitably sympathetic expression.

Sidebottom was still now, with two officers kneeling alongside him, checking his vital signs. Then I saw the wires and a flood of relief swept through me. He hadn't been shot; he'd been Tasered.

CHAPTER EIGHTEEN

Ten o'clock next morning I had him to myself. He'd been fed and watered, had eight hours rest and was wearing a pale-blue disposable oversuit and a totally confused expression. He looked like someone who'd been hit by a thunderbolt, which he had. The Taser gun shoots out two fine wires tipped off with supersharp barbed points. After they strike home fifty thousand volts are blatted between the wires and the unfortunate target has all his Christmases, birthdays and orgasms in one mighty kick in the head. His nervous system blows a fuse and he loses all interest in whatever illegal activity he'd been involved with. One day we'll lose someone – the electric chair only uses three thousand volts – but at the moment the Taser is the preferred alternative to the Heckler & Koch.

At first Oscar had adamantly refused a solicitor but I

persuaded the duty man to have a word with him and eventually Oscar relented. I was concerned about his mental state and didn't want any repercussions. Maggie was assisting me in place of big Dave, to create a less threatening atmosphere, and we were being videoed. The doctor assessed him as being fit for questioning, gave him some aspirin for his headache and we were off:

'When did you last see Mrs Threadneedle?' was my first real question, after the niceties had been performed. He said he couldn't put a date on it.

'Was it before or after the murder of her husband?'

'Before. I think it was the day before. I had a music lesson with her.'

I resisted the temptation to ask if the lesson involved any actual piano playing. That would come later, after we'd demolished his resistance.

'What was being Tasered like?' I asked.

'It was terrible. I thought I'd been killed.'

'One of our assistant chief constables volunteered to be shot by one, before we went over to them. He said much the same thing.'

'He must be mad.'

'That's what we thought. I wouldn't dare. How well did you know Arthur George Threadneedle?'

'Not at all; I'd seen him a few times, at the Centre.'

'That's the Curzon Centre.'

'Yes.'

'You worked there, I believe.'

'Not full-time. I had part-time release from my college course, and I worked there in the vacations.'

I kept it informal and chatty, slipping the occasional leading question into the conversation. The duty solicitor, who'd been on duty all night, looked bored and his notepad remained unsullied. When I decided the time was right to step up a gear I produced the gun from my briefcase and laid it on the table, saying: 'DI Priest produces gun and offers it as evidence. It is an Entwistle humane killer fitted with a silencer, as used to despatch horses in accordance with BHB recommendations.' It looked evil, lying there on the Formica, and the tension in the room ratcheted up several notches.

'Tell me, Oscar,' I said, 'when was the last time you saw this gun, or one like it?'

The solicitor was more awake than I'd given him credit for. He said: 'Come off it, Inspector; you can do better than that.'

I dipped my head in acknowledgement and tried again. 'Have you seen this gun before?' I asked.

'No, never,' Oscar replied, his eyes fixed to the weapon. I'd been thinking that fifty thousand volts had made him a more compliant interviewee, but now I could see his old belligerence returning.

'Were you at a party in the grounds of Curzon House on the evening of Wednesday, May thirtieth?'

'I don't remember.'

'Do you deny being there? It was to celebrate your twentieth birthday.'

'I neither deny or admit being there.'

'Or that you were playing Russian roulette with a similar gun?'

'Same answer.'

'There are witnesses willing to say that you were.'

'Name them.'

'All in good time. What was your relationship with Mrs Janet Threadneedle?'

'She was my music teacher.'

'Were you in a sexual relationship with her?'

'That's one way of putting it.'

'How would you put it?'

He had to think about that, but the opportunity to boast about his prowess was too much to resist. He said: 'She was a sex-starved old biddy who couldn't get enough of me, so I gave her one whenever it was mutually convenient.'

'And how often was that?' I asked. It wasn't relevant but I'm as interested as the next *Daily Mirror* reader. Out of the corner of my eye I caught Maggie giving me a quick glance.

'About three times a week,' he told us, the memory causing him to grin.

'And this was in lieu of a piano lesson,' I suggested.

He liked that, and laughed out loud. 'Yeah, in lieu of a piano lesson. That's good, that is.'

I wanted to ask him if he liked her, but it wouldn't propel the enquiry forward whatever the answer. I wanted to know if there was the slightest spark of affection in him for a sad but talented lady. I wanted to put my hands round his throat and finish the Taser's job, but instead I said: 'When did you last see your father?'

That stunned him slightly, but he quickly recovered. 'Years ago,' he said.

'Your parents split up, I believe.'

'Yeah.'

'Why did you think that was?'

'At the time? I didn't know.'

He didn't want to talk about it but he was going to have to. 'Did you love your parents?' I asked. He nodded and I said: 'Tell me about your dad. Did he take you places?'

'Yeah, all over.'

'Such as?'

'All over. Silverstone, Oulton Park, Cadwell. Everywhere.'

'Car racing?'

'No, bikes.'

'Motorbikes.'

'Yeah, except that he said if you had one it was a bike, if you didn't, they were motorcycles, not motorbikes. He was always telling that to people. He liked being awkward. He was great fun.'

'At the time, why did you think he left?'

'At the time? Mum said he'd gone to Portugal, to work for Uncle Dennis. He has a bar there. She said Dad had got himself a new girlfriend.'

'And you believed her?'

'To start with, yeah.'

'So what changed?'

'Mum and Threadneedle, that's what.'

'Go on, please. You're doing well.'

'I thought it was all Dad's fault; that Mum was, you know, the injured party. But after the divorce came through she'd found herself a boyfriend before the ink was dry. That made me a bit suspicious but I thought she was, you know, making the best of a bad job; or maybe she was making Dad pay for what he'd done to us. She started buying expensive clothes and wearing lots of makeup; and going out a lot more, dressed to the nines. And underclothes. Sexy stuff you don't expect your mother to wear. She'd leave it strewn about her bedroom, as if...as if...as if they couldn't wait.'

'Did you know it was Threadneedle at this point?' Maggie asked.

'No. The name didn't mean anything to me. But the more I learned the more I decided that Mother wasn't as blameless as I'd thought. I started writing it all down to give to Dad. Thought it might bring him back and I could live with him. I was learning the guitar, in a bit of a group, but wanted to be a bit more serious, learn the piano. I told Mum and one day she said she'd found me a piano teacher. I didn't know for quite a while that she was the boyfriend's – Threadneedle's – wife, Janet. She let it slip, once or twice, that she was unhappy, but I just thought it was, you know, mid-life blues, or something like that. She was a good teacher. I had one or two lessons a week, was doing reasonably well, until...'

Until... We all waited, hanging on to his every word.

'Until... one day last summer. It was a hot day and Janet had it all planned. First of all, she spiked my drink. And she'd had one or two herself. She took me upstairs; said I'd never seen the rest of the house, had I? We didn't make it past the front bedroom; screwed each other brainless on top of the duvet. Afterwards, lying in bed, she told me about Mum and her husband, said they were the reason Dad left. I went mad, started crying. She said not to worry; we could get revenge in our own sweet way.'

We sat in silence, wondering if he'd finished, until Maggie said: 'And did you?'

'Yeah,' he replied. 'Well, she thought so. College was out, so we stepped up the piano lessons to three a week. She had a thing about doing it – sex, I mean – in every room in the house. Said she wouldn't feel she'd had revenge on her husband until she'd betrayed him in every room in the home he'd bought for them. It's a big house, but we did it in two days, while he was away on one of his golfing breaks, doing something similar with Mum in one room at the Holiday Inn.'

All the time he was speaking his eyes were flicking towards the gun, then at his own hands as they gripped the edge of the table. 'When did you first meet this chappie?' I asked, giving it a tap with my knuckle. The DS stirred in his chair but remained silent.

'About three weeks ago,' he replied.

'What were the circumstances?'

He thought about it: thought about a life sentence; thought about how old he'd be when released; thought about the girls he'd miss; thought about his chances of walking out of court with a non-custodial; thought about everything in a crazy whirlwind of emotions and facts and figures, lies and half-truths, that swirled round in his brain. A snatch of a nonsense poem came into my mind, began to dominate my thoughts. *The time has come, the walrus said, to talk of many things.*

'She had it,' he told us.

'She?' I queried.

'Janet. Mrs Threadneedle. I was going to the supermarket, early on, and saw her loading the back of her car. I parked next to her, which was about as far away from the doors as you could get. She was excited, glad to see me, kept saying she'd done it, she'd finally done it. 'Done what?' I asked, and she told me that she'd shot her husband earlier that morning and he was dead.'

'So what was she doing at the supermarket?' Maggie asked.

'That's what I wanted to know. She said she was establishing an alibi and was going to find somewhere to dispose of the clothes she'd worn, and the gun. I told her she'd no chance. The police would find her clothes and arrest her, so I offered to help. We put the bag holding them in my car and I told her to go home, as she normally would have done, and report the murder. I said I'd get rid of everything. I drove to the campus at York and hid them in a dumpster. It was Monday, and they empty them on a Monday.'

'But you missed the collection.'

'Yeah.'

'And the following Monday was a bank holiday and the bin men weren't working.'

'Refuse disposal technicians,' Maggie said.

'Of course,' I agreed. 'The refuse disposal technicians weren't working, and we eventually got round to examining the dumpsters and found the evidence. So how come you had the gun?'

'I...just kept it. Thought it might come in useful one day, you know...'

So that was the way he wanted it to go. He'd sold her down the river. Their stories overlapped, but he'd blamed her for doing the deed herself. He was simply the knight in slightly tarnished armour who'd helped out a fair maiden. If the price he had to pay for his gallantry was a small term in custody, so be it.

Did he keep the gun in case he wanted to top himself? Doctors and farmers have the highest incidence of suicide, simply because they have the means at their disposal. Doctors take a few pills; farmers run over themselves with the muck spreader.

'What are your feelings towards Janet now?' I asked.

He hadn't thought about it, had to have a think. He'd reached the stage where he wanted to talk, but this was a new one. The barriers were down and he held the stage. Unburdening oneself, it's called, and it really does exist.

'She's a bit of a nympho,' he said. 'A right raver underneath. You wouldn't think butter would melt in her mouth until you get to know her. If you close your eyes she's a decent shag.'

And suddenly the thought of locking away a promising student who'd been let down by his parents didn't bother me. He could have said she was nice; she'd been kind to him; helped him through a difficult patch. He could have said that she'd loaned him the use of her body, against her instincts and moral code, and he'd always be grateful to her. He could have said she'd given him some of the best times of his life. He could have said nothing. But he didn't, and I didn't care if we threw the key away.

We can't interview a prisoner once he's been charged, so we charged Oscar with a lesser crime of assisting an offender, so we could hold him, and passed the tapes to the Crown Prosecution Service. They would decide what we could hit him with.

While I was trying not to be titillated by Oscar Sidebottom's confessions, Dave and Serena were hot on the scent of the pit bull gang. 'We went to see Terry Bratt,' Serena told me when I'd finished talking to the CPS lawyer who has an office on the premises, 'and showed him the list of probable pit bulls we'd gathered from the public appeal. I told him that we wouldn't dream of asking him to grass on a member of his extended family but we were slowly working our way through the list and it might be in his and Bruno's interest if he could possibly point us in the right direction. He looked at the names and said: "Him. He's Carl's nephew. He's got Bruno's brother. Nasty piece of work." I said: "The dog or him?" and he said: "Both of them."'

Dave said: 'It's Serena's show but no doubt she'd like you in the team.'

I looked at her. She said: 'Let's go.'

He worked a scrapyard from a run-down site on the poorer side of town, where the travellers pitched up for the summer when they'd been run off their traditional camping grounds. It was a symbiotic relationship: the tinkers brought in wrecked and abandoned vehicles that they found (and, some would say, occasionally engineered), and he paid them a tenner and separated the wreck into its component materials. The council and the police looked the other way until their collective necks hurt and were grateful that someone was doing the dirty work. He was called Chick Shillito and had a reputation for being an ex-boxer and a hard man. Rumour had it, Dave told me in the car, that he'd fought Richard Dunn, who was later beaten by Muhammad Ali.

'Presumably he lost to Dunn,' I said, 'otherwise he'd be the one who fought Ali.'

'Um, yes, I suppose so,' Dave agreed, but I didn't feel any happier about it.

The yard was surrounded by an eight-foot-high galvanised fence topped off with razor wire. Serena wondered what was in the yard that warranted such precautions, but Dave put her straight. 'Nothing's safe with that lot living next door,' he told her. 'They'd steal the dog, given half a chance. And he probably got a council grant for it.' He yanked the handbrake on and we climbed out.

Fifty or more years of oil drippings and comings and goings had sterilised the surrounding ground into a compacted surface that was waterproof and dust-free. You just left oily footprints wherever you went for the rest of the day. A large wooden structure, reinforced with several assorted doors, appeared to be where the work was carried out, and two windowless ex-British Rail goods vans completed the buildings inventory. A flatbed Ford lorry with a tow hook on the back was ready to go, come nightfall, and a rusting 1989 Range Rover stood with one hub supported on bricks. Several mangled car bodies, unrecognisable to anybody but the most sad enthusiast or a traffic officer, were piled in the far corner. As yards go, and considering the nature of the enterprise, it was reasonably tidy.

'Anybody home?' Dave shouted, reinforcing his question with a side-footed kick at the wire mesh gate.

Two and a half seconds later a black and tan ball of spitting fury came skittering round the end of the garage and hurled itself against the fence, inches from Dave. Serena took several steps backwards. I said: 'Did anybody bring the dog scarer?'

The man himself wasn't far behind and was about what we expected. Earring, tattoos too numerous to record, shaved head, dressed by Adidas. He took in the three of us at a glance and realised we weren't the judges for the Best Garden competition. He said: 'How can I help you?' and shouted for the dog – Banjo – to calm down. It settled for snarling at Dave, slavering copiously, with lips curled back to display as fine a set of molars and canines as you'd see anywhere. We flashed our IDs and Serena told Shillito who we were.

'Got a warrant?' he asked, pulling on his roll-up and flicking the stub into space.

'It's on its way,' Dave told him. 'Tie the dog up and let us in.' Banjo realised he was being talked about and started barking at Dave again.

'He doesn't like being tied up.'

Dave's hand delved into his jacket. I thought he was putting his ID away but when he pulled it out again he was gripping the nickel-plated 0.38 Webley revolver we'd relieved a Yardie of some months earlier. His arm was straight, pointing the gun down at the dog's head. 'I said tie the dog up and let us in or I'll blow its pea-sized brain out.'

He was talking Shillito's language. The man turned on his heels and went to fetch the dog's chain and the keys to the gate. Dave looked at me, saying: 'And before you ask, yes, he knows.'

I said: 'I would never have thought otherwise, Dave. Not for one minute. Not for a single second. And it worked better than the dog scarer would.' I telephoned the nick and asked them to organise a search warrant and some assistance, *muy pronto*. In half an hour we had two pandas, a SOCO, the dog unit and a mechanic armed with a generator and angle grinder, all eager to help. In another fifteen minutes we had the warrant.

Shillito was swearing that he didn't know what was in the goods vans. He hired them out as safe storage, that was all. They were solidly constructed of a double layer of hardwood planks, running east to west and then north to south, built to withstand the rigours of a steam-age shunting yard. The big side doors were held closed by a system of sliding rods and levers secured by a pair of massive Chubb padlocks. When the mechanic started the generator and approached the first lock with his angle grinder, the thought of the £100 Chubbs falling uselessly to the ground was more than Shillito could take. He remembered where he kept the spare keys.

The possibility of a long jail sentence for aggravated burglary helped his amnesia even further. Suddenly it came back to him whom he'd hired the wagon to: Carl and Sean Pickles, his distant relatives. He'd even, on a couple of occasions, allowed them to take Banjo for walkies. They'd borrowed him to try to impregnate a bitch owned by another member of the family but she was never in season. There was good money to be made that way. No, he'd no idea what the overalls, baseball caps and surgical gloves were doing in the wagons, or whom the flat-screen TVs and various other electronic goodies belonged to. Serena arrested and cuffed him, and thoughtfully placed her hand on top of his head so he didn't hurt himself as he struggled into the back seat of the panda.

I left them to it. The late nights were catching up on me and I started to recognise the symptoms of sleep deprivation: a nervous tick; nosebleeds; eczema; general weariness; headaches; seeing imaginary things out of the corners of my eyes; making mistakes. OK, so three out of seven might not be life-threatening but I wasn't at my best. I told Dave that I wasn't feeling very well; was taking the rest of the afternoon off; would he please let Gilbert know. We'd have a big meeting in the morning, but meanwhile I was off duty.

When it looked as if I'd be spending more time in East Yorkshire I asked Driffield if they could arrange a bed for me in a spare cell, preferably one unit of comfort higher than that provided for their normal clients. They gladly obliged and I'd thrown my lightweight sleeping bag in the boot just in case the Home Office issue sheets were unappetising. I had loose ends to tidy over there, so I headed east again.

First call was Driffield nick to confirm my bed for the night and let my opposite number know that the Threadneedle investigation was now in the slippery-fingered hands of the CPS. He'd cooperated without interfering, and I was grateful. I told him as much as I could about the Peccadillo case but he could see no future in pursuing it and was happy to leave it with me. *Not in the public's interest* saves us more rainforests than green wheelie bins ever will. We swapped anecdotes about old-timers until we found someone we both knew and I set off on the next leg of my odyssey.

The combination of rainfall and sunshine over the last month was what my father would have called *good growing weather*. Unfortunately his love of things herbaceous hadn't been passed on to his son. All I knew was that I was losing the battle being waged in my little plot.

It was being lost on the Curzon estate, too, but they were putting up a decent fight. Just beyond the barrier I was stopped by a character clad in safety gear that made him look like a samurai warrior: helmet with wire mesh visor; leather apron; knee pads; gauntlets and big boots. Weapon of choice: the chainsaw. He halted my progress with an extended arm while a tractor crossed my path, then urged me on with a flourish. Blue smoke from a bonfire drifted between the trees and the rise and fall of a chainsaw's exhaust gnawed into the afternoon.

I emerged into the car park and the sunshine and made an extravagant turn that brought me to my usual place, facing the house but some distance from it. I locked up and walked towards what I'd come to regard as the tradesmen's entrance.

Toby and Aspen were sitting on the steps, backs against the wall, enjoying what was left of the sunshine. Their school rucksacks were lying nearby and they were both reading books. As I approached they lowered their books and gave me a wave. Aspen had her white Goth face on and Toby had borrowed her Moto-X boots.

'Hello, Charlie,' Toby called to me. 'Have you come to arrest someone?' They looked like two clothes-peg dolls propped against the wall, with pipe cleaner legs sticking out.

'Not today. What are you reading?'

She held the book so the front cover faced me. '*Dracula*. It's Aspen's. We've swapped books.'

'Are you enjoying it?'

'No. It's a bit heavy going. She says wearing her boots will help me understand it.'

I turned to Aspen. 'And what literary masterpiece has Toby passed on to you?' She held it towards me and I said: '*Harry Potter and the Giblets of Fire*.'

Toby fell over sideways, laughing, and Aspen spun the book round in disbelief. 'It's "*Goblet* of Fire",' she asserted.

When Toby had recovered and was back with us, I asked her if her father was at home. She produced a handset from her pocket and said she'd find him.

'This is Mr Curzon's number one personal assistant,' she told him when he answered. 'There's a Mr Priest to see you. No... No... Yes... No. I haven't, honest.' Then, to me: 'He's on his way.'

Curzon shook my hand with vigour and took me into a room I hadn't seen before. I'd call it the gentleman's study. Leather, deep-buttoned easy chairs, a huge desk, more bookshelves than the village library and portraits of ancestors and various other pampered animals on the walls. Only the flat-screen computer monitors added a note of incongruity. He invited me to take one of the easy chairs and I managed to sit down without shooting off its highly polished cushions.

He told me my visit was an unexpected pleasure and made the usual offer of coffee. I declined, saying I had places to go, had called in to tie up a few loose ends and answer any questions he may have.

'Toby's in fine fettle,' I said, 'back to her old self'

'For the moment,' he replied, adding, 'Aspen has come round for her tea. They make a good double act.'

'I had noticed. Does the CF go into remission or does its severity vary day to day?' It wasn't the most diplomatic question I'd ever asked, but hiding from Toby's illness, as if it didn't exist, wasn't doing her any good, and I earned a reaction.

Curzon sat up straight, folded his arms and planted his feet firmly on the carpet. 'Yes,' he replied.

Yes, what? I thought. Try harder. 'It goes into remission?' I suggested.

'It's difficult to say,' he told me, relaxing a little. 'There are so many variables, like pollen count, humidity, cold weather. Even Toby's state of mind appears to have an effect. It's a terrible illness, Charlie. Terrible. I wouldn't wish it upon an enemy.'

'Is a heart and lung transplant an option?' I'd done my research and Google said it was.

'Just about the only option for the foreseeable future, but she won't entertain it. It's her complaint, she says, and she'll deal with it her way. We're respecting her wishes.'

'What about the genetic approach? Is anything happening on that avenue?'

'Not really. You know how it goes. Lots of teams all over the world claiming to have made a breakthrough, but they're all chasing funding from the same pot of money.'

I wanted to talk to him about genetics, but wasn't sure how to go about it. After an awkward silence I jumped in with: 'I understand it's a single-gene disease, whatever that means.'

He didn't flinch. A fly landed on the table in front of him and he wafted it away. 'That's right. What it means, basically, is that only one of a pair of genes is healthy and the other is wonky. We can live with that, but it's possible to pass on the faulty gene. If you inherit a good gene from one parent and a faulty one from the other you will have no symptoms but will be a carrier. Laura and I were carriers, although we didn't know it, until...until poor Toby drew the short straw and inherited a bad gene from each of us.'

'But the disease skipped Ghislaine.'

'That's right, but she hasn't had the tests so we don't know if she's a carrier.'

I wondered what the royal family would make of it. They'd bred out haemophilia and the Hapsburg lip and now they had a sporting chance of introducing cystic fibrosis into their illustrious gene pool. I said: 'No, I don't think I'd have the test, either. Not until it became an issue.'

The fly found me and flitted around my head. I took a few swipes at it and it flew off to find somewhere more welcoming. 'One of my reasons for coming was to tell you about Janet Threadneedle. I'm not sure how well you knew her, but if you could call yourself a friend I think she'd be pleased to hear from you.' I told him that she'd been arrested and charged with the murder of her husband. I didn't go into detail about the bloody clothing we'd found, or mention the affair with her teenage pupil.

'Thanks for that,' he said. 'I'll write to her. Is it conclusive that she did the deed?'

'I think a court will find the DNA evidence overwhelming.'

'Ah, DNA again. It must have made your job much easier.'

'In some ways,' I agreed, 'but it works both ways.'

'Certain criminals must be cursing its discovery.'

'I know.' I've always felt a little sorry for Dr Crippen. He committed what he thought was the perfect murder and boarded a ship to the United States. When it set sail he must have thought that he was in the clear, but what he didn't know was that Mr Marconi had been busy perfecting his radio machine, and the law was waiting for him on the other side. That was bum luck in anybody's book. Since the invention of DNA profiling in the late 1980s cold cases are being resurrected almost every day. Old men, barely able to walk, are standing trial for rape, while others, now found to be innocent, are finding a kind of freedom.

I said: 'Did your new knowledge of genetics help with your horse racing exploits?'

He looked uncomfortable, took a swing at the fly, then stood up to find a newspaper, which he fashioned into a fly swat. 'Help with the horse racing?' he repeated, giving himself time to think. 'Is this what it's all about? Are we talking about Peccadillo?'

'I believe you had a share in him.'

'Are you wearing your policeman's hat, now, Charlie?'

'I'm always wearing it, James. You're under no obligation to answer my questions.'

'But if I don't you'll invite me down to the station for an interview.'

'I doubt if it will come to that. So did you?'

'Yes, if you must know. I was a member of the syndicate. I fell for Threadneedle's promises. I blamed my wife, Laura, but I was as enthusiastic as she was.'

'What did a share cost?'

'Fifteen thousand pounds, plus my share of vets' fees, training fees, entry fees. It goes on and on.'

'It was a drain on your income.'

'You can say that again.'

'But you were hoping to recover your money by

winning races and putting the horse to stud, riding on the doubtful rumour that it was descended from the legendary Shergar.'

'Got it in one, Charlie. Put nothing in writing, Threadneedle told us. Just show them the photos, mention Shergar, nudge nudge, wink wink, and let them know it came from Ireland. Leave the rest to their imaginations.'

'Who's us?' I asked.

'Me and Motty. He was sucked in, too. Threadneedle was his boss so the poor man didn't have much choice. He put his life savings into it. I felt guilty about that, afterwards.'

'Anybody else?'

'Not that I know of. I didn't sell any shares and I'm sure Motty didn't. I think Threadneedle brought one or two of his cronies into the syndicate, but I don't know who.'

'Didn't you have reports or a balance sheet? You sound to be very trusting.'

'He was a smooth talker, Charlie, and events eventually overtook us.'

'What events? What brought them about?'

'I think you know the answer to that, Charlie. I think you've suspected all along. Toby brought them about, or her illness did. Ghislaine and I read everything we could about the complaint. It didn't help Toby one iota, but I came away with a decent grounding in elementary genetics. Unfortunately for us some, veterinary students had taken samples from Shergar and his DNA is on record. There was talk of all thoroughbreds having to have passports.

I realised then that there was no way we could pass Peccadillo off as a descendant of Shergar. I could run as fast as he could. He was a liability. This house was costing a fortune – I looked like losing it – and I didn't know where to turn. I told Threadneedle about the passports and he said to leave it to him. I think he was attracting some heat from the other people he'd sold shares to. They wanted their money back and so did I. Next thing I knew, the stables had burnt down and Peccadillo was dead.'

'Did the insurance pay out?'

'Not to my knowledge.'

The fly landed on the table in front of me. My hand came down like a striking cobra and squashed it flat. I brushed the corpse on to the floor. Curzon, lost in his own world, didn't notice.

'That just about coincides with what Motty told me,' I said.

Curzon jerked himself awake, back to the here and now. 'Motty?' he echoed. 'You've talked to Motty?'

'As much as it's possible to talk to him, yes. I'm going back there now, to get a final statement from him about the gun. That should wrap it up.' I stood up and we shook hands. I asked him to say goodbye from me to his daughters and said I'd try to get over for the village fete in August, when his dolls' houses would be launched. He walked me to the door but didn't come outside. I strolled to the car, parked in the middle of nowhere, and took in my surroundings. The sun was dropping and flocks of swifts – I'd decided they were swifts – were screeching overhead, gorging themselves on the clouds of midges that towered into the sky. As I swung the car round I saw his face at the window, watching me leave.

Motty had been to one of the functions that pensioners fill their days with: dining club; bingo; card games or line dancing, so he was smartly dressed and alert. The evening was warm but the light was fading, so I accepted his invitation to step inside. Once again he was pleased to see me, and when we shook hands he clung to my fingers for a few seconds longer than I felt comfortable with. His bungalow was tiny, the living room just about big enough to qualify for that description, with a bedroom and galley kitchen visible through half-open doors. It must have been heartbreaking, moving here after all those years in the head lad's cottage attached to the stables. But it was warm and comfortable, and monitored by a warden who lived nearby. No doubt other professional carers were on hand to help him through his declining years without having to bother the rest of us. I wondered how often the undertaker's hearse visited the little precinct.

I did most of the talking. I told him that Threadneedle had kept the gun and his wife had found it. She'd probably shot him with it and her boyfriend had assisted her. Motty listened, wide-eyed, and nodded in appropriate places.

'We've done some measuring,' I told him, 'and come to a conclusion. We've decided that you couldn't have shot the horse by yourself, Motty. You're just not tall enough.' His dark complexion grew even blacker, and he sat there, nodding slowly, rocking backwards and forwards.

'You had some help,' I said.

'Some help,' he agreed.

'Your loyalty to your employer is admirable, Motty,' I told him, 'but the time has come to tell the truth. Do you understand what I'm saying?'

'Tell truth,' he replied.

'I think the *meister* was there when Peccadillo was killed. Am I right?'

'Aye,' he confirmed, not looking at me.

'The horse was standing up,' I said. 'You'd need some help to shoot it. Somebody to hold it steady while somebody else used the gun. You're the expert,' I told him. 'You're the horse whisperer. I suspect you held his head, calmed him down, while the *meister* pulled the trigger. Is that about how it happened?'

'Aye.'

I stood up and walked over to the window. I'd led the witness, no doubt about it, but he was an honest man and I believed him. The lady who lived across the lawn was watering her pansies and Puccini's 'Nessun Dorma' could be heard faintly playing next door. A car drew up two doors away and a man and a small boy carrying a bunch of flowers got out, visiting grandma. I said: 'I don't suppose it matters now. You were the legal owners of the horse and you, Motty, were licensed to use the humane killer, so I don't suppose the law was broken. The *meister* may have pulled the trigger but it was under your supervision. We're checking if he made an insurance claim but if he did we think it was unsuccessful. As he's dead now there's not much point in pursuing it.'

I turned to face Motty, expecting him to be relieved that the case was as good as solved and he could go back to his memories, but his eyes were wide and his mouth hung open. 'Who...dead?' he asked. 'Who dead?'

'Threadneedle,' I replied. 'Arthur George. He's dead. Have you forgotten?'

'Not the *meister*,' Motty came back¯ at me. 'Threadneedle...he not *meister*. He not...shoot. He not shoot.'

Now it was my turn to be shocked. 'Threadneedle is not the *meister*?' I echoed. 'Is that what you're saying? So who is? Tell me, Motty, tell me who was there when you killed Peccadillo. Tell me who pulled the trigger.'

CHAPTER NINETEEN

It was nearly dark when I rang Gilbert to tell him that the cases were solved and his number one detective would probably call in sometime tomorrow morning. 'I told you it was a private murder,' he said, 'and as for all this gallivanting off to East Yorkshire...just a waste of resources. Nothing much ever happens over there. It's the sticks. Sleepyville. Get yourself back here and do some real detective work.'

After that I rang Phyllis Smith to book whatever she could rustle up at short notice, with a bed for the night, but she wasn't answering her phone. I tried one of the Dunkley numbers but a woman with a can't-be-bothered voice told me she had no vacancies and put the phone down on me. It looked like it would have to be a curry in Driffield and my cell at their nick. I'd driven away from

Motty's at Dunkley somewhat aimlessly and parked in
my usual place, facing Curzon House. I don't know why.
It was one of those habit things. After a few visits we
become possessive about seats in restaurants, or coat pegs,
or urinals. I always use the second one from the left at
Heckley nick; feel I've been cheated if someone beats me
to it. So there I was, in the middle of an acre of block
paving, while the night grew darker around me.

I pretend it was the stars that drew me there. I
remembered that night a couple of weeks ago when I
followed Toby to Low Ogglethorp, with the heavens ablaze
with starlight. It was magical. Why do the stars all look
the same size, I wondered? Not *exactly* the same size, but
near enough when you consider how different they are:
red giants and yellow dwarfs; galaxies and gassy planets;
lumps of rock and blazing fireballs. They all look similar
from down here on Earth, reduced by distance and time
to insignificant pinpricks in the sky. I could've been an
astronomer if I hadn't made it as a cop.

I didn't really want to sleep in a cell at Driffield.
There'd be the same old leg-pulls; the same smells and
noises; the same repeated explanations. It would have been
worth twenty pounds to have a bed at Phyllis's, but she
still wasn't answering the phone. If I got to Driffield after
midnight the place might have quietened down a bit by
then. I switched off and decided to go for a walk.

I'd miss Toby, no doubt about it. There'd be a fresh
case in a day or two, with a different cast, but Toby
would be a difficult act to follow. I took the same path
again but this time there was no moonlight and I stumbled

here and there, wondering if I was mad. There was something uplifting about her. Something life-enhancing. Her indomitable cheerfulness knocked you sideways, made you feel good to be alive.

I was there, wherever *there* was. Left for the hidden village of Low Ogglethorp, right for Coneywarren Field with its fake stone circle. I decided that the chances of breaking a leg were lower at Coneywarren and turned right.

My night vision had come good and I was seeing clearly now. And hearing. It was a small laugh, followed by the sound of footfalls on dry grass and someone humming, very softly. I stopped and listened, thinking about withdrawing, not wanting to interrupt someone's lovemaking. But I thought I knew who it was, and felt myself being drawn slowly towards the sounds.

There were two of them, performing some sort of courtly pavan. He was leading her, pulling her along, his steps slow and stately, his gait high as they swayed in harmony around the newly restored silver birch. They were both as naked as the day they were born. I held my breath and watched the two figures, their whiteness luminescent, as they performed a ritual known only to them. Six times they went round in a clockwise direction, then they switched hands and made six more turns to the widdershins. They weren't young people and they weren't fine specimens of our race. Time had ravaged their bodies, but there was something innocent and ageless about their dance and I felt privileged to be witnessing it. They turned to each other and embraced, slowly sinking to the ground, and I sneaked away. Their laughter followed me down the trail: his like a cawing jackdaw, hers like breaking glass.

I had a long talk with Maggie in the morning. Banjo the pit bull had donated a saliva sample, and his owner, Chick Shillito, had put the finger on Sean and Carl and they were going down, no doubt about it. Young Oscar Sidebottom had decided that playing the white knight was not for him and had put all the blame on Janet Threadneedle. Janet, meanwhile, prompted by Oscar's savage testimony, had blamed him for the whole thing. He wanted Threadneedle dead and had persuaded her that it was the right thing to do. She'd loved her young paramour and had been swept along by him. I said I'd see her later.

As soon as the streets were aired I drove to Curzon House again. I decided I was in danger of becoming neurotic and parked near the tradesmen's entrance, just to demonstrate that I was a free spirit. Grizzly answered the bell.

'Good morning,' I said, hoping I didn't look as if I'd spent a sleepless night in the cells. 'This is a surprise.'

'Good morning, Charlie,' she replied. 'Yes it is. We thought you had solved all your cases and gone home. What can we do for you?'

'Loose ends,' I explained. 'There are always loose ends. I was hoping to speak to your father. Is he available?'

'I'm afraid not. He's taken Toby birdwatching. They had an early start. Can I take a message?'

'No, not really. Any idea when they'll be back?'

'Lunchtime, at a guess.'

'Where will they have gone?'

'Sorry. No idea.'

'OK.' I wished her all the best and climbed back in the car. Something was troubling me, and it wasn't the supercool, unhelpful Ghislaine Curzon. Toby had gone birdwatching with her father. Early in the morning. I wondered whose idea it was. I picked up my phone, then put it away. I switched on the Airwave, then switched that off, too. Motty had told me, in his own way, that it was Curzon who had shot Peccadillo. That it had been Curzon's idea. When I told him, the day before, that I was about to take a statement off Motty, he must have realised that he'd be exposed as the killer. Perhaps he hadn't broken the law, but there was an attempted insurance fraud to consider, plus the dodgy syndicate, and he'd killed a perfectly healthy horse. With a daughter engaged to a royal prince it was a tabloid's dream story.

Puffins. I remembered the painting above Toby's bed. She'd painted it herself because they were her favourites. 'Daddy was going to take me to see them at...' That's where my memory ran out. I pulled the road atlas out of the seat pocket behind me and thumbed through it until I reached the Yorkshire coast. The background to the painting was a series of sheer cliffs. I'd seen photographs of them many times, on calendars and in magazines, but never visited them. They were our answer to Beachy Head, except Beachy Head has an unenviable reputation. Beachy Head hosts a fair number of suicides every year. There it was: Bempton, just up the coast from Flamborough Head.

God, it was miles away. I switched on the Airwave and once more switched it off again. Bridlington was nearer to Bempton, but how could I explain? And if they arrived there first, lights flashing, they might aggravate the situation; precipitate some rash action by Curzon. I lay the open map on the passenger seat, slammed into first gear and put my foot down, hard.

There was a network of narrow lanes between me and my destination. The B1253 threaded through them but took me into Bridlington. I risked it and was lucky, traffic was light and soon I picked up the B1255 towards Flamborough and then the RSPB signs for their reserve at Bempton.

It was a pay and display car park, divided into neat bays by low wooden rails. Three people were at the ticket machine, trying to help each other find the right change, but I didn't bother with a nicety like paying. I drove straight past them and went on a tour of the park, looking for Curzon's elderly Volvo. I was beginning to think I'd guessed wrongly when, suddenly, there it was. I parked tight behind it, blocking him in.

They weren't in the shop so I set off down the limestone path towards the cliff and its viewing points. The place was buzzing with lesser-spotted birdwatchers. Some were obvious amateurs, with the wife and kids, hoping to see a puffin; others dripped with hundreds of pounds worth of cameras, binoculars and telescopes, and you just knew they could tell an Arctic warbler from a Greenland chiffchaff at five hundred metres and would sniff with disdain at anyone who couldn't.

The RSPB information board said that there could be up to a quarter of a million seabirds there, including the largest colonies of gannets and kittiwakes in the British Isles. By the smell of the place I'd say they were all at home. I walked down the grassy field towards the sturdy fence that protected the edge of the cliff, and the thought of it, there in front of me, gave me a nervous feeling in my legs.

It took your breath away. Four hundred feet, dead vertical, and every square foot inhabited by a screaming, cawing, gaping mouth, demanding attention. The air in front of the cliff was filled with wheeling and swooping seabirds looking for their own offspring. I stood mesmerised, my mind completely boggled, and almost forgot why I was there.

There were five observation points where the fence was designed to give the birdwatcher a view of the cliff face. It was elbow to elbow at the first one but I guessed that number five, half a mile away, would be relatively quiet, so I struck out towards it.

When I was nearly there I saw Toby coming towards me, cleaning her spectacles, binoculars hanging round her neck. They were those green rubberised ones that have lens covers dangling on them. When she was right up to me I said: 'Good morning, Toby. Fancy meeting you here.'

She peered up at me, thrusting her face close to mine, like short-sighted people do. 'Charlie?' she said. 'Is that Charlie?' She hooked her specs around her ears. 'It is!' she declared. 'What are you doing here?'

'I came to count the gannets,' I told her. 'It's part of my job.'

'How many did you get?'

'Five thousand seven hundred and ninety-seven.'

'I got five thousand seven hundred and ninety-six. You must have counted one of them twice.'

'Never. You must have missed one.'

'Rubbish! Have you seen them dive in?' She made a diving motion with her hand, terminating in a *splosh*.

'Spectacular, aren't they. Where's your daddy?'

'He's following me. Must have stopped to look at something.'

'You walk on, Toby. I'd like a word with him.'

'Without me there. I get the message. Is it true you've solved the murder?'

'You ask too many questions, but yes, we think we've solved it.'

'Will you get promoted?'

'No! Now go!' I pointed down the trail and she skipped away.

He was meandering, stopping to use his binoculars, then consulting a bird book to try to identify something he'd seen. I leant on the fence and watched the aerial ballet being performed before my eyes. The gannets were special, folding their wings for the last fifty feet of their dive and entering the water with hardly a splash. They rose out of it a few seconds later, not a feather out of place, their painted heads as immaculately drawn as the Clinique girls at the mall.

'Hello, James,' I said, 'I didn't know you were a twitcher.'

Curzon shook his head to break out of the reverie.

'Hello, Charlie,' he replied. 'A twitcher? No, not me. This is a surprise. What brings you to Bempton?'

'Grizzly said I'd find you here, and I just wanted to fill you in before I went back to Heckley. Are you heading home?'

'Yes, I think Toby's seen all she wants. But haven't you work to do? I think we know enough about the whole sad case, don't you?'

'Possibly, but I'd like to clarify a couple of points. Can we have a chat back at the house, if you don't mind?'

'Fine,' he replied, but his expression indicated that he'd prefer to have his fingernails pulled out.

At the cars I suggested that he lead the way because he was more familiar with the lanes. 'Do you mind if Toby rides with me?' I asked. 'We've some catching up to do.' Toby looked delighted with the idea.

He led us along back roads, skirting the Wolds with their wide, lush valleys, through villages with names as unlikely as Grindale, Thwing and Octon. Sledmere, with its ornate Victorian architecture, demanded closer inspection, but we drove straight through. It would have to wait for another day. I asked Toby how the tennis serve was going and she told me that her father had promised to buy a serving machine, so she'd have something to play against.

'I'm going to call it Rafael, after Rafael Nadal,' she told me.

'Sounds fun,' I said. 'Some of those machines are so realistic they grunt and spit.'

'Rafael doesn't grunt and spit,' she protested.

'No, but some of the women players do.'

'Ha ha! Perhaps I should start. When we get one will you come over and have a go on it?'

'Ooh, we'll see.'

'It's not just me. Grizzly would like you to, as well.'

'Ha! I doubt it.' Curzon had stopped at a narrow junction, waiting for a tractor and trailer to go by. The farmer gave us a wave and we were off again.

'She's not going to marry Kevin, you know.'

I said: 'Toby, you should keep things like that to yourself. It's personal.'

'She told me last night, in bed.'

'Did you hear what I said?'

'Yes, it's personal.' She twisted in her seat until she was facing me, her knees drawn up. 'She's on the shelf, now,' she declared, 'so you could marry her, and that would make me your sister-in-law. Would you like me for a sister-in-law?'

I nearly drove into the ditch. 'Over my dead body,' I told her.

Curzon took me into the room with the deep-buttoned easy chairs and then vanished for several minutes. He reappeared carrying a tray laden with coffee and biscuits.

'No milk, I believe.'

'Thank you.'

He fussed about, placing my coffee on the Queen Anne table at the side of my chair, leaving me a napkin, neatly folded and geometrically positioned. I didn't mind the time-wasting: I wasn't looking forward to our conversation any more than he was. Eventually he took his place in the easy chair facing me.

'So what's it all about?' he asked.

'I think you can guess,' I replied. 'I went to see Motty Dermot last night, as you know, and we had a long conversation. I say conversation, but I did most of the talking, asking direct questions that required simple answers. Unfortunately, that caused me to make some mistakes with his replies in the past, to jump to false conclusions. Motty told me that he was assisted by the *meister* to kill Peccadillo, and I was led to believe that this meant Threadneedle, but I was wrong, wasn't I?'

He sat in silence for a long while, then chose his words carefully. 'Motty goes back a long way,' he said, 'and he's lived a sheltered life, surrounded by horses and racing folk, like his father and grandfather before him. He, and others like him, are like conduits going back two hundred years, with language and values that stretch back that far. Because I live in the *Big House* he credits me with some sort of respect. Respect that I don't deserve. When he talks about the *meister*, he means me.'

'Do you want to tell me about it?'

'Not particularly.' He pushed himself upright, saying: 'Biscuits. Please, have a biscuit.'

I sat patiently waiting until we were both furnished with a side plate and a home-made crunchy cookie. 'I think you've worked it all out by now, Charlie,' he said. 'You're a good cop.' I took a bite of biscuit and sipped my coffee. 'I was in big trouble,' he continued. 'Big financial trouble. The gales had taken off much of the roof and the rain was doing the rest. First estimate was quarter of a million, going up every day. We were running as fast as we could just to stand still. We applied for grants everywhere imaginable, tried to do a deal with the local council, but nobody was interested.'

I sneaked a look at the clock on the wall and thought I'd better speed things up a little. I said: 'And then along came a white knight in the form of Arthur George Threadneedle.'

'Something like that. We knew him quite well, through the musical evenings and the horse racing. Put it down to naivety, greed, desperation, what you will, but we fell for the spiel and invested fifteen thousand pounds in the Peccadillo syndicate. It was peanuts, really, but it was just about my last fifteen grand. If the rumours could be believed – that Peccadillo was descended from Shergar – it would win a race and then earn us a fortune in stud fees. It all sounded so simple.'

'But you'd learnt about genetics, and genetic fingerprinting.'

'That's right. The horse couldn't run, wouldn't even cut the mustard as a selling plater, and the new techniques would prove it wasn't descended from Shergar. I took Threadneedle to one side and spelt it out to him. He thought about it and came up with the idea of the fire. I went along with it and Motty came in with us. I thought Threadneedle would do the deed and I'd be a mere spectator, but at the last minute he said he'd be under suspicion as he was the owner. We'd have a better chance of success, he said, if he had a good alibi and Motty and

I did the dirty work. He swore there was no paperwork to link either of us to the horse, so we did it. We shot the horse first, then broke its leg, then started the fire. It was the dirtiest night's work I've ever done.'

'Who fired the shot?'

'I did. Motty was supposed to, but he couldn't reach. I was more or less forced into it.' He sat quietly for a while, then added: 'I'm not offering that as an excuse. I was just as culpable, whoever fired the shot.'

'Did you start the fire?'

That took him by surprise. He thought about it for a few seconds, looking embarrassed, then took the line of least resistance. 'Yes,' he admitted. Another long, awkward pause before he enlarged upon and tried to excuse his admission. 'Right from the beginning that was supposed to be my role in the job – starting the fire. Threadneedle had laid a trail of straw soaked in paraffin or petrol, and brought a box of cook's matches, just in case I forgot mine. It was slow to start; I thought we'd blown it, then it went up like a bomb.'

I took a sip of coffee, then said: 'But it was all unnecessary, wasn't it, because the country homes people stepped in and offered you a lifeline?'

'Yes, I suppose it was. Two days later, would you believe. Their letter came two days later. We thought they'd forgotten us – they'd been sitting on our application for a year – but then, out of the blue, they came to the rescue.'

'Sighs of relief all round.'

'You can say that again. We'd have gone under, no

doubt about it. Funny thing is, that doesn't sound so bad, now. I'd have lost this place but we'd have stayed a family. Now I'm scared stiff I'll lose the girls. I can't see Pumpkin ever forgiving me. Losing her love is a price I can't afford.'

I'm normally immune to moral blackmail, but he had a point. And I don't believe in the confessional approach. All that does is transfer the pain to someone else. Someone who doesn't deserve it. I'll go to my grave with my heart filled with black secrets, and they'll all go with me.

'What happens now?' he asked.

'I'll go back to Heckley,' I replied. 'Tomorrow I'll have a word, off the record, with our prosecution service lawyer. I'll tell him about this hypothetical case involving a humane killer, a racehorse that couldn't run and a deliberately started fire. He'll tell me that no crime was committed other than a fraudulent insurance claim, but as the chief claimant was dead it was not in the public's interest to pursue it. Case closed. We're short of filing space at the nick, so we'll probably destroy the file.'

'Really?'

'I think so. I'll probably fail big Dave's Gaitskell Heights test, but you won't be doing anything similar in the future, will you?'

'Gaitskell Heights test?'

'It's a long story.'

'Right. Well, I can safely say no to that. You've been... It's more than I deserve, and I'm grateful. You know you'll be welcome at Curzon House any time you like, and I speak for the girls as well as myself.'

'Thank you,' I said, but I knew that when I drove down that lane again it would be for the last time. I placed my empty mug back on the tray and manoeuvred myself to a standing position. 'Say goodbye to Toby for me, please. I've enjoyed her company.'

'She'll be sorry you've not said it yourself.'

'Oh, she'll get over it,' I told him. Most people do.

He invited me to the village gala at the end of August. I said it was a busy time for us but I'd try to make it, then it was back to the car. I wound the window down so I could hear the *plunk plunk* of Toby's demon serve for as long as possible.

Gaitskell Heights are a pair of Sixties tower blocks at the heart of the Sylvan Fields estate in Heckley. They quickly became run-down and neglected, and because of this they were used by the council as a dumping ground for poorer tenants, meaning anyone who fell behind with their rent. Then they widened the qualification requirement to include single-parent families, immigrants, druggies on rehabilitation programmes and all the other unfortunates, misfits and bone-idle dropouts that wash up on the edges of society. The locals call the flats Gaza.

When I'm lenient with someone like Curzon, when I'm dealing with someone I might like under different circumstances, Dave always asks me if I'd pass the Gaitskell House test. If they lived in a tower block and not in a six-bedroom town house, would I treat them with the same consideration? Of course I would, I tell him, but he doesn't believe a word of it, and neither do I.

* * *

Sean and Carl pleaded guilty to aggravated burglary and robbery and are awaiting sentence. The kidnapping charge was dropped. They are remanded in custody and have been told to expect custodials. Janet Threadneedle is out on bail, living at her sister's in Harrogate, awaiting trial for murder. She'll be given life, but life can be short. Oscar Sidebottom was briefly sectioned and is now awaiting psychiatric reports prior to his trial for attempting to pervert the course of justice. Terry Bratt was sentenced to community service for offences against the Dangerous Dogs Act, but allowed to keep Bruno on condition he had him neutered and microchipped. Dave's canine friend, Banjo, wasn't so lucky, which resurrected the usual joke: 'Was it mad?' 'Well, it wasn't too pleased.'

Buckingham Palace issued a statement saying that Ghislaine and the prince had parted amicably, each to pursue their own career. The weather changed at the end of May and we had a dreadful summer. All over the country, barbecues, bought during the first flush of spring, stood dripping and rusting on block-paved patios, monuments to the Englishman's eternal optimism. I didn't make it to the village gala, and the rain lashed down all that weekend, so I doubted if Curzon sold many houses. In September a postcard arrived on my desk, addressed to: *Detective C. Priest, Number One Policeman, Heckley, Yorkshire.* It was a photograph of Mont Blanc, sent by Toby. The message was brief, saying that the treatment was doing her good and she was feeling a lot better. I guessed that she was at some sort of clinic. I took the card home and pinned it on my board in the kitchen, between last Christmas's Age Concern raffle tickets and the washing machine settings.

Dave, Jeff and I had been for a walk, taking in the Derwent reservoirs. Dave offered to bet me a pound that Jeff would tell us that the Dambusters trained there, but I didn't take up his offer. On the way down Jeff said: 'The Dambusters trained here, y'know.'

'Really,' we replied, giggling with silent glee.

It was a miserable day – autumn had come early – so we didn't hang about. I'd had a bath and my M&S ready meal and was just about to start watching *In Bruges*, which Jeff had loaned me, when the phone rang. It's usually bad news when the phone rings at nine o'clock on a Saturday evening so I answered it like the professional I pretend to be.

'It's me,' said a female voice from the not-too-distant past.

'Hello, me,' I replied. 'This is a surprise. How are you?'

'I'm fine. How are you?'

'I'm fine, too. I was just about to watch *In Bruges*. I'm told it's good.'

'It's brilliant. Look, Charlie, why don't you bring it round here and we could watch it together. I was about to open a bottle of Lindemans but didn't want to drink it by myself. I'd love to see you.'

'Oh, what a shame,' I said. 'I've been out for a walk and am well knackered. I won't be very good company, I'm afraid.'

'Well, it doesn't matter if you fall asleep.'

'And...' I added, thinking on my feet, 'and...there's the little matter of the three cans of Foster's I've just downed. I can't afford an OPL rap.' Actually, the three cans were in the fridge, still chilling.

'Oh, that's a pity. I just felt like some company. Tell you what: how about if I brought the bottle round to your place?'

This was becoming worrying. I said: 'Much as I'd like to see you, I don't think you should drive. You sound as if you've had one or two already.'

'Just a little one, that's all. I could always take a taxi.'

Sometimes, I feel as if I'm the victim of circumstances. I said: 'A taxi?'

'That's right. They're cars that take you where you want to go, for a small fee. Shall we say half an hour?'

'Right,' I replied. 'Half an hour. I'll look forward to seeing you.'

'Will you, really?'

'Of course. More than you'll imagine.' I can smooth-talk for Heckley when it suits me.

'I'm on my way.'

'Bye.'

Ah well, I thought. Bruges will still be there tomorrow. I was climbing the stairs to clean my teeth and have a squirt of Givenchy *Pour Homme* when the phone rang again. It's a murder! I thought, my hopes raised. Please be a murder!

'Hi, it's me again,' she said. Her voice had developed a certain huskiness since our previous conversation, thirty seconds earlier. 'I've been thinking.'

'Thinking,' I repeated. 'That sounds dangerous.'

'No! It's fun, not dangerous. How about if I wore my uniform? Would you like me to wear my uniform, *Inspector*?'

Ah well, I thought, in for a penny, in for a pound. 'Yes,' I replied. 'I think I'd like that. I think I'd like it very much, *Superintendent*.'

AUTHOR'S NOTE

This story is fiction and all the relevant characters in it are imaginary. I have used some real places and institutions to create a sense of location and distance, but any implied criticism of these is without foundation. Throughout the writing of this book I was received as always with courtesy and cooperation wherever I made my enquiries.

The real Alice Hawthorn is in the village of Nun Monkton, and well worth a visit.